Beau muttered a curse and captured her mouth with his.

Elizabeth sighed and settled against him. The kiss was soft and sweet. His skin was warm and smelled of his cologne, and she inhaled it deeply into her lungs while her mouth caressed his.

Under other circumstances she would rather have her derriere tattooed with a snake than be caught in the middle of an embrace like this where any stranger might see them.

But how could she step away when she had thought about being in his arms like this, secretly yearned for it, for so many months now? When she had imagined this kiss so many times—and was discovering that the reality of it far, far exceeded any fantasy?

She would have to go back to her dull, insular existence soon enough. For now, she wanted to savor every second.

Dear Reader,

This month we have something really special in store for you. We open with *Letters to Kelly* by award-winning author Suzanne Brockmann. In it, a couple of young lovers, separated for years, are suddenly reunited. But she has no idea that he's spent many of their years apart in a Central American prison. And now that he's home again, he's determined to win back the girl whose memory kept him going all this time. What a wonderful treat from this bestselling author!

And the excitement doesn't stop there. In *The Impossible Alliance* by Candace Irvin, the last of our three FAMILY SECRETS prequels, the search for missing agent Dr. Alex Morrow is finally over. And coming next month in the FAMILY SECRETS series: *Broken Silence,* our anthology, which will lead directly to a 12-book stand-alone FAMILY SECRETS continuity, beginning in June. In Virginia Kantra's *All a Man Can Be*, TROUBLE IN EDEN continues as a rough-around-the-edges ex-military man inherits a surprise son—and seeks help in the daddy department from his beautiful boss. Ingrid Weaver continues her military miniseries, EAGLE SQUADRON, in *Seven Days to Forever*, in which an innocent schoolteacher seeks protection—for starters—from a handsome soldier when she mistakenly picks up a ransom on a school trip. In *Clint's Wild Ride* by Linda Winstead Jones, a female FBI agent going undercover in the rodeo relies on a sinfully sexy cowboy as her teacher. And in *The Quiet Storm* by RaeAnne Thayne, a beautiful speech-disabled heiress has to force herself to speak up to seek help from a devastatingly attractive detective in order to solve a murder.

So enjoy, and of course we hope to see you next month, when Silhouette Intimate Moments once again brings you six of the best and most exciting romance novels around.

Leslie J. Wainger
Executive Senior Editor

Please address questions and book requests to:
Silhouette Reader Service
U.S.: 3010 Walden Ave., P.O. Box 1325, Buffalo, NY 14269
Canadian: P.O. Box 609, Fort Erie, Ont. L2A 5X3

The Quiet Storm

RAEANNE THAYNE

INTIMATE MOMENTS™

Published by Silhouette Books

America's Publisher of Contemporary Romance

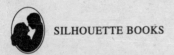 SILHOUETTE BOOKS

ISBN 0-373-27288-X

THE QUIET STORM

Visit Silhouette at www.eHarlequin.com

Printed in U.S.A.

Books by RaeAnne Thayne

Silhouette Intimate Moments

The Wrangler and the Runaway Mom #960
Saving Grace #995
Renegade Father #1062
*The Valentine Two-Step #1133
*Taming Jesse James #1139
*Cassidy Harte and the Comeback Kid #1144
The Quiet Storm #1218

* Outlaw Hartes

RAEANNE THAYNE

lives in a graceful old Victorian nestled in the rugged mountains of Northern Utah, along with her husband and two young children. Her books have won numerous honors, including a RITA® Award nomination by the Romance Writers of America. RaeAnne loves to hear from readers. She can be reached through her Web site at www.raeannethayne.com or at P.O. Box 6682, North Logan, UT 84341.

To speech therapists everywhere.

Special thanks to Robert Hale, editor of the *Waggoner Cruising Guide*, for his invaluable help to this dedicated landlubber about all things nautical.

Chapter 1

The ice princess was nervous.

From his post by the door of the precinct break room, Beau Riley watched the woman perched on a plastic molded chair in front of his desk. She sat prim as a schoolgirl, with spine-cracking posture—knees perfectly aligned, shoulders back, those huge blue eyes focused neither to the right nor the left.

He might have thought she was carved from a thin glacial sheer except for her hands, which trembled ever so slightly.

No. Scratch that, he corrected himself, looking a little closer. She was more than nervous. She was scared to death. Elizabeth Quinn, multigazillionaire publishing heiress, looked ready to jump right out of her skin.

He had to admit he wanted to let her stew in it a little longer, let her sit there until perspiration popped out on that lush, perfect lip, until she was as jumpy as a grasshopper on a hot sidewalk.

The vindictiveness of the impulse startled him. Was his ego really so fragile?

Maybe. He had plenty of reason to dislike this particular rich bitch.

Still, curiosity was a far stronger element of his psyche than petty vengeance. He had to find out. What the hell was she doing perched at the desk of one of Seattle PD's finest? What would possibly make the ice princess come down from her crystal palace to mingle with the rest of the world?

Whatever she was doing here, he wouldn't find out unless he talked to her. With one hand fisted around the handle of his favorite Sonics coffee mug, he sauntered to his desk and loomed over her.

As he neared, she drew a deep breath as if gearing up for a firing squad, then she lifted her gaze to his. He wanted to think he saw an instant of shocked recognition in those cool-blue eyes, then she shielded whatever emotion might be lurking there.

"May I help you?" he asked, his voice sharp as an ice pick.

She blinked a little at his tone, and those pretty white hands fluttered just once then tightened on the strap of a slim little nothing of a purse he was willing to bet cost more than his month's salary.

"Are you…" Her voice faltered and she closed her eyes. After a few seconds she opened them again. He was intrigued to see that the nervousness had given way to determination. "Are you Detective Riley?"

So it wasn't a mistake. She was here looking for him. He narrowed his eyes as his curiosity kicked up a notch. Last time he'd seen her, she hadn't been nearly as eager to talk to him.

"Yeah. I'm Riley. Who wants to know?" He couldn't resist asking the question, even though he knew exactly who she was.

Muscles worked in her throat as she swallowed. "My name is Elizabeth Quinn. I'm a…friend of Grace Dugan's.

She gave me your name and said you might be able to help me.''

Ah. Suddenly things began to make more sense. He should have known Gracie had her meddling little fingerprints all over this somehow. His temporarily sidelined partner damn well ought to have enough on her plate with a husband like Jack Dugan, a new baby, an energetic seven-year-old and that big house out on Bainbridge Island.

But Gracie wasn't content with that. Oh, no. She wasn't happy unless she was coming up with new and creative ways to tangle up his life.

He swallowed a frustrated growl and turned his attention back to the latest complication perched in front of him. Damn. Why did it have to be Elizabeth Quinn? She probably needed a traffic ticket fixed or some other piddling thing.

He wanted to order her away from his desk. Wanted to snarl that he had real police business waiting for him and didn't have time for this today. Before he could open his mouth, though, he caught sight of her hands again. Those long, slender fingers looked strangely vulnerable clasping that ridiculous bag. Closer inspection showed that instead of the glossy polish he might have expected, the nails were bare and looked as if they'd been chewed almost to the quick.

The sight shouldn't have moved him. He was a hardened police detective who had seen the worst life had to offer. Still, a funny little twinge caught in his chest.

''How can I help you?'' he finally asked.

Elizabeth Quinn pursed those lush lips, so at odds with the rest of her prissy, back-off demeanor. She followed his gaze to her hands, then looked back at him, and the sudden pain etched into her eyes like acid on glass took him by surprise.

It had been there all the time, he realized, just buried beneath all the nervousness.

"I need you to find a murderer," she whispered.

Okay. He wasn't expecting that one. He edged back in his chair and frowned. "We have a chain of command for these kinds of things, Ms. Quinn. If you're here to report a crime, I can point you in the right direction. Other than that, I'm not sure how I can help you."

Her chin lifted. "I've been through just about every link in that chain of command, Mr. Riley. I'm ready to hire private investigators, but Grace suggested I come to you first."

Lucky him. He made a mental note to wring Gracie's pretty little neck the next time he saw her, and blew out a breath. "What is it you expect me to do?"

She had an odd habit of pausing before she spoke, as if weighing the wisdom of every word. Beau caught himself leaning forward so he didn't miss anything.

"I'm here to ask you to reopen a case that has been closed."

"We don't close murder cases until a suspect is convicted."

"This case was closed because the death was ruled a suicide. But it's not. I know it wasn't. You people have it wrong, no matter how damning the evidence might seem. Tina never would have killed herself. *Never.* She might have been depressed and…and in trouble but she would never have done anything that drastic."

Whoa. Where did all this intensity come from? The ice princess had suddenly vanished, leaving behind a passionate woman with snapping blue eyes and flaming color.

He wouldn't have expected that such emotion lurked inside the brittle shell of Elizabeth Quinn. He had to wonder what other heat might be hidden there.

"I'm sorry. You're going to have to give me a little more than a first name to go on here. Tina who?"

It was fascinating to watch her control click back into

place. One minute she radiated fire, the next she sat before him composed and cool. She waited just a heartbeat more, then she spoke softly. "Tina Hidalgo. My friend. Three weeks ago she was found dead in her apartment. Shot."

Her mouth with its elegant pink tint gave a tiny quiver and straightened again. "There was no sign of forced entry, no fingerprints but her own on the gun, and she left a note."

"Sounds pretty cut-and-dried."

"Yes, that's what the other detectives—Speth and Walker—concluded. But they're wrong."

He had seen this reaction before. Suicides were often the toughest cases a cop had to work. In their grief and denial, the people left behind often struggled to face the fact that their loved one would ever take such a final step. They often preferred to focus their anger not on the deceased but on the cops with the nerve to put such a stark label on their loss.

He didn't want to add to her grief, but it would be cruel to give her any hope that he could help her. "Ms. Quinn, I'm sorry about your friend. But Marc Walker and Dennis Speth are both fine detectives. They wouldn't have closed the case unless they had ruled out any possibility of homicide and unless the medical examiner signed off on their findings. I'm not sure what you would like me to do."

"Grace seemed to think you might consider taking another look at the facts in the case."

No fair dragging Gracie into it again. He was definitely going to have to have a talk with her.

"Are you party to any facts in the case that Detectives Speth and Watson don't know?"

She was quiet for several beats. "I don't think so. But I'm not sure they gave proper...proper consideration to some of those facts."

"Such as?"

Again that little pause, then she drew a deep breath.

"Tina has a son. A beautiful little boy, Alex. For reasons I won't go into, he lives with…with his grandmother and with me, but Tina loves him."

Raw grief swam in her eyes for just a moment, then she composed herself. "She loved him," she corrected. "Tina was a good mother who loved her son. She never would have left him like that. I *know* she wouldn't. She was trying to get her life straightened out so Alex could live with her again. We just talked about it the evening before she… before she died."

"Ms. Quinn—"

"Please. Will you at least look at the facts of the case and see if you can find anything the other detectives might have missed? Grace said she would do it herself if she could access the files."

Beau ground his back teeth. If he didn't agree to help Miss Priss, he could just picture Grace storming the precinct to comb through the report herself, dragging her newborn and her stepdaughter, Emma, along with her. Gracie wouldn't let the fact that she was supposed to be on extended maternity leave for at least another six months stop her.

Whether he wanted to or not, he was going to have to help Elizabeth Quinn. Damn. For anyone else in the world, he wouldn't mind agreeing to take a look at the file—what could it hurt?—but it stuck in his craw like a bad piece of haddock that he had to humor someone like her.

He pictured her the last time he'd seen her, at the event Grace had conned him into attending by using a potent combination of guilt and blackmail.

Society benefits weren't his thing. He would never have agreed to go to that one if it hadn't been a fund-raiser for Grace's pet project, an after-school program for troubled inner-city kids—and if she hadn't thrown in the reminder that she was eight months pregnant and needed all the moral support she could find.

He had been standing by one of the food tables on Jack Dugan's vast, pine-shaded deck overlooking the Sound, munching on some kind of lobster thingy that barely made a mouthful and wondering when the hell he could finally leave, when he spotted her. The Grace Kelly look-alike in an ice-blue sweater, matching slacks, designer shoes and one row of discreetly elegant pearls that made her look as if she'd just walked out of some exclusive photo shoot for *Town & Country.*

Just another bubbleheaded, self-involved socialite, he figured. Still, something about her intrigued him. *Rear Window* had always been one of his favorite movies.

He watched her from the other side of the huge deck for a long time: the furrow of her forehead as she concentrated on what the elderly matron in the garish purple suit was saying; the way she tucked her smooth blond hair behind her ear with slender fingers; the soft smile that captured her mouth at something the older woman said.

After a moment he watched her excuse herself and wander to an empty spot on the deck facing the water. She stood there for a long time, gazing out at the Sound. She looked lonely. Isolated, removed from the crowd, just as he felt. Unable to help himself, he finally began to move purposefully through the milling people toward her.

When he reached her side, he had murmured something inane about the sunset, just as an opener. He didn't even remember what, but he knew she had to have heard him. She froze but didn't respond at all and an instant later she turned abruptly and walked away from him, leaving him astonished and uncomfortably aware that his face was burning.

He'd never considered himself a particularly vain man but he sure as hell wasn't used to women completely ignoring him. As brush-offs went, this one had been particularly brutal.

It still stung, he had to admit. Two months later.

He didn't want to help her. He wanted to tell her to take a dive right into the Sound. But she had Grace on her side. What the hell else was he supposed to do? After a moment, Beau blew out a breath. The only way he was going to get rid of her was to humor her.

"Look, Ms. Quinn, I'll check out the file. I don't think I'll see anything there that Speth and Watson missed, but I'll take a look. That's all I can do."

As Elizabeth registered his words, she felt as if a weight the size of the Cascades had just been hefted from her shoulder.

He was going to help her find who killed Tina! She wasn't going to have to do this alone.

Ohthankyouthankyouthankyou. The words jumbled up in her head, in her throat, shoving together like boxcars on a derailed train. She froze for an instant, painfully aware he was watching her, expecting some response. *Slow down. Think.* With fierce concentration, she managed to sort the words out, after what she hoped wasn't too awkward a pause.

Thank. You. Thank you.

She murmured the words, then rose. She had to get out of here. Soon. She could feel her composure begin to crack apart like fragile antique glass. If she wanted to get through this meeting without it completely shattering, she was going to have to wrap things up quickly.

Coming here, facing Beau Riley, had taken every ounce of strength she possessed. More. Her insides were shaky, hollow, and her head pounded from trying so hard to concentrate.

She didn't do at all well with strangers or with confrontations. But she had to remember Alex. This was all for him. She couldn't let that sweet child grow up with one more strike against him, the stigma and pain of believing his mother had committed suicide. As she well knew, he would have enough to deal with throughout his life. He didn't need this, too.

Tina did not kill herself. Elizabeth knew it better than she knew the blasted alphabet.

If she had to face a thousand gorgeous police detectives to prove it, she would do it for Alex.

She wasn't sure exactly how, but by some miracle she managed to say goodbye and to hold the fraying edges of herself together until she could escape from the dark-eyed, intense Beau Riley.

Somehow she made it out of the precinct and through the echoing parking garage to her car. She unlocked the door and slid inside, then sagged against the leather, wanting nothing but to stay right there in a boneless, quivering heap.

Beau Riley. She pressed a hand to her stomach, finally admitting that not all of the fluttering there stemmed from stress and nerves. An unmistakable sizzle of awareness was there, too, along with a huge dose of mortification.

She should have known. Beau Riley, the detective Grace swore would help her, was the same man she had encountered at the Dugans' party a few months earlier.

Beau Riley was the man she had treated with such abominable rudeness, only because every single word in her head had vanished when he approached her, looking male and gorgeous and terrifying.

Rather than stand in front of him gaping like an idiot, she had chosen escape.

Did he remember her? Of course he would. Not many men could forget a major-league rejection like that. For one fleeting moment she wished she could rush back into the police station and explain why she had turned her back on him. If only she could assure him her behavior had nothing to do with him, but with her.

She couldn't, of course. Even if she managed to find the right words, she could never explain to someone as self-possessed as Beau Riley how stupid and awkward she was. She could never tell him that no matter how hard she tried, she didn't understand every word he said to her.

How could she blurt out to a stranger that the wiring inside her head sometimes decided to go haywire and when it did, she couldn't even find a simple word like hello?

She blew out a breath. He must think she was the rudest person on the planet. The ice princess. She knew people called her that. It was a far better label than the ones she'd heard as a child.

Freak.

Moron.

Stupid.

She would take ice princess any day. The hand still pressed to her stomach clenched into a fist. She would just have to let him go on believing her cold. If he was willing to help her find who killed Tina, she didn't care what he thought of her.

She closed her eyes but his image still burned in her mind, as it had far more often than she cared to admit since the night of the fund-raiser, until Tina's violent death three weeks ago had pushed away anything as frivolous as thoughts of a gorgeous man.

Tina would have called him a major hottie. Elizabeth managed a smile even as grief pierced her again whenever she thought of her friend.

He was very different from the polished, smooth executives her father had paraded home in the months before his death a year ago, eternally hopeful that one of them would take his dimwitted daughter off his hands.

Beau Riley had little in common with those tame, docile

men like her one-time fiancé, men who cared more about their manicures than about things like truth and justice. She knew it instinctively.

The bleat of her cell phone shattered the quiet inside the Lexus before she could dwell more on the detective.

She gazed at the phone as it rang a second time, tempted to ignore it. Talking on the phone was always a challenge when she couldn't use body language and facial expressions as cues.

One look at the incoming number told her she had no choice but to pick it up. Luisa never called unless it was important.

"Hello?"

Silence answered her for a moment, then Luisa's melodious, soothing voice reached her. "*Mi hija?* I worry for you."

Elizabeth didn't need to see the older woman's sweet, plump face to comprehend the concern and love in her voice. Some of the tension in her shoulders began to seep out. "I'm fine. I'll be heading for the…" Big. Water. Float. She could see the blasted thing in her mind but the slippery word evaded her.

"I'll be home soon," she finally said.

Ferry! That's what she meant. The ferry. She almost blurted it out but she knew Luisa had enough experience with her conversational idiosyncrasies after all these years that the occasional lurch didn't faze her at all.

"How is Alex?" Elizabeth asked instead.

"Taking a nap," his grandmother answered. "Did you talk to the *policia?*"

"Grace's friend agreed to look at the file. I think he will help me."

The other woman didn't answer and Elizabeth swallowed her sigh. Luisa wasn't convinced that her daughter had been murdered. She wanted Elizabeth to let the whole thing drop, to allow the police ruling to stand. As painful as it was to think her daughter had ended her own life, Elizabeth suspected Luisa feared digging too deeply into Tina's wild, troubled world.

"I'll be home soon," she finally repeated. "Give Alex a kiss for me when he wakes up and tell him I'll take him down later to watch the..." Swim. Quack. This time she forced herself to concentrate until the word came to her. "To watch the ducks."

She hung up the phone and stared out the windshield at the dim, unnatural light inside the garage. Despite Luisa's reservations, Elizabeth knew she was doing the right thing by pursuing this investigation, no matter how difficult she might find it.

For Alex and for Luisa.

And for Tina, who had never called her stupid.

An hour after Elizabeth Quinn walked out of the precinct, Beau could swear her subtle perfume like just-ripe peaches still lingered in the air, sweet and fresh and oddly innocent.

Like her.

He frowned. Now why the hell would such a thought enter his head? He didn't know about the innocent part but he knew for sure she wasn't sweet. She was cold and snobby. The ice princess, who didn't have the time of day for a cop unless she wanted something from him.

Somehow the nickname didn't jibe with the quiet, solemn woman who had faced him with trembling hands and chewed-to-the-quick fingernails.

There was more to Elizabeth Quinn than her reputation. He had a feeling she was far more complex than the facts of the case she had asked him to look into.

With a sigh he turned back to the file. What did she expect him to find that the other detectives couldn't? The file told a grim story of a troubled woman who had hit rock bottom.

Tina Hidalgo, age twenty-eight, had been found by a nosy neighbor peeking through open blinds. She was dead of a gunshot wound. The Glock with only her fingerprints on it—the Glock she had purchased illegally the day before she died—was on the floor, underneath her dangling fingers. The medical examiner said the bullet entry and exit were consistent with a self-inflicted injury.

She had powder burns on her hand.

And she had left a note, short and succinct.

I'm sorry.

He looked at the copy of the note included in the file. Her girlish handwriting with its big loops and rounded letters looked shaky, but that was only to be expected by someone under severe emotional strain. It definitely matched other samples of her writing, also included in the file.

Elizabeth Quinn had left out a few interesting little tidbits during their meeting. Like Tina Hidalgo's drug problem. The night of her death, she had enough heroin in her system to launch the space shuttle.

Elizabeth had also neglected to tell him her friend had been fired the week before from her sometime-job as a stripper for frequent absences from work—and even more damning, this wasn't her first suicide attempt. Seven years earlier, she'd had her stomach pumped after swallowing a bottle of painkillers.

It was a clean case. Speth and Watson hadn't missed anything. He set his pen down and rubbed at the ache between his eyes he always got when he read too much.

He wasn't going to enjoy telling Elizabeth Quinn his conclusions. He could just picture that devastated grief in her pretty blue eyes again.

"What's all this?"

Beau looked up from the file. He'd been so engrossed in

trying to figure out how to break the news to Ms. Money-bags Quinn he hadn't noticed the return of his temporary partner.

"Hey, Griff," he greeted the clean-cut, scrubbed detective. Fresh off patrol, J. J. Griffin was eager to learn the ropes in the violent crimes division. He was a little too idealistic, maybe, but Beau figured that shine would wear off after another month or two.

"How was the dentist?"

Griff flashed his teeth. "Great. Not a single cavity, as usual. I'm telling you, it's all about flossing."

"Thanks for the tip."

The kid ignored his dry tone and picked up the case file. "This is that Hidalgo case Speth and Walker caught, isn't it? I thought they told the lieutenant in yesterday's briefing they were signing it off as a suicide."

"They did. I'm just taking another look for a friend of the victim's."

"That classy piece I saw sitting at your desk before I took off?"

Beau decided he didn't like the slightly besotted look in Griff's pretty-boy eyes. He grunted an assent.

"What are you looking for?" his partner persisted.

"The friend doesn't agree it was self-inflicted. She thinks we're missing something."

"Like what?"

"If I knew that, the case wouldn't still be closed, now would it?"

In his relentlessly cheerful way, Griffin didn't appear to take offense at Beau's curt tone. He pulled a chair over. "Mind if I take a look?"

Beau shrugged. If the kid wanted to waste his time, too, he wasn't going to stop him.

He was examining the medical examiner's report again

when Griff plopped a photograph on top of it. "What's this smudge here?"

"Where?"

The kid pointed it out. Beau frowned and reached into his desk drawer for a loupe for a closer look. What he saw through the magnifier sent red flags flashing all over the whole case.

"I'll be damned," he muttered.

"What is it?"

"Her wrist is bruised. See? Right there?"

"Like she was tied up?"

He looked carefully at the autopsy photo. "No. They're not deep enough for that. And only the right hand is bruised." The writing hand, the trigger finger.

As if someone had held her wrist just long enough to force her to write that brief note. And then held it tight and helped Tina Hidalgo commit suicide.

Why hadn't CSI picked up on it? And why wasn't it in the ME's report? Maybe because the rest of the facts in the case pointed so overwhelmingly to suicide.

It still might be, he reminded himself. Tina Hidalgo could have gotten those bruises hours—or even days—before her murder.

But all his cop instincts were warning him that everything in this case wasn't as it appeared at first glance.

It looked like Elizabeth Quinn would get her way after all, probably just as she always did. Her friend's case would go back into the active pile, which meant he was going to have to see the ice princess again.

He didn't even want to *think* about whether his tangle of emotion at the thought was dread or anticipation.

Chapter 2

Several hours after her visit with the terrifying police detective, Elizabeth still couldn't quite seem to catch her breath.

She sat on a bench near the water's edge watching Alex toss stick after stick into the shallows in the hope that his new puppy would chase after it.

He wasn't having much luck. Although she was a yellow Labrador, Maddie either didn't have the retriever instincts of her breed or she didn't quite catch the concept of *fetch* just yet. Instead of bounding into the water after the stick, she planted all four of her gangly legs on the rocky beach and watched the boy with a bemused expression on her jowly face.

Probably the same expression Elizabeth had worn at Beau Riley's desk earlier—that slightly panicked what-am-I-supposed-to-do-now? look.

The detective's opinion of her shouldn't matter at all. She knew it. But she hated imagining what he must have thought of her sitting in front of him with her thoughts and words atangle. Pathetic. He must have thought she was absolutely pitiful, and he had probably agreed to help her only so he wouldn't have to deal with her anymore.

She sighed, angry with herself for continuing to dwell on this. Was she so narcissistic, so desperately eager for approval, that she really cared why the man had agreed to help her? His motives didn't matter. Finding Tina's killer was the important thing.

Still, she couldn't help wondering with bitter regret why he seemed to bring out the worst in her, first the night of Grace Dugan's fund-raiser and then today at the police station.

Most of the time she was far more composed. She could go days without stumbling over her words or missing more than the occasional conversational beat.

If she did start to have trouble, she had learned over the years that she could invariably hide the worst of it behind a veneer of chilly reserve.

It was just her bad luck that Beau Riley—the first man she'd been attracted to since Stephen—made her forget all her usual defenses, made her feel just like a stupid, stuttering girl again.

And there was the real trouble, she admitted. She was attracted to him, to that masculine combination of dark wavy hair, green eyes and lean, dangerous features.

She knew better. Experience could be a cruelly effective teacher. A man as brash and confident as Beau Riley would want nothing to do with someone like her.

Alex grunted suddenly, and she looked up from her grim thoughts in time to see him throw the last stick from the pile he'd collected so carefully into the water with more pique than precision. He made a garbled series of sounds, each more frustrated sounding than the last as he glared at the dog he had adored until now.

Elizabeth mentally kicked herself. Usually she was far more attuned to Alex's moods. Why hadn't she noticed his mounting frustration over his inability to make Maddie do what he wanted? If she had been paying attention—instead of brooding over her encounter with Beau Riley—she would have picked up on the signs and headed this minitantrum off at the pass.

She, of all people, should have sensed it. Heaven knows, she had enough experience herself with that same suffocating frustration over the past twenty-seven years.

Rising swiftly from the bench, she touched Alex's shoulder so he would face her. As soon as he turned, she had to fight the urge to kiss that adorable scowl off his little face.

Don't give up, she signed.

Maddie's a stupid dog, he responded, his hands that were still chubby with baby fat a little clumsy with the signs.

No she's not. We need to work a little harder to teach her what we want. I'll help you.

Alex's bottom lip stuck out. *I don't want to. Maddie's a stupid dog,* he repeated.

Not stupid. Young. She won't learn unless we take the time to teach her. Come on, I'll help you.

For the next half hour they worked with the dog, trying to teach her to obey the hand signal for *fetch.* Elizabeth was tempted several times to use verbal commands with the dog but she resisted, remembering the advice of Alex's speech pathologist.

Maddie was Alex's dog, a birthday gift from her and Luisa a month ago, just a week before Tina's death. As her master, he should be able to command her. Since the boy's oral speech was unreliable to nonexistent, his speech therapist thought it best to use only hand signals with the dog.

With a little instruction, Maddie was a smart thing, Elizabeth thought as the dog finally managed to figure out what they wanted from her. At last, she eagerly bounded after the stick and brought it back to Alex, who giggled and let her lavish doggie kisses on his face.

His frustration forgotten, the boy and dog wrestled happily in the thick carpet of grass above the shoreline. Elizabeth returned to her bench, content to watch them, her love for this sweet child a thick ache in her throat.

She remembered that first moment she had seen him, shriveled and red and already squalling his little heart out. Tina had asked her to be her labor coach, so she had been there throughout that miraculous day he entered the world.

Every time she thought about seeing him born, she wanted to weep with joy that she had been allowed to play such an important role in his life.

She'd been there, too, at the routine six-month well-baby check with Tina when his pediatrician first suggested the child couldn't hear. And at the subsequent specialist appointments when the doctor's suspicions had been confirmed.

She loved him as fiercely as if he had been her own child, and she wanted to do all she could to make sure he lived a happy life and grew up to be a confident, self-assured young man who would never look at his hearing impairment with any kind of shame.

While they worked with the dog, storm clouds had begun to gather over the water. It was getting late, and Luisa would probably have dinner ready soon, she realized.

She had waited just a moment too long to herd the boy and dog inside. By the time she managed to get Alex's attention to sign that it was time to go in, the first drops of rain began to pelt them.

She and Alex raced for the house, laughing as Maddie jumped around them with excitement. By the time they made it to the back door off the kitchen, the skies had opened in earnest and they narrowly escaped getting drenched.

Inside the vast, gleaming kitchen, they were met by the luscious aroma of oatmeal chocolate chip cookies baking and by Luisa holding out the cordless phone to Elizabeth.

"For you." Luisa didn't bother to hide her disapproval. "I was taking a message when I heard you come. It's the *policia*. That detective."

Elizabeth froze, gazing at the phone as if it had suddenly barked at her like Maddie. She hated the funny twirling in her stomach but she couldn't seem to control it.

She wasn't at all sure suddenly if she could handle another encounter with Beau Riley just yet. Maybe in a few days.

She almost instructed Luisa to take his number so she could call him back after she had a chance to muscle up the courage. Then Alex brushed past her, caught in the gravitational pull of the cookies, and the words tangled in her throat.

Alex. She had to remember Alex. Maybe Detective Riley already had new information about Tina's death. He didn't strike her as a man who wasted any time. She had no choice but to talk to him and find out if he'd learned anything.

She wiped suddenly clammy hands on the jeans she'd changed into after she returned from the city, then took the phone from Luisa.

With a grim feeling that she would need all the concentration she could muster to hold her own with him, she slipped out of the kitchen and into the music room down the hall.

"Hello?" she finally said, despising the thready edginess in her tone.

"I thought maybe we were cut off."

In contrast to her own nervous squeak, the detective's voice was deep and commanding, a smooth, rich bass. He had shades of the South in his voice, she discovered. Not much, just a hint of a drawl, like a slow-moving Georgia creek hidden in thick timber.

Her mind went blank for a moment but she fought hard to regain composure. "No. I'm sorry. I needed to find a…quiet spot to talk."

"Big party going on?" Not exactly cordial in the first place, that voice dropped several degrees. He must not have a very high opinion of her if he thought she could come to the police station one minute speaking of her best friend's murder, then return home to throw a soiree.

Of course he didn't have a high opinion of her. The first time they'd met, she had given him the coldest of shoulders and the second time she had sat at his desk all but wringing her hands like the helpless heroine of some silent film. He must think she was a complete idiot.

Stupid cow. Stupid, tongue-tied cow.

"No party," she said finally, trying her best to silence the taunting ghosts of the past. "Just the usual chaos." A boy, a puppy and Luisa, with her mournful eyes and disapproving frowns. "Has something happened?"

"Yeah. Something's happened. My partner picked out something in the crime-scene photographs the other detectives must have missed. It might not mean anything, but it's worth checking out."

Excitement flickered through her. "What is it?"

There was just the slightest delay before he spoke. She wouldn't have noticed it except it was the same pause she employed while she concentrated on trying to pick her words carefully. She had the impression the detective didn't want to answer her question but he finally spoke. "Some unusual bruising on one wrist."

"Bruising? What kind of bruising?"

Again he hesitated. "What you might expect to see if someone were to grab your wrist tightly."

Oh, Tina. Elizabeth drew a sharp breath as a host of terrible images slithered across her mind, of fear and violence and a terrible death. She sank down onto the piano bench. What had happened to the sweet, innocent girl who had loved to dance and to swim and who used to sit at this same piano for hours with her picking out "Chopsticks" and "Heart and Soul"?

"Ms. Quinn?"

"Yes. I'm here."

"I'm sorry. I thought you'd want to know."

"Thank you. I…I did. I do." She drew a ragged breath. She had known this wouldn't be easy. "So what now?"

"I'm still trying to figure out how this slipped past the medical examiner and what else they might have missed. I've got a few other leads on this end. I'd like to talk to neighbors, co-workers, that kind of thing. I have to warn you, I don't know how far we're going to get. Coming in cold to a three-week-old murder is about as easy as trying to find hair on a frog. The trail cools a little more with every passing day."

"I know. But thank you so much for helping me. I…can't tell you how grateful I am."

There was another pause, then he cleared his throat. "I'd like to take a look at her personal effects, too. See if she left an appointment book or address book or something that might give us a little more to go on. Can you tell me where I might find her belongings?"

"Here. Everything is here. The landlord wanted her apartment cleared so he could make it ready for another tenant but we…we weren't ready to go through her things yet. Luisa and I had them packed into boxes and brought here after the other detectives cleared the scene."

"Mind if I take a look at them?"

"No. I…of course not." She rested a hand on the sudden fluttering in her stomach. He wanted to come here, to her home. "When would be convenient for you?"

"What about tomorrow afternoon?"

So soon? The fluttering turned into a whole flock of nervous butterflies. But she couldn't very well refuse, not when she had practically begged him to investigate the case. "Yes," she finally said. "Tomorrow would work."

She gave him directions to Harbor View from the Dugans' house just a mile away, and a few moments later they ended the conversation.

After she hung up the phone, she rose from the bench and crossed the thick carpet to the tall, mullioned windows overlooking the Sound. Rain still battered against the glass and stirred the water into a choppy froth. The sun had almost set and the lights of the city across the water had begun to twinkle and dance.

She watched them for a long time before she realized slow tears were trickling down her cheeks like the rain against the window. She swiped at them, grateful she'd had the wisdom to come in here away from Luisa and Alex.

It didn't escape her attention that she had grieved far more for Tina in the last three weeks than she ever did throughout her father's long, lingering death from cancer or after he finally died last year.

She had grieved a long time ago for what would never be between her and Jonathan Quinn. Maybe by the time he died she had no more tears left inside her for the cold, exacting man who never had any interest in trying to understand the daughter who tried so desperately to please him.

Luisa and her daughter had been far more of a family to her than her own father. Of course Tina's death would hit her hard.

Knowing she was justified in her pain didn't ease it at all. She stood in the dark music room for a long time, until the rain slowed and her cheeks were dry once more.

Beau glared at the phone. "I don't care about your backlog, Marty. That's no excuse for incompetence. Any first-year medical student would have picked up on bruising like that. How could your guy have missed in an hour-long autopsy something my rookie partner saw after thirty seconds of looking at a grainy crime-scene photograph?"

He listened to the medical examiner give the old familiar bull about his staff being overworked and underpaid. On the surface Marty Ruckman might seem like the consummate politician trying to cover his rear, but Beau knew him well enough to know the coroner cared as deeply as the detectives about finding justice for the dead.

"Whatever the reason, Marty," he finally said, "we both know this was a major screw-up and it's up to you to make it right. I want you to personally go over the autopsy records and see what else this guy missed. I'll call you tomorrow."

He hung up without saying goodbye and thumbed an antacid off the roll in his desk. He didn't need this today. He and Griff had a dozen other active cases, and he really didn't have time for this kind of bureaucratic baloney first thing in the morning.

And where the hell was his partner? Every time he turned around, the kid disappeared.

He was about to send out an APB when he saw a curly-haired blond dynamo heading toward his desk. His mood immediately lifted.

"Hey, it's my best girl. This is a surprise!"

Emma, Gracie's seven-year-old stepdaughter, launched herself into his arms. "Hi, Beau. Grace said I could come back and see if you were here while she talked to her boss. I didn't have school today so Grace and me are gonna have lunch downtown and go shopping for new clothes and maybe go to the park if Sean's not too grumpy. Hey, guess what? I lost another tooth last night and the tooth fairy brought me two whole dollars and I'm saving it for a new Barbie."

When she slowed down to take a breath, he dutifully admired the hole where her tooth used to be, handed her one of the candy bars from his secret emergency stash and asked her how her new baby brother was working out.

She gave him a disgusted look. "He's boring. I thought he would be able to play by now. Mom and Dad and Lily say Sean's just about the smartest baby in the world but I think he's dumb as a rock. All he does is sleep and eat and cry.''

He laughed—he couldn't help himself—and kissed her blond curls. "He'll grow out of it. Trust me. Pretty soon he'll be picking the lock to get into your bedroom and inventing all kinds of ways to tease you.''

He thought again that Emma was by far the best thing to come out of Grace's marriage to Jack Dugan two years earlier. Beau was still withholding judgment about the cocky millionaire flyboy who had captured Gracie's heart. Dugan had lifted her out of a dark, desolate place when no one else could reach her and he made her happy, so that counted for something. But he was also a reckless, arrogant son of a bitch.

His daughter, on the other hand, was a complete doll. Almost as cute as Marisa had been at that age.

Unexpected pain punched him hard in the chest at the thought of Grace's daughter, and he glanced at the framed picture on his desk of a laughing, beautiful girl with dimpled cheeks and long glossy braids. Three years she'd been gone. Sometimes he could hardly believe it had been that long since they'd taken a trip on his boat or shared a picnic at the beach or played one of their fiercely competitive games of Horse at the basketball hoop hanging from Gracie's little garage.

It had been three years since she'd been killed in a drive-by shooting outside her school, and he still missed her fiercely.

Jack Dugan and his daughter had forced their way into Grace's life and helped ease her grief and guilt. He should be grateful to the man, and he was. But a part of him still felt small and selfish for wondering why he couldn't seem to find the same kind of peace.

"You want some paper to color on while you wait for your mom?'' he asked Emma.

Little lines fanned up between her eyebrows as she tried

to decide. "How about if I make you a paper airplane? My daddy just taught me how."

"Great. I've been needing one of those."

He handed her some scratch paper out of his drawer and grinned at her frown of concentration as she folded the paper with the precision of a laser surgeon performing a frontal lobotomy.

She was almost finished when he spotted Gracie heading toward them. As usual, the air around her seemed to crackle with energy as she made her way through the squad room to his desk. Despite her lack of height and delicate appearance, she was a fierce cop who cared passionately about her cases.

Just now she looked far from that hardened detective, loaded down with a baby carrier and a Winnie the Pooh diaper bag. He relieved her of both and urged her to sit down.

Emma looked up and flashed her gap-toothed grin. "Hi, Grace. I'm making Beau one of my super-duper high-flyer airplanes Daddy taught me to make."

She grinned at her stepdaughter as she pulled little Sean out of the baby carrier. "And I'm sure Beau will find some way to make trouble with it. Like launch it at the lieutenant when his back is turned." She turned back to Beau. "Sorry I took a little longer than I'd expected. I didn't mean to let Em just run free. Were you in the middle of something when she came back?"

"No. I was all done yelling by the time she got here, so she missed all my better cuss words."

"Uh-oh. Trouble with a case?"

If Emma hadn't been there with her wide eyes and her avid curiosity, he would have unloaded on Grace about it. Hell, she ought to be working the case with him, since this one was her baby. Besides, Grace had always had a way of seeing patterns and flags that evaded everybody else.

But since she couldn't very well pack that cute dark-haired new baby on her hip while she went out on interviews, he was on his own.

He shrugged and chose to change the subject. "How's the kid? Is he sleeping through the night yet?"

Grace sighed. "Not yet. He still thinks he needs to eat every two hours. Kind of like someone else I know," she said pointedly.

"Hey, we're both healthy, growing males. We need our food."

She snorted and he grinned back. He and Grace had been partners on and off for a dozen years, first on patrol and then as detectives. They knew each other inside and out and loved each other deeply, just not in a romantic way. She'd always been like an annoying little sister to him, but he couldn't imagine his life without her.

"What brings you down here?" Beau asked. "I didn't think we'd have to see your ugly mug for at least another few months."

She made a face with features that were small and delicate and, he had to admit, far from ugly. "Keep it up and you won't have to see it for longer than that." She paused. "Actually, Beau, I just talked to Charlie about extending my maternity leave by another six months. I'm going to fill out the paperwork."

He stared at her, grim images of spending more time with an eager puppy of a partner like J. J. Griffin. He did a quick mental calculation. "A whole year? You're taking a whole year off? You were just getting back in the groove!"

"I'm sorry, Beau. I should have told you before I talked to Charlie and filled out the paperwork."

"Why do you need a whole year?" He knew he probably sounded like a spoiled little kid whose best friend was moving away but he couldn't seem to help it.

"When you have children, maybe you'll understand. I didn't have many choices with Marisa. You know what it was like for us. I was all she had and she was barely a few weeks old when I had to go back to work just to pay the rent. This time everything is different. I've discovered I'm not in a big hurry yet to rush back to all this. I just need a little time with Em and the baby. But I'll be back, I promise."

"Not for a whole year!"

"Come on, Beau. J.J.'s a good cop. You'll break him in. Besides, you still have to promise to keep me up-to-date on what you're working on. I'll still be around so you can bounce cases off me. What put you in such a temper earlier?"

He held up the Hidalgo file. "This."

She read the name on the tab. "Tina Hidalgo. Why does that sound so familiar?"

"You should know since you're the one who sicced her friend on me. Elizabeth Quinn, remember? You told her I would look into the closed case for her."

She caught on quickly. "You saw Elizabeth? Are you reopening it?"

He nodded with a glare.

"She must be so relieved."

"I don't know about that. She's a hard nut to crack."

"She's just quiet. When you get to know her a little better, you'll find out she's a real sweetheart."

He wasn't so sure. He had a feeling sitting in an ice-cold stakeout car in the middle of January would be warmer than spending any more time with Elizabeth Quinn.

Grace frowned at him as she settled the baby back into the carrier. "You've got that look on your face again, Beau. She *is* a sweetheart. She's just a little reserved with people she doesn't know. Be nice to her, okay?"

"I'm nice to everyone," he growled.

Before Grace could answer, the lieutenant's booming voice carried through the whole squad room.

"Riley! What the hell do you think you're doing?"

Beau sent a quick glance to Emma, still folding what was

turning into a whole fleet of paper airplanes. She had stopped working and was looking at him wide-eyed.

"Uh-oh." Gracie stood up. "Sounds like you've stepped in it again. This looks like a good time for us to run. We have a lunch date, anyway. See you later, Beau. Why don't you come out for dinner next week? I'll call you."

She kissed him on the cheek, then waited for Emma to do the same before leading her by the hand toward the door, the baby carrier in the other hand, just before Charlie reached his desk.

Short, thickly built and in his midfifties, Charlie Banks was just about the best cop Beau had ever known. He had sharp instincts and a pit bull's temperament when it came to investigations. A native of Boston, he still spoke with a hard New England accent and had little patience for stupidity.

"I just got off the phone with the medical examiner," he growled. "Imagine my surprise when he informs me you have reopened an investigation two other fine detectives of this department ruled a suicide. You mind telling me when the line-of-command fairy dropped by and granted you a free pass?"

Beau winced. He supposed he should have told Charlie what he was up to. "I told a friend of Gracie's I would look into the matter for her. I spotted a red flag or two so I'm just double-checking some things."

"Riley, how many damn times do I have to tell you? You can't just hotshot around here, picking and choosing the cases you want to work on. You've got twenty active case files on your desk as we speak. Until you clear a few of those, you don't have time to run around digging up self-inflicted gunshot cases."

"What if it wasn't self-inflicted? Look at this photograph. Doesn't that look like a bruise on her wrist?"

Charlie squinted at the autopsy photo. "It's a smudge on

the film. That's it. Certainly not enough to warrant any more use of this department's time and energy.''

The lieutenant saw a smudge on the print; Beau saw a woman who loved her son and inspired deep loyalty in her friends.

''Charlie, I've got a hunch about this one. You mind if I work it on my own time?''

His boss looked at him for a moment, then rolled his eyes. ''You need a life, Riley.''

''Yeah, tell me something I don't know. So are we good on the Hidalgo case?''

''Your time is none of my business. Do what you want. Just don't do it when you're supposed to be working other investigations. You come up with something besides a hunch and a smudge on a photograph and we can talk about reopening the case. Until then, you're on your own.''

Beau watched Charlie walk back to his office, then looked once more at the driver's license photo clipped to the manila folder. Tina Hidalgo had been pretty. He could see the signs of it even in the grainy picture. Underneath the hard, brittle shell of worldliness, her mouth was sweetly curved, like a ship's bow, and her eyes were the same color as cinnamon sugar.

Maybe she did kill herself. Maybe he was wasting his time. But everyone deserved somebody to stand up for her, even a junkie stripper like Tina Hidalgo.

Chapter 3

Elizabeth Quinn's house was exactly as he expected—huge, elegant and imposing.

Later that evening, Beau paused outside immense wrought-iron gates and studied the place. The massive structure was redbrick with rows of black shutters marching across the face. It was set back from the road amid glossy, perfectly manicured lawns on a chunk of waterfront property that must have set dear old Dad back a few bucks.

He turned down the volume on an old Emmy Lou Harris CD and pressed the buzzer, flashing his badge and a curt wave to the security cam. A few seconds later the gates slid open, and he drove up a smooth-as-black-silk driveway.

The Quinn estate—Harbor View, according to the sign out front—had probably never seen anything as disreputable as his old pickup, he thought with a small grin. Maybe it was about time they did.

Old money had never impressed him like it did some cops, although very few people in Seattle except Grace

knew why. Beau didn't want it spread around that he had
seen more than enough of it in his lifetime to know how
controlling and corrosive too much of it could be.

He walked to the door and rang the buzzer, listening to
the low murmur of chimes inside the house. A small, plump
Hispanic woman in her late forties opened the door almost
before the last echo faded away. He was glad to see she
wasn't in one of those pretentious little black-and-white uniforms like the help in his grandmother's home had been
forced to wear. Instead she was dressed in jeans and a
brightly patterned cotton T-shirt.

"Welcome, Officer. Please come in."

Something about the tightness around her mouth warned
him she wasn't exactly thrilled to have him there. He wondered why but didn't have time to dwell on it before she
led the way through an elegant foyer down a confusing
series of hallways and finally to a large room at the rear of
the house.

The first thing he saw was a wide bank of floor-to-ceiling
windows with a killer view of the downtown Seattle skyline
across the water.

The second thing was Elizabeth Quinn.

Wearing jeans and a thick, cream-colored turtleneck
sweater, she sat on the floor with her back to the door,
plopped down right in the midst of what looked like a whole
convoy of toy trucks involved in some massive pileup. In
front of her was a dark-haired little kid who looked to be a
couple of years younger than Em. Both Elizabeth and the
kid were gesturing wildly.

It took Beau a few beats to figure out what she was doing
waving her hands around like that. Sign language, he realized. The boy was hearing impaired, at least judging by
those aids in his ears, and the ice princess was communi-
cating with him.

In a million years he never would have expected to find

her like this, cross-legged on the floor playing with a little kid. He suddenly remembered a flash of their conversation from the day before.

Tina has a son. A beautiful little boy. He lives with his grandmother and with me.

This must be the kid. The file hadn't even mentioned him, so of course it wouldn't have included the information that he had a hearing impairment. Was the woman who answered the door his grandmother, then? Tina Hidalgo's mother?

Why did she fairly crackle with animosity toward him? Didn't she want her daughter's case reopened? What did she have to hide? the cop in him wondered.

In a cool, emotionless voice the older woman announced his presence. "The policeman is here."

Elizabeth whirled around and looked up at him, two bright splashes of color scorching her cheeks. "Oh. You're early."

"A few minutes. The ferry wasn't as crowded as I expected."

"I…come in."

She scrambled to her feet. The boy rose, too, watching him out of huge, thickly lashed eyes that didn't appear to miss anything. Beau started to greet him, then remembered the boy wouldn't hear the words. Unsure if the boy could read lips, he finally opted for a wave and a smile.

"This is Alex," Elizabeth said, signing for the boy's benefit as she spoke. "Alex, this is Mr. Riley."

The boy smiled shyly and held out his hand like a perfect little gentleman. Beau tucked his grin away and crouched to his level, shaking the offered hand solemnly.

"I need to talk to our visitor for a while so you can go play with your…" Elizabeth paused for a moment as if her mind wandered or she forgot the words she was signing while she spoke aloud. "Grandmother," she finally said.

"*Abuela.* Can you do that? I'll try to tell you a story before bed."

The boy nodded. Picking up one of the trucks—a miniature blue Peterbilt with bright orange flames licking down the sides—he hurried past Beau with another shy smile and slipped his hand into the older woman's.

A young, leggy yellow Lab Beau hadn't noticed before bounded up from a corner and padded after them, leaving Beau alone with Elizabeth in the surprisingly comfortable, lived-in room at odds with the formality he'd seen in his quick glimpse of the rest of the house.

Elizabeth nibbled her lip for a moment then blew out a breath. "Alex is…was Tina's little boy."

"And his grandmother?"

"Luisa. She's been housekeeper here since I was a baby. She and Tina lived in an apartment above the kitchen."

The woman was a tangle of contradictions. She wore what was probably a three-hundred-dollar sweater to play trucks on the floor with her housekeeper's grandchild and she spoke of them more like family than servants. He had to admit he was intrigued in spite of himself.

"Nice digs," he finally said, scanning the recreation room's plump leather couches surrounding a huge flat-screen TV. Watching Sonics games here would be almost as good as courtside seats.

Not that he would ever have the chance for either, he reminded himself. This was business. Strictly business.

She shrugged. "It's too big for just me and Luisa and now Alex. I'll probably sell it eventually but I hate to give up the view."

He shifted his gaze reluctantly from the TV to the city landscape across the water. "I can see why."

"I'm sure you're anxious to begin," she said after a moment. "Tina's things are stored in…"

Her voice trailed off, and she paused for a few seconds.

The color that had begun to fade now returned. "A room upstairs," she finally finished. "If you'll follow me, I'll show you the way."

He gestured to the door and she led him without a word to retrace the route he and the housekeeper had taken from the front door, then up a long, curving flight of stairs rising from the entry.

She wasn't much of a chatterer, he couldn't help but notice. Was it snobbishness or just reserve, as Grace had said? He followed her up the stairs, trying hard not to ogle her long, luscious legs in whitewashed blue jeans. They weren't designer threads, he observed, just plain old off-the-shelf Levi's that looked as if they'd been well-worn. Another piece to the puzzle.

At the top of the stairs she took off to the left and he followed her past at least ten closed doors.

How the hell many rooms were in this mausoleum anyway? he wondered. If the Quinn publishing fortune ever took a downturn, she could always open a medium-size hotel.

Finally they reached the end of the hallway and she opened the door. Inside he found a good-size bedroom where a small huddle of cardboard boxes had been stacked neatly against a wall. Not many boxes, he noted, maybe not even a dozen. A pitiful legacy for a woman who had walked the earth for twenty-eight years. The thought made him sad.

Elizabeth seemed to be on the same wavelength. "It's not much," she said, her voice small and sorrowful. "I'm not sure what you hope to find here."

"I'm not, either. I'll know when I see it."

"Would you prefer if I left you alone?"

He smiled a little at the barely concealed eagerness in her expression. Obviously, something about him made Miss Millionaire Quinn nervous. He had to admit he liked the sensation.

If it was true what Grace said, that Elizabeth was only reserved around people she didn't know, maybe she just needed to spend a little time with him to thaw some of that ice.

"No, stay. You might see something out of place, something I would otherwise miss."

Elizabeth stared at that small smile, at the way the sun-bronzed skin creased at the corners of his mouth and the sparkle in those green eyes. That smile was entirely too appealing for her peace of mind. It made him seem far too approachable, not nearly as terrifying, and she wondered what he would do if she snapped at him to knock it off, to just keep his blasted smiles to himself. She couldn't, of course. Not if she didn't want to appear any more ridiculous than she already did with her awkward pauses and jerky, stop-and-go conversation.

Staying here with him was the last thing she wanted to do. Every instinct in her shouted for her to escape while she could, to put as much distance between them as possible, which in a house as sprawling as Harbor View was a fair span. But she couldn't do that, any more than she could politely ask him to please refrain from smiling in her presence.

Instead she forced herself to pull a low ottoman nearer the boxes. She perched on it with her hands folded in her lap and tried hard not to stare at the way the powerful muscles in his back flexed under his casual black golf shirt as he hefted a large box from the stacks and lowered it to the floor.

They lapsed into silence as he unfolded the flaps of the box and began sorting through the contents. It was so difficult seeing these things of Tina's that she had used and loved lying forlorn, jumbled together in boxes.

Neither she nor Luisa had been able to bring themselves

to sort through the boxes yet to decide what they would keep and what they would give to Goodwill.

She found it disconcerting—heartbreaking, even—to see these bits and pieces of Tina's life examined by a stranger, no matter that she had brought him into this, no matter how well meaning his motives.

I'm sorry, she mouthed, with a prayer that Tina could hear her.

"So the victim—Tina—was the daughter of your house-keeper?"

Caught up in her thoughts, it took her a moment to register the sudden question. She blinked. "Yes," she answered carefully. "I was only a few months old when they moved in. My mother died a short time after I was born and Luisa raised me."

"Luisa, not your father?"

She thought of her father and the wide, unbreachable chasm between them. "He was…" *Distant. Cold.* "Busy. He had little time for a young child." Especially one who tried so hard to please her father that when she finally did start to talk, years past the normal time, her words never came out right when he was around.

Beau Riley raised one of those dark eyebrows as if to encourage her to say more, but she stubbornly resisted, choosing to change the subject instead. "Tina and I were only a year apart so we were constantly together. Really, we were more like…like sisters than anything else."

"How long did she live here?"

He was subtly interrogating her. She knew it and fought a burble of panic at having to answer a long string of questions. But if it would help him get a better idea for Tina's life, she would try. "After high school we both moved to L.A. We shared an apartment while I attended college and she tried to find work as a model."

That was where the wildness in Tina had first emerged,

while Elizabeth had been desperately trying to pass her classes. She hadn't noticed the changes at first, too consumed with her own struggles, trying to focus on her schoolwork with the awful specter of one more failure looming over her shoulder every second.

As the months passed, they had grown further and further apart until they would go days without their paths crossing even though they shared living space. Elizabeth spent every waking moment at the library and Tina had a jampacked social life and worked two jobs while she waited for the big break that never arrived.

"But you both came back?"

"Yes. My father was ill. I returned to care for him." Though he didn't want her here, even at the end.

"And Tina?"

She relaxed, discovering it wasn't so very difficult to talk with him after all. For all his disconcerting abruptness the other day in his office, Detective Riley obviously must have a great deal of practice listening to people. "Her modeling career wasn't going well. She came home to find work and it was during that time she became pregnant with Alex. After that, she stayed so Luisa and I could help with him."

"Is the boy's father involved in his life?"

Elizabeth shook her head. "I don't know who he is. I wish I did, but Tina would never tell us."

That had stung, she had to admit. But it was just another in the tangled web of secrets her friend had kept from her and Luisa, secrets she had ultimately taken to her death.

"Tina was…troubled, Detective. Angry."

"Angry at who? The kid's father?"

She thought about it then shook her head. "I don't think so. She loved her son very much. 'He's a gift,' she used to say. 'A sweet and precious gift.'" To her chagrin, her voice broke on the last word. Sudden tears choked her throat, burned her eyes.

Her heart ached to think what Tina would miss as her son grew up. She wouldn't see his baby fat melt away or send him off to his first school dance or be able to buy him his first razor. She would miss teaching him to drive and arguing with him about curfews and preparing him for college.

She wouldn't miss those things, though, Elizabeth vowed fiercely even as she wiped at her tears with a handkerchief she dug out of her pocket. She and Luisa would take care of Alex. They would love him and teach him and never, ever make him feel as if his disability made him any less of a person.

She looked up and found Detective Riley watching her out of those intense dark eyes that seemed to see right past her defenses.

"I'm sorry," she murmured.

"Don't be," he answered, his voice gruff, then he turned back to sorting through Tina's belongings. He might have only been trying to avoid an overemotional woman but she didn't think so. He was giving her time and space to compose herself. The unexpected kindness warmed her far more than she wanted to acknowledge.

As a hardened detective he must have seen many grieving friends and relatives, she thought. And perhaps some who didn't grieve. That was probably harder.

Why did he do it? she wondered. Grace Dugan said he was one of the best detectives in Seattle. *When he works a case, Beau is relentless, like a junkyard dog with a bone. He'll gnaw it and gnaw it until he shakes out the truth.*

She was suddenly very grateful to have this particular fierce detective on her side, no matter how nervous he made her.

They worked through several boxes with only the occasional comment or question from Beau as to whether she recognized items or noticed anything missing.

After they opened most of the boxes containing the average flotsam and jetsam of a person's life—a pitifully few knickknacks, some dishes, Tina's collection of hatpins—he opened one that sent color climbing up Elizabeth's cheeks.

These were Tina's work uniforms. Her feathers and leathers, she had called them—the costumes she had worn while working as a stripper, albeit a well-paid one.

Beau cleared his throat and pulled out a minuscule nurse's uniform that wouldn't have concealed a single thing on any self-respecting female over the age of six, complete with thigh-high sheer white stockings and a perky little cap.

An odd, glittery heat uncurled inside her at the sight of such a silly, frilly thing in his masculine hands.

"You didn't tell me your friend was in the medical profession."

Oh! He had to know perfectly well what Tina did for a living. She couldn't think how to respond to his tongue-in-cheek observation, even if she could find the right words.

At her silence, he looked over at her and his teasing grin slid away. "Sorry. I shouldn't have joked about it. Given the circumstances, it was in bad taste, and I apologize."

Finally she managed to smile. Tina would have laughed out loud at his comment. And under other conditions, Elizabeth would have joined in. "No. It's…it was a joke to her. That's all it was. She thought it was hilarious that she could make so much money for a few hours' work." She paused. "She didn't like being a stripper, but it was helping her improve her life. She was taking computer classes, going to Narcotics Anonymous meetings. Looking for a better apartment."

He watched her out of those probing green eyes for a moment, then finally spoke. "She had heroin in her system the night she died. Did you know that?"

Elizabeth nodded. "The other detectives told us. She must have had a…" She had to scramble for the right word.

Difficulty? Backtrack? No. Those words fit but they weren't what she was looking for. She hit on it after what she hoped wasn't too noticeable a pause. "Relapse. She must have had a relapse. Before that, she had been clean for almost six months."

"Do you know why she would have purchased a gun the day before she died?"

"I don't. I'm sorry. She didn't say anything to us. Maybe she was being threatened about something. Debts, maybe. I know she had quite a few. I tried to help her with…with money. A hundred times I tried to help her but she would only get angry."

"That must have been difficult."

"Yes," she answered, hoping the simple word would conceal the world of pain behind it. When they were children, the disparity between their financial situations hadn't existed. Only as they grew older had Tina begun to resent that Elizabeth would never want for anything.

Nothing financial, anyway, she thought with old, familiar bitterness. Her father had paid her bills—her tuition, her car, her apartment. Or rather, the trust fund he and her mother had set up for her before her birth paid her expenses. But Jonathan Quinn had given her little else.

To her relief, the detective didn't seem inclined to pursue that line of questioning. He opened the last box. Halfway through, he found the soft burgundy Coach handbag she had given Tina for Christmas the year before. Another harsh sliver of grief jabbed into her. Tina had adored that purse and had used it constantly.

"Pay dirt." Beau pulled it from the box. "Just what I hoped to find."

"Why?" She managed to squeeze the word out around the lump in her throat.

"I don't mean to sound sexist here but most of you women carry your lives around in their purses. All the little bits and pieces that give a clear picture of who you are, what you do with your days. Makeup, credit cards, appointment books. Everything. I'm willing to bet that somewhere in here hides the key to unlocking the mystery of what really happened that night. We just have to find it.''

Chapter 4

Elizabeth couldn't contain a small gasp as the detective dumped the contents of Tina's purse out on the bedspread in the guest room. It seemed a terrible invasion of privacy, letting him paw through the contents. Like reading someone's diary or opening another person's mail. A woman's purse was sacred!

I'm sorry, she whispered again to Tina. Even as she thought the words, she knew Tina wouldn't have objected. Not if it meant finding out the truth about her death.

"A lot of cops think working a case is like trying to put together a jigsaw puzzle with half of the pieces missing. To me, it's more like a big, dead-serious scavenger hunt. The clues are there, you just have to know where to look for them. Then work your tail off to figure out what they mean."

"Is there something I could do to help?"

He glanced over at her and she was startled again by the green of his eyes. "While I read the entries in her planner, why don't you look through her address book here and put a small check by the people you might know in common? If you see anything unusual in there, make a note of it.''

Elizabeth nodded and took the slim address book from him. Only after she perched next to him on the edge of the guest bed did it occur to her to be uneasy at working in such close proximity to Beau Riley. Despite the solemnness of the task ahead of her, she was suddenly intensely aware of him, his broad shoulders just a few feet from hers, the masculine scent of his aftershave, of pine and sandalwood, the lock of unruly dark hair dipping across his forehead like a comma.

How many women had been tempted to smooth that lock of hair back into place? she wondered. And how many had acted on the temptation? Well, she would most certainly *not* be among their number.

If not for this case, she would be doing everything she could to stay as far as possible from Beau Riley. He made her so nervous. She couldn't remember the last time she had been so edgy and off balance. It wasn't a sensation she cared for at all—especially when she knew she should be focusing on finding out who had killed Tina, not on gorgeous police detectives with intense eyes and tousled hair.

Reining in her wild thoughts, she forced her attention back to the book in her hands and began poring through the pages. Most of the names were unknown to her and she assumed they were co-workers or men Tina might have dated. A few names seemed vaguely familiar, as if Tina had mentioned them in passing, but Elizabeth had never been very good at remembering names, especially when she didn't have a face to assign to it.

By the time she reached the end, she had made small checks by a few dozen names, schoolmates of both of them or acquaintances from their time in Los Angeles but nothing seemed out of the ordinary. If only she had some clue what she was supposed to be looking for. She was terribly afraid she would miss something important and just be too stupid to recognize it.

She turned the last page, to the Zs, then stared at the page. "This is odd."

She hadn't realized she'd spoken aloud until the detective looked up from the day planner.

"What?"

"Tina has the name of Dr. David Zacharias listed here. I had no idea she knew him."

Beau sat back. "Zacharias. That rings a bell." He thumbed back through Tina's planner. "Yeah. Here it is. She had an appointment with him listed a few days before she died."

She gaped at him, questions whirling through her mind. "Are you sure? She never said a word!"

"Yeah. It says Dr. Zacharias, three in the afternoon, Tuesday the first. What's the big deal? What kind of doc is he?"

"He's a..." Drat, the word escaped her. She closed her eyes for just a second while she tried to find it again, reeling from a complicated mix of astonishment, disbelief and an odd sense of betrayal.

Tina had never said a word. Nothing! How could she have kept it from them?

"He's a doctor who specializes in treating hearing impairments in children," she finally answered. "She must have been looking for a consultation for Alex. But this doesn't make sense. I don't believe Tina would make an appointment with Dr. Zacharias without telling her mother or me."

"Well, Alex was her son. Maybe she didn't feel the need to consult you about his medical care."

Elizabeth wished she had the words to adequately convey to Beau how unsettling this discovery was. "For three years

Luisa and I have been begging her to let us take Alex to Dr. Zacharias. He's a surgeon whose clinic specializes in cochlear implants in children. It's one of the best of its kind in the country."

"Oh, right. I saw a documentary about those a few months ago. Isn't that a pretty controversial procedure?"

She nodded. "Some people oppose them because they say they're eliminating the…the culture of the deaf. Some advocates think children with hearing impairments are better off simply adjusting to their challenges, learning ASL and lip reading instead of trying to change the way God made them."

She respected the point of view, but life experience had shaped her own strong opinions. As a person who had spent most of her life trying to make herself understood, she believed children with hearing impairments deserved the chance to communicate with the entire world, not simply others who were deaf or those who had learned ASL.

"So why didn't Tina want you to take her kid to see this guy? Did she agree with the anti-implant sentiments?"

"No. It wasn't anything like that. Her health insurance wasn't the greatest. It wouldn't cover the procedure and Tina could be…stubborn. She refused to even consider allowing me to pay for it."

Oh, how that had hurt. By default, since he had no place else to leave it, Elizabeth's father had bequeathed her more money than she could ever spend in a dozen lifetimes.

She had wanted so desperately to do everything she could to help Alex, but Tina had been adamant. Alex was her son and she would find a way to take care of him herself.

And yet before her death Tina had made an appointment with Dr. Zacharias without informing her or Luisa. Elizabeth couldn't even begin to comprehend why. She hated to think this would be just another in the web of secrets Tina took with her to the grave.

"You have any idea why she would make an appointment with this doctor if she wasn't planning on Alex having implants?"

"I don't know." Baffled frustration simmered through her. "Maybe she changed her mind about accepting my help. Or maybe her insurance changed its coverage policy, although I'm sure she would have told us if that were the case."

"Maybe she found the money to pay for it somewhere else."

"Where? With hospital costs and follow-up, a cochlear implant costs at least fifty thousand dollars. Where would she find that kind of money?"

He didn't answer and Elizabeth drew in a sharp breath. He didn't *need* to answer. She could tell exactly what he was thinking—if Tina had somehow come up with the money for Alex's surgery, it had probably come through means either illegal or immoral.

Oh, Tina. What did you do?

"Do you know where she banks?" Beau asked gently.

She had to blink back the hot sting of tears at the compassion in his gaze. He knew how terrible this was for her, digging into all the sordid details of her friend's life, she realized.

He knew there was a very real possibility they would find out Tina had been involved in something illegal. He probably expected it. This was the very thing Luisa feared, that any investigation would unearth information about Tina's death—and her life—they would be better off not knowing.

For one wild, anxious second she wanted to tell Beau Riley she'd changed her mind about doing this, that she had been mistaken to pursue the investigation. How would she ever break the news to Luisa if she and Beau uncovered criminal activity by Tina beyond the substance abuse they already knew about?

She couldn't back out now, though. She had dragged the detective into this and she had to see it through to the end, no matter what the cost. "I believe she had accounts at First Federal."

"That's a starting point, anyway."

Beau fought an absolutely insane urge to place a comforting arm around her delicate shoulders, to try everything he could to take that pain from her wide, expressive eyes. How had he ever thought Elizabeth Quinn was cold and unfeeling? In just one afternoon with the woman, he was discovering she had a whole sea of emotions churning just below the surface.

He cleared his throat. "I'll see if I can get a financial statement from them Monday when the banks reopen. And while I'm there, I can see if they know anything about this." He pulled Tina's key ring off the bedspread and selected the small, unusually shaped key he'd noticed earlier.

A frown appeared between her delicate brows. "What is it?"

"A key to a safe-deposit box. A First Federal safe-deposit box, if I'm not mistaken."

"How can you possibly know that?"

"Because I'm a crack detective." He grinned at her, wondering what it would take to get her to smile back. "Actually, because it says First Federal right there on the shaft."

He didn't add that his instincts still hummed at him. Whatever was inside that box had something to do with Tina Hidalgo's death, he could feel it in his bones. Ordinary people didn't go to all the trouble and expense to obtain safe-deposit boxes unless they possessed something significant— or secretive—they wanted to keep in a secure place.

From all he'd learned about the woman so far, Elizabeth's stripper friend didn't sound like the sort to keep a box full of jewels on hand.

"Will the bank let you open her safe-deposit box without

some kind of…'' With another of those intriguing pauses of hers, she left her sentence hovering between them while that trio of lines between her brows deepened. After a few beats she continued. ''Permission. Without a…a warrant or something.''

''You're right, ordinarily I would need a warrant to get in, something I might have a hard time finagling since I'm working this case on a purely unofficial basis. But they should let you or her mother open it in my presence if one of you is her executor.''

''I am. She named me legal guardian of Alex and executor of her will. Tina was afraid her mother would have trouble with the…the legal system because she isn't a native English speaker. Ironic, isn't it?'' she mumbled under her breath.

''Why's that?''

A blush colored those high-society cheekbones. ''Nothing. I was thinking aloud. Sorry.''

He waited for her to say more but she closed those delectable lips, so he let the matter drop. ''If you have the legal paperwork and her death certificate, you shouldn't have any trouble getting into her box.''

''I believe she used the…downtown branch most since it was only a few blocks from her apartment. If she had a safe-deposit box anywhere, it would probably have been there.''

''Good thinking. See, your mind is already working like a detective.'' He smiled at her again, and this time he was elated to see a little answering lift at the corners of her mouth. ''Monday I'll be tied up in court all morning, but I should be able to meet you around one at the bank.''

''That would be fine. I volunteer at Alex's school in the morning. I should be done by then. Thank you.''

Uncomfortable with her gratitude, especially in light of

his less-than-enthusiastic attitude toward the whole case, he shrugged. "I haven't done anything yet."

"You're here. You listened to me."

The soft words shouldn't have affected him so much, but he had to again fight the urge to comfort her, to pat that silky Grace Kelly hair and pull her close and hold her until the pain left those blue eyes.

He blew out a breath and shoved the impulse away. He had to get away from her before he did something completely insane. "I think I'm done here. We've looked through all her belongings, right?"

"Yes. This is everything from Tina's apartment. Luisa might have some older things stored in the attic. I can ask her."

"Maybe eventually, but I have a feeling we're on the right track here." He paused, compelled to honesty. He couldn't let her get her hopes up because he wasn't sure he'd be able to sit by and watch those hopes dashed against the rocks of hard reality. As he knew all too well, sometimes bitter truth was far more difficult to live with than a comfortable lie.

"You realize this may all be for nothing, right? No matter how badly you might wish otherwise, there's a chance your friend's death was exactly as it appeared to the other detectives."

She was quiet for a moment and she looked fragile and a little lost as she gazed at the pitiful pile of belongings scattered around them. "I know. If all we find are…are dead ends, at least I'll know I tried. I can live with that as long as I know I did everything I could."

He hoped for her sake that would be enough. He rose, more to put distance between them than anything else. "I'd like to take her address book and her date book with me if you don't mind so I can start running interviews with anybody who might have seen her in the days before she died."

Before she could answer, a knock sounded at the door. Elizabeth rose from the bed with what he sensed was her inherent grace and opened it to the housekeeper.

The woman looked as stern and unsmiling as before. "Dinner is ready if you want to stop for *un momentito*."

Elizabeth made a small exclamation and glanced at the slim gold watch at her wrist. "I'm so sorry, Detective. I hadn't realized it was so late. I meant to invite you to stay but I forgot."

No way. The last thing he needed was to spend more time with the all-too-intriguing ice princess. He didn't like discovering all the layers hidden underneath her cool exterior. He started to refuse, but she gave him an imploring look.

"Luisa is a wonderful cook. Please stay. At least let us feed you for all your trouble."

His refusal tangled in his throat and he shrugged and dutifully followed them down the stairs. Not a good sign. The only other women in his life he had a tough time saying no to were Grace and Emma, and just look how wrapped around their meddling little fingers they had him.

Dinner at Harbor View wasn't at all the grand affair he would have expected. Place settings were jumbled haphazardly around one end of a huge mahogany table in the formal dining room—by Alex, he assumed, judging by the boy's proud face. Beau was seated next to Elizabeth on one side of the table while Luisa and her grandson sat across from them.

He had to admit, the food was divine, the best home-cooked meal he'd had since the last time he ate with the Dugans. With that distant, vaguely unapproving look still on her lovely round features, Luisa filled his plate with some kind of spicy casserole, full of peppers and cheese and tamales.

He had two helpings and was trying hard not to make a pig of himself by asking for a third while he watched the three of them converse in the mysterious, gracefully beautiful language of the hearing impaired.

They laughed suddenly, all three of them. He had no idea why and he thought this might be a little like what the hearing world was for a deaf person. Perhaps they were always a little afraid they had missed some kind of joke.

As their laughter faded, Elizabeth glanced at him. That expressive, telltale color climbed her cheeks. "Oh, Detective Riley. We're excluding you. I'm so sorry. We're being terribly rude."

He smiled. "Don't worry about it. I find it fascinating to watch. What was so funny?"

She signed the words she spoke for the boy's benefit. "Alex was telling us a story about what one of the other children did at school yesterday."

"This is the sign for school?"

Whatever he did must have been way off. The three of them shared a look, then the kid burst into laughter. He could see Elizabeth trying hard not to join him, but eventually she lost the battle. She smiled first, something that completely transformed her solemn features, then she gave in to full-fledged laughter.

Her laugh was magic, he thought, entranced by it. By her. It was like walking through a dark, brooding forest and suddenly stumbling onto an enchanted, exquisite waterfall.

Now where the hell did that come from? Beau blinked, astonished at himself for the fanciful image. He wasn't at all the sort to wax poetic, especially not over a woman in a completely different stratosphere like Elizabeth Quinn.

"What did I say?" he asked gruffly, embarrassed more at his thoughts than by any sign language faux pas he might have committed.

"That's the sign for cracker. They're similar but not the same. See, here's school."

She showed him and he repeated the sign until he had it right.

"Now how would I say dinner was fantastic?" he asked Elizabeth.

She showed him and he turned to Luisa and copied the signs exactly as she had demonstrated, feeling all thumbs at how much more difficult it was than they made it look.

The housekeeper unbent enough to give him a small smile and touched her left fingers to her chin then brought her hand downward away from her face with her fingers together and her thumb extended.

"That's *thank you,*" Elizabeth explained. She repeated the same motion. "And that's also one of the ways you can say *you're welcome.*"

He turned to Luisa again and mimicked her actions. "Now how do I say I like your puppy?" he asked Elizabeth.

This time the signs were a little more complicated but he managed to repeat them to Alex.

The boy smiled with delight, and for an instant Beau was struck by how something in his large brown eyes reminded him of Marisa. Before he could analyze why, Alex's pudgy hands flew rapidly through a series of a dozen signs, none of which Beau had any clue about.

He laughed a little. "Whoa. What was that?"

Elizabeth smiled again. "He said the puppy's name is Maddie and she's learning to play fetch but she's not very good yet."

"My favorite game."

Alex signed something again, words that made Elizabeth give a hard shake of her head and respond quickly. The little boy looked stubborn as he repeated the signs, and Beau was consumed with curiosity.

"What did he say?"

She paused and color flared on those delectable cheekbones again. "He wants you to come outside and play with him and Maddie for a while. I told him no, that you were very busy. I'm sure you have other things to do.''

He ought to say no right now before this complicated woman and her taciturn housekeeper and the cute little boy managed to dig any deeper under his skin. But Alex was gazing at him eagerly out of flashing dark eyes that were painfully familiar and Beau knew he couldn't disappoint him.

''Tell him I can't think of anything I'd rather do.''

Chapter 5

Elizabeth sat on her favorite bench overlooking the Sound and the city lights watching Alex and Beau play with Maddie.

Beau stood on the pebbled shore looking strong and masculine while he threw Maddie's favorite ball far into the water, much farther than either she or Alex would have been able to throw it. Maddie loved the exercise. She would joyfully paddle after it and then Alex would summon her back to shore with the hand signals they had worked out.

All three of them seemed to be having the times of their lives. The communication barrier between Beau and Alex didn't appear to bother either of them. A few times Beau stopped what he was doing to ask her the sign for a word or a translation of something Alex had said, but they didn't seem to need many words between them.

Maddie bounded out of the water and shook to dry herself, sending a flurry of water droplets flying onto both of them. Beau laughed, deep and rich, and Alex joined him with his sweet little giggle.

Her heart twisted with love for him. Tina's son was such a sweet, happy boy, despite his challenges. The two of them made quite a picture in the golden light of the setting sun—the big, gorgeous detective and the dark-eyed little boy.

Seeing Beau interact with Alex was a revelation. She wouldn't have expected Beau to be so good with small children. The day before at his desk he had struck her as someone too impatient, too forceful to have much time for the pesky questions and inevitable dawdling that come with children.

That impression had probably been created out of her own nervousness, she acknowledged, and her embarrassment at finding out he was the same man she had treated so rudely at Grace Dugan's party.

Whatever the reason for her misperception, he and Alex seemed to be dealing together famously.

This was so good for Alex. With no father in his life, he had spent nearly his entire five years surrounded by women. His mother, Luisa, herself, his schoolteachers and speech-language pathologists. All women.

Even though men had certainly come and gone through Tina's life, Elizabeth knew she'd worked hard to keep that part of her world separate from her son.

Heaven knows, the times he spent here at Harbor View with her and Luisa had been virtually male free, except for the gardener and occasional visits by old friends of her father.

Although he hadn't objected to the child's presence at Harbor View, her father had shown no interest in him, even though Alex had stayed frequently at the house in the months before Jonathan's death. As long as the child stayed out of his way, Jonathan hadn't minded his presence.

As a result of that dearth of male companionship, Alex was soaking up Beau's attention like a corner garden seeing sunlight after weeks of rain.

It couldn't be healthy for him to live completely under female influence. She was going to have to do something about that, she realized, though she wasn't exactly sure about her options.

Maybe she could enroll him in a Big Brother program of some sort or hire a male tutor when he was a little older. She didn't need to worry about it right this moment. She and Luisa had plenty of time to discuss the best options and come up with a plan.

Whoever they ended up bringing into Alex's life would have to be far less threatening to her psyche than Detective Riley or she wasn't sure she would survive.

After the next throw, Beau leaned down to Alex and held out the ball. "Do you want to throw it now?" He gestured toward the water, and Alex understood immediately. He took the ball and with his little face screwed up in fierce concentration, he heaved with all his might.

Maddie lunged after it, joyfully jumping through the baby waves that licked at the shore before emerging victorious. At Alex's signal, she bounded back to them and dropped it at his feet, then flopped to the ground, panting heavily.

"Looks like she's worn out. We should probably give her a break," Beau said, then turned back to Elizabeth. "How do I sign that Maddie is tired?" he called.

She showed him the sign for tired and he repeated it. Alex responded and Elizabeth laughed at the little rascal.

"What did he say?" Beau asked, joining her at the bench.

"He said he's tired of throwing balls, too. The one time that he threw it in must have just been too much for him."

He smiled, his gaze on Alex, now poking at the pebbles with a stick looking for crabs or other stray sea creatures sometimes washed up by the tide. "He's a great kid. Does he have any functional hearing at all?"

"Not much. The aids help a little so he can hear loud

noises but most spoken conversation isn't within his range, even with the hearing aids.''

"What caused the loss?"

"Doctors aren't sure. It was probably something he was born with." Just as she had been born tongue-tied and stupid as a result of brain damage suffered during a difficult delivery.

"How long has he lived here with Luisa and you?"

"On and off throughout his life. Whenever things got rough for Tina she would send him to live with us until she could straighten herself out. About six months ago she went into rehab and she signed custody of him over to me. That's the longest he's ever been here."

"Why not make his grandmother his legal guardian?"

"She said I could protect him better than her mother."

"Protect him? From what? His father?"

She shrugged. "She never said. I always assumed she meant from herself. Tina was a wonderful mother but when she was using, she didn't..." She faltered, but plowed through anyway. "She wasn't always aware of things. When she was coming down she would sleep for hours. If something happened when she was like that, Alex wouldn't have been able to use the phone to call for help or go to a neighbor. Tina finally realized he would be much more safe here."

Had she really gotten through that whole thing without stuttering or dropping a word, with only that one little pause? She couldn't believe it. Maybe she was finally beginning to relax around the man.

"You seem to have adapted well to the challenge of raising a child with a hearing impairment. I imagine it's not always easy."

He couldn't know that she had always felt a powerful bond with Alex, even before he ever came to live here at Harbor View. Few others would understand the connection.

"I feel blessed every day for the chance to be a part of his life. Alex is my son now in every way, the only child I expect to have."

She hadn't meant to let that last part slip but the detective immediately picked up on it. "Why would you say that? You're a beautiful woman. You have plenty of time to meet some smooth country-club type and have an estate full of little blond tennis players."

"No," she murmured, gazing out at the Seattle skyline. "That's not going to happen." *So she's not the sharpest tool in the shed. Who needs conversation with that hot body of hers and all that beautiful money that goes with it to keep me warm?*

Elizabeth closed her eyes as fragments of that terrible, overheard conversation seeped underneath the cracks of the closet in her mind where she usually tried to keep the memory hidden.

No, she would never marry. She had long ago resigned herself to the inevitable fact that she would spend the rest of her life alone. She didn't particularly like it but she wasn't foolish enough to dream again of happily-ever-afters. Her silly fantasy of one day having a family of her own had been shattered that day into tiny, jagged pieces.

Even if some man was somehow willing to take on a tongue-tied half-wit for a wife, she would never be sure whether he wanted her for herself or for her father's millions.

Why was she thinking of her broken dreams now? Two years had passed since she broke her engagement to Stephen Pembroke, an engagement largely orchestrated, she saw now, by her father in that last year when he knew he was dying.

It all seemed another lifetime ago. Yes, she had suffered terrible pain and betrayal at hearing the man she thought she loved—the man she thought had been just as in love with her—dismiss her so cruelly. It had hurt bitterly but she had survived and was stronger for it.

She would have changed the subject to something safer—maybe politics or religion—but Beau wouldn't let her. "You're a beautiful woman, Elizabeth," he repeated. "I seriously doubt I'm the only man in King County who's dying to find out if that mouth of yours tastes as good as it looks."

Heat curled seductively through her insides at his low words. She didn't want to look at him. She *couldn't* look at him. There was no denying his meaning. Even an idiot like her could figure out the man was attracted to her, that he wanted to kiss her.

Oh, heavens. What was she supposed to do now? She sought frantically for some kind of witty comeback, some light and harmlessly flirtatious response like Tina might have said.

Nothing came to her.

Absolutely nothing.

Oh, heavens.

It was just a silly, banal comment. Not a proposal. Still, panic started spurting through her veins and she couldn't seem to catch her breath. *Come on. Think.*

She was painfully aware of him next to her on the small bench, his leg just inches away, his broad shoulder brushing against hers whenever he moved. The silence stretched between them, thin and taut. He seemed content to wait for her response, but anything she might have said in reply was tangled in her head, in her throat, in her mouth.

As the seconds ticked away, she felt heat scorch her face. Finally she couldn't bear the thick tension between them another instant. She had to get away. Like the idiot she was—the stupid, terrified little girl—she scrambled to her feet.

"Excuse me. I...I need to do something."

She tapped Alex on the shoulder. *Time to go inside,* she signed, then she grabbed his hand and hurried toward the house, her face burning with humiliation and her mouth filled with shame.

Well, that was certainly as clear as a damn church window.

Beau watched Elizabeth rush away as if he'd just lit her sweater on fire. All the way to the door, the kid cast baffled looks over his shoulder toward Beau, still sitting on the bench at the water's edge.

Twice now she'd shot him down, abruptly and brutally. He didn't need any kind of damn interpreter to figure out Elizabeth Hoity-Toity Quinn wasn't interested in anything he might have to offer besides his keen investigative skills.

He frowned. No, it was more than that. He'd like to think she was just a cold-hearted ice princess, but somehow the image didn't mesh with the woman he'd come to know a little better this afternoon.

Something else was going on. He didn't claim to be the world's greatest authority on women but he'd never yet seen a woman go so completely cold so fast.

What the hell had he said? He went back over the conversation, wincing a little as he realized he probably had sounded like some balding, middle-aged loser, gold medallion and all, trying to pick up a hot date in a singles bar. But his own inept come-on couldn't have been enough to put that wild, cornered look in her eyes.

The ice princess was encased in a few more layers than he thought. He had too many self-protective instincts to try thawing them again. He'd just have to leave that to some other man.

Damn shame, though. She had the most incredible eyes, a pure brilliant blue that reminded him of the time he'd gone on a once-in-a-lifetime fishing trip to northern Alaska with some fellow detectives and had encountered clear, crystal mountain lakes exactly that color.

Gorgeous eyes and a sweet smile, he admitted. The few times he'd gotten a glimpse, he'd been completely entranced by the way her features softened and seemed to glow from the inside out, by the rare beauty of it.

But not for him.

He sat there a few more moments, not sure whether he ought to climb into his pickup and drive away or wait around to see if she came back out of the house.

It seemed bad manners to just leave. But then, it wasn't exactly proper etiquette to leave a guest practically in mid-sentence.

To hell with this, Beau decided. He rose and turned to leave when he spotted Elizabeth walking across the flagstone verandah, her lovely features set in hard, tight lines. He met her halfway and saw that her hands were trembling slightly, just as they had done the day before at his desk.

She looked at the ground as she finally spoke. "I'm sorry I…left like that. It was…unforgivably rude."

He noticed she didn't give any explanation for her strange behavior, just those stiff, tight words that jerked out of her mouth like jagged little rocks striking the ground.

"No problem. I'm sorry if I was out of line."

She opened her mouth to answer, then he had the distinct impression that she changed her mind about whatever she was going to say. After a beat, she answered. "I'm sure you have other things to do this evening. Thank you for your help."

Now why did her tone of voice remind him of his grandmother dismissing her houseboy for the day? Damn but he'd always hated that tone of voice.

He was trying his best not to be seriously teed off but it was getting tougher by the second. She was the one who had come to him for his help. She was the one so desperate to find her friend's killer—if indeed such a killer existed. He was doing her a favor and he didn't appreciate being treated like the hired help just because he'd dared overstep the serf-princess boundary for a teensy second.

"Don't mention it," he muttered.

Something in his tone made her gaze flash quickly to his, then she looked back to the ground looking even more distressed. But still she didn't respond.

Something was definitely going on with her. His cop instincts wanted him to interrogate her until she told him what it was, but he didn't have any rights to probe into her life. He was here as a favor to Grace, to find out what happened to Tina Hidalgo, and he'd do well to remember that.

"So I'll meet you on Monday, right?"

"M-Monday?"

"Yeah, Monday. At First Federal, to check out the safe-deposit box, remember?"

"Oh. Right. The bank. Yes. Of course. I'll see you then."

She paused for a moment, then finally met his gaze. "Thank you again and I'm…sorry," she murmured. "It means a great deal to me that you're willing to help me."

Just don't cross the line into any kind of personal arena again. She might not have said the words but he had no doubt whatsoever that she meant them.

Well, she didn't have to worry, Beau thought as he walked to his truck. No matter how attracted he was to Miss Elizabeth Quinn, from here on out he'd keep it to himself. He'd damn well bite off his own tongue before putting himself through that kind of rejection again.

Chapter 6

Two days later Elizabeth's stomach still burned with mortified shame whenever she thought about Beau Riley and those moments by the water, an image that popped into her head far too frequently for the sake of her peace of mind.

She sat in Alex's classroom with its drawings on the wall and its crayon-and-paste scent, grimly aware that the gorgeous detective and the whole complex mix of fluttery awareness and mortification he sparked in her should be just about the last thing on her mind during her weekly volunteer stint. She knew it, but still she could think of nothing else, nothing but the way she had run away and left him sitting alone by the shore.

Maybe if she wasn't meeting the detective later that day she might be able to concentrate on helping Alex's teacher cut out construction paper shapes for the next day's activities, but with every tick of the clock, her nerves tightened more.

How could she have behaved so stupidly? At the very

least she could have changed the subject or laughed off what she could see in retrospect was a very mild flirtation. Instead, what did she do? She panicked. She bolted from him as if she was a frightened doe in hunting season and he had a big, bad rifle trained on her.

What must he think of her?

She didn't think she wanted to know.

With all her heart she wished she never had to see the man again. But she was meeting him in just—she checked her watch—a little more than two hours. She drew in a shaky breath. She had two hours to figure out how she could face him, to come up with a way to smile and be polite and act as if nothing had happened.

Nothing *did* happen, she reminded herself. She had certainly made a fool of herself but it wasn't as if *that* had never happened before, more times than she could count. She had survived humiliation before and she could do it again.

But, oh, how she wished just once she could carry on a normal conversation with him without sounding so foolish. That she could be glib and funny and unselfconscious.

She sighed again and glanced up to find Alex's teacher watching her out of concerned eyes. "Is something wrong, Elizabeth?" Jennifer McKay asked. "You've been distracted all morning."

Elizabeth summoned a smile. "Sorry. I've got a lot on my mind."

Jen grinned. "You've got that man-trouble look in your eyes. Want to talk about him?"

The two of them were alone in the classroom as the eight children in the special education preschool class had gone outside to enjoy the weak sunshine on the playground for a few moments with the two classroom aides. For one crazy moment she was tempted to take this chance to spill all to Jen.

She couldn't, though. Jen was a wonderful friend and a devoted teacher. Since he'd been in her classroom, Alex had made amazing progress and Jen had helped steer Elizabeth to ASL material to broaden her own vocabulary. She was someone Elizabeth both liked and respected. How could she tell her what a fool she'd made of herself without telling her of her own communication problems?

Elizabeth had chosen to keep that part of her life a secret. Very few of her friends knew about her speech impairment. Although she was sometimes afraid she was only deluding herself, she wanted to believe it was never even noticeable to most of the people she talked to. She had come a long way from that silent little girl and could now converse with Jen or with Grace or the others in her small circle of friends for hours without more than the occasional slipup.

So why did Beau Riley bring out the worst in her?

She knew the answer to that. He made her nervous because she was wildly attracted to his dark good looks and his solid strength, even though she knew how foolish it was.

Jen grinned again. "Now that was definitely a man-trouble sigh. Come on, spill. Who is he?"

"No one," she lied. "You happily married new brides just can't believe any woman in the world could possibly be content without an H-word of her own."

"Don't knock it until you try it. Married life is fabulous."

"You're lucky. You found a good one."

Jen smiled, a slightly besotted look in her eyes, and Elizabeth returned her smile thinking of Jamie McKay, Jen's husband, who had red hair and a boyish face and taught math at the high school. He was kind to children and puppies, likely never cheated on his income taxes and didn't make Elizabeth the slightest bit nervous.

Jamie McKay wasn't Beau Riley, though. When Jamie looked at her, she never once felt as if she'd been thrown headlong into the current of a wild, raging river and couldn't manage to find a single safe handhold.

"Okay, if you're not thinking about a man," the teacher said, "does whatever's troubling you have anything to do with Tina's death?"

Jen knew about the circumstances of Alex's mother's death. She had been at lunch with them the week before when Elizabeth had spilled all to Grace Dugan and asked for her help, which had led to Beau.

"How's the investigation going?" Jen asked.

"Fine. After class I'm meeting the...the detective who is looking into the case."

Rats. She could feel the heat seep into her skin just mentioning Beau Riley and knew she must be blushing for the whole world to see. Jen was too sharp not to notice.

Sure enough, the teacher grinned. "This detective. Anyone I know?"

"He's that friend of Grace's she mentioned at lunch last week. Her partner at Seattle PD."

"Oh yes, I believe I met Detective Riley before Grace had her baby. Bedroom eyes, hunky shoulders, calls everyone 'ma'am' in that slow, sexy drawl. Is that who's helping you?"

"Yes," Elizabeth mumbled. "That would be Beau."

"It's all making sense to me now." She gave Elizabeth a teasing grin, then turned serious. "This detective, is he as convinced as you are that Alex's mom didn't commit suicide?"

"No. But he's keeping an...an open mind, which is more than the other detectives were willing to do. They saw a stripper with a...drug habit and automatically assumed the worst. But they didn't know her."

"Neither did I. But she must have been someone pretty special."

Elizabeth lifted her gaze from the construction paper

pumpkins, astonished. The bare facts of Tina's life that Jen had heard sounded sordid and harsh. "Why would you say that?"

"A few reasons. First, she gave birth to a sweet little boy like Alex, and when she found out she was in trouble, she had the courage and strength to find a better situation for him at Harbor View with you."

She paused, then smiled gently. "And because something about her inspired such loyalty and devotion in her friend, who would go to any lengths to find out what happened to her."

The pumpkins blurred to orange blobs as tears burned her eyelids. Oh, she needed that reminder. It didn't matter how nervous Beau Riley made her, how much of a fool she made of herself over him, how awkward she felt. Tina mattered. Tina and Alex.

"Thank you," she murmured to Jen.

"For what?"

"Giving me a little much-needed perspective."

"Anytime. Now why don't you tell me more about this gorgeous cop."

To her vast relief, Elizabeth was spared the necessity of answering by the return of the children to the classroom.

She was late.

Beau took another bite of the chili dog he'd just bought off a street vendor and scanned the sidewalk in front of First Federal. No sign of any champagne-blond high-society types. Maybe her limousine had a flat or her round of golf at the country club went long.

No, that wasn't fair. Yeah, he had a deep-seated prejudice against the rich and famous. He had his reasons. About twenty million of them, give or take a few million—the money his grandmother had loved above all else, the fortune she had sacrificed everything to protect.

The fortune she had left to her only surviving relative, despite the fact that he'd walked away from her when he was sixteen and never once looked back.

It all sat gathering interest in some fund administered by his grandmother's trustee in Big Piney, Georgia, waiting for Beau to claim it. He never would. At least not for himself. He didn't want it. He just had to find the right charity to dump it into and then he would be free of that monkey on his back.

No, it wasn't Elizabeth's fault that he'd come to associate wealth with amoralistic elitists who thought their money gave them license to get away with whatever they damn well pleased.

As much as he'd like to, he was having a hard time placing Elizabeth in the same category as his grandmother. Not when she played trucks with her nephew and cared so passionately about what happened to a tired, drug-addicted stripper.

He found a convenient pillar in front of the bank to lean against, then scanned the street for her again. He could wait a few more moments for her, then he'd have to get back to work or face Charlie's wrath.

He was just about to check his watch again when he spotted a familiar figure. His squeaky-clean, eager-beaver partner was crossing the street toward him—at the light, of course. The kid had probably never jaywalked in his life.

"There you are!" Griff exclaimed, juggling a bowl of what looked like blobs of white goo. "Why did you run off? One minute you were there picking up that tube of nitrate poisoning, the next you were pulling a disappearing act on me."

Beau scowled. It probably hadn't been too nice of him to try to ditch the kid. Gracie would have his butt if she found out about it. The kid was his partner and they were supposed to stick together.

But damn it, he was meeting Elizabeth on his own time. This was his lunch break, and he sure as hell didn't feel like baby-sitting for someone who ate bean curds and dressed like a young, upwardly mobile stockbroker.

"You're a detective now," he answered. "Trained to locate missing persons. Maybe I just wanted to give you a little test. See how well you would do."

"Hate to break it to you, but you were fairly easy to find. All I had to do was follow the smell of congealed beef lips and here you are."

"This is a work of art." Beau took another bite of his chili dog and made a big show of enjoying every mouthful.

"Right. And that sound I hear is your arteries hardening."

Griff leaned against the other side of the pillar. He wasn't a bad cop. For a relative rookie, he had pretty spot-on instincts. Hell, under other circumstances, Beau might have even enjoyed being the senior partner, pushing his weight around, showing the kid the ropes.

But no matter how hard the kid tried, Griff wasn't Gracie.

"So you want to tell me why we're casing a bank? You got a night job I don't know about? Like maybe moonlighting as the inside man to a bank heist?"

He waited to answer, not sure how much he wanted to tell his partner. "I'm waiting for someone," he finally admitted.

"By any chance does that someone look like Grace Kelly and have legs a couple miles long?"

Beau followed the direction of Griff's besotted gaze and found Elizabeth making her graceful way through the lunchtime crowd of businessmen with briefcases and women in suits and gym shoes.

He didn't like the little hitch in his heartbeat at the sight of her. Didn't like it one bit. He also didn't like this urge he had to order his partner to keep his damn puppy-dog eyes off Elizabeth Quinn's legs.

"You're late," he growled at her.

She nibbled her lip and looked away. "I-I'm sorry. After school Alex couldn't find one of his favorite toys and he wouldn't settle down for Luisa or eat lunch until we found it and by the time I changed my clothes we were too late for the f-ferry and had to wait for the next one and then we ran into road construction..."

She paused to take a breath, color high on her cheekbones, and he felt like a major hard case.

"I do appreciate your help and I'm very sorry to keep you waiting," she finished.

"Did you bring the death certificate and the executor paperwork?"

Again she nibbled that scrumptious-looking lip. "Yes. I have them right here."

She extracted them from a slim burgundy leather attaché and handed them over.

He studied the papers for a few moments, aware of the censure in his partner's gaze at his abrupt tone. Looks like as long as they were teamed up, Beau would always be the one who got to play the bad cop. Griff just didn't have it in him yet.

"This should do the trick," he said after examining the documents. "I have the key here, so let's get this over with."

"Somebody want to fill me in?"

Beau glanced over at his partner. "Not really. You were supposed to be occupied with your tofu crap while I help Ms. Quinn here with a little business."

"My tofu crap can wait. Ms. Quinn, I'm J. J. Griffin, partner to this ill-mannered primate. What kind of business?"

Elizabeth took his offered hand. "A friend of mine, Tina

Hidalgo, was killed a few weeks ago under suspicious circumstances. Detective Riley has been kind enough to help me look into her death.''

"Oh, the strip—'' Griff winced as Beau cut off his word by the simple but brutally effective method of grinding the heel of his boot over Griff's preppy loafers.

"The exotic dancer,'' Griff dutifully corrected himself.

"Yes,'' Elizabeth murmured. "We found a safe-deposit key in her belongings and we're here to see what's inside.''

"Mind if I tag along?''

"Yes,'' Beau growled at the same time Elizabeth shook her head.

"Of course not,'' she said, with a warmer smile than she'd ever bestowed on him. He wasn't sure why that smile made him so cranky—and he wasn't sure he *wanted* to know.

Annoyed and out of sorts, he led the way inside the bank and asked the first available teller who handled the safe-deposit boxes.

"That would be Teresa Myers. Over there.'' She pointed to a woman of about forty with a teased red dye job and thick eyeliner sitting at a desk across the bank.

Again he took charge. "I'm Detective Beau Riley, Seattle PD. This is my partner, Detective Griffin, and Elizabeth Quinn. We need to look at the contents of a box belonging to Tina Hidalgo. I don't have a number but we believe it's located at this branch.''

She took the key from him and examined it. "Yes, this is one of ours. But, Detective, you know I can't allow you access to any safe-deposit boxes unless you have a warrant or are accompanied by the box holder.''

"Ms. Hidalgo is deceased. And, yeah, we have her death certificate and this is the executor of her estate.'' Impatient, he cut off the clerk before she had a chance to give her spiel.

After that Ms. Myers was all too eager to help. "What was the name again? Hidalgo, did you say?"

At his nod she typed a few keystrokes on her computer then pointed to her monitor. "Here we go. Tina Hidalgo, box 1684. It's one of our smaller boxes. According to our records, she hasn't been using it long. Ms. Hidalgo only registered for her box four weeks ago. On the first of the month. Does that information help?"

Two days before her death. He saw the fact as even more of an indication that whatever was inside the box was significant. "It could. Thank you. Can you let us in the vault now?"

"Yes, but I'm afraid I can only let two of you in at a time. I'm sorry, those are the bank rules."

He smiled at her. "That's no problem at all. Detective Griffin won't mind waiting for us outside. It will give him a chance to finish his delicious lunch. Isn't that right, Detective?"

His partner made a face but didn't press the issue. The clerk picked up a master key then led them to a thick metal door, which she unlocked and held open for them.

Elizabeth hadn't said anything since they approached Ms. Myer's desk. She looked tense, apprehensive, her mouth in a tight line and her shoulders stiff. Probably scared to death about what they might find inside. He wanted to comfort her—at least give her arm a reassuring squeeze or something—but he wasn't about to get kicked in the teeth again.

"Let's see, 1684. That should be on the south wall, near the bottom," the bank clerk said. "There it is, three rows down, fourth box from the left. As I'm sure you know, Detective, it takes two keys to unlock the box, the one you have and my master key here. After we open it, I'll leave you alone to look through the contents. Ready?"

He saw Elizabeth draw in a deep breath and hold it as he stuck the key in the slot and twisted. Ms. Myers did the same with her master key, and he heard the snick of the tumblers releasing, then the small door swung open.

Chapter 7

"I'll just leave you two alone now so you can look at whatever is inside. I'll be right outside if you need anything else."

Elizabeth barely heard the bank clerk. All she could focus on was the stutter of her heart in her chest and Beau's hands on the small metal tray inside the safe-deposit box.

She was vaguely aware of the woman leaving them but she couldn't see anything but Beau pulling out the contents of the box with what seemed like excruciating slowness. She wanted to tell him to hurry at the same time she wanted to tell him to shove it all back inside.

Within this simple container might lie all the answers to whoever had killed Tina, and Elizabeth suddenly wasn't at all sure she had the strength to look inside.

The air was cool inside the small vault, probably to protect any heat-sensitive documents, and she shivered as Beau pulled out the contents. She couldn't stand not knowing so she peered over his shoulder, then blew out her pent-up breath, deflated.

A few papers. That was it. Not money, not jewels, not rare coins. Just a letter and what looked like a bank savings account passbook.

"Oh. Is this all?"

Her disappointment must have filtered through into her voice because Beau sent her a small smile that managed to make her feel considerably warmer in the cool air. "Whatever they are, they have to be important somehow. Tina obviously was concerned enough about them to go to all the trouble of placing them here. If nothing else, it helps us draw a picture of the last few days of her life. At some point she visited this bank and opened a safe-deposit box to protect something she considered valuable."

He paused and studied her for a moment then handed her the box. "Maybe you ought to have first crack at looking through whatever's inside. She was your friend. She might have left you a message or something."

These rare bouts of thoughtfulness from such an abrupt man completely disarmed her. The small, steady heat from his slow smile kindled to something considerably warmer.

"Go ahead," she murmured. "You know the kinds of things that might be…pertinent to the investigation."

He crossed to a small table and two chairs set up against one wall for patrons and took a seat. After a moment Elizabeth joined him across the table, focusing on steady breathing to calm her nerves.

She was suddenly painfully conscious of the fact that she and Beau were alone in this small, cramped space, and he seemed to be using up every available liter of oxygen.

She took a breath to settle herself down as Beau pulled out the passbook first. "Looks as if she had an account at a different bank. Washington Federal." He opened the first page. "It's in the name of Alex Hidalgo."

Elizabeth frowned. "Alex? She had an account for Alex? She never said a word about it."

"Maybe she started a college fund or something."

Before she could answer, Beau turned the page to the most recent transaction on the account. His dark eyes widened and his jaw sagged. "Whoa! Hell of a college fund. According to this, there's a hundred grand in the account. That should be some serious interest by the time the kid graduates from high school."

"A hundred thousand dollars? That's impossible! Where would Tina get that kind of money?"

Even before she finished asking the question, she knew the answer. Not precisely, maybe, but she knew Tina wouldn't have been able to come up with that kind of cash through any legal means.

She and Beau had had a similar conversation a few days earlier, she remembered, when going through Tina's things at Harbor View, about the appointment Tina had apparently made for Alex with Dr. Zacharias and the cochlear implant clinic.

She gasped. "Wait! Maybe this was the money she was going to use to pay the hearing clinic."

"Maybe. But where did it come from? There's only one deposit listed here, for the full amount. It was deposited the same day she secured the safe-deposit box, two days before her death."

"It might have something to do with the letter."

Again he paused, his gaze on her. "Do you want to read it?"

She shook her head. "Go ahead."

As Beau pulled a single sheet of vellum from the envelope, something about the stationery niggled at her but she didn't have time to think about it before Beau began reading in his deep voice with the soft, barely perceptible drawl.

"My dear,
I can't tell you how your letter stunned me—and then filled me with indescribable joy. How I wish you had

come to me earlier, at least once in the past five years. If only I had known, I would have done everything in my power to help you. You have to know I would never have left you to deal with such an outcome alone. I must tell you, Tina, you were a shining ray of joy during a dark time for me, and I am sick indeed that I repaid you so cruelly by abandoning you at such a critical hour. Still, I'm elated that you've decided to tell me the truth now. Of course I'll help you, in any way possible. I've deposited the amount you requested in the account set up in the child's name. I will respect your wishes to stay away for now and not complicate matters further, but I beg of you to reconsider. I want nothing more than to have a relationship with my son. And with you, if you can ever find it in your heart to forgive an old fool.

> With kind regard,
> Andrew

Oh, dear heavens. This was a letter from Alex's father, the man Tina steadfastly refused to identify for all these years. Apparently, he was a wealthy man named Andrew, someone Tina had petitioned for help in the days before her death.

Andrew. She frowned. She didn't remember Tina ever mentioning an Andrew....

Suddenly her breath caught and she felt the blood leach from her face as the pieces fell into place. All her thoughts and words became a tangled, jumbled skein, and for several long seconds she couldn't manage to pick up a single thread.

"What's wrong?" Beau asked.

"No," she finally managed. The metal chair clattered back and hit the floor with a clang as she jumped to her feet. "No. It's impossible."

"What, Elizabeth? Come on. Tell me. You look like somebody just socked you in the gut."

That described precisely how she felt. Queasy and breathless and stunned. "The...the letter is signed Andrew. My g-godfather's name is Andrew and he uses exactly this kind of paper for his personal correspondence. Handmade Italian parchment. I buy him a supply every year for Christmas. He's Alex's father! Oh, I think I'm going to be sick."

"Sit down." Beau grabbed her arm and righted the chair, then guided her back into it. "Take it easy. This is all speculation. We don't know if the guy is the same Andrew."

"It has to be! Beau, he was my father's closest friend. How could he do this to Tina? He's more than thirty years older than she was!"

"What can you tell me about him?"

She closed her eyes and drew a shaky breath. "He and my father grew up together near Boston. They attended the same prep schools then lived together while they both went to Harvard, Andrew at the law school and my father at the business school. He's a judge now and has a daughter around my age."

Just the thought of Leigh Sheffield was enough to send her straight into panic mode.

Stupid cow. Stupid tongue-tied cow. You're such an idiot you can't even say your own name.

Despite all the efforts of their fathers to throw them together as children, Leigh had despised and mocked Elizabeth from the cradle, it sometimes seemed. She had been relentlessly cruel, spurred on by her selfish, shallow mother, who had run away with a tennis pro six or seven years ago.

Right before Alex must have been conceived, she realized.

"You said he's a judge?"

"Yes. His name is Andrew Sheffield. He's a..." She couldn't remember the title for a moment but concentrated until it came to her. "He's a superior court justice here in Seattle."

She jumped as Beau's sudden pungent oath echoed in the small vault. "What's the matter?"

"Hate to break it to you, sweetheart," he growled, "but this case just got a hell of a lot more sticky."

"Why? Do you know him?"

"Yeah, you could say that. Andrew Sheffield has presided in any number of cases where I've been the primary investigator. I've testified in his courtroom half a dozen times. Right now he's sitting the bench over a murder case I worked, one of the worst cases of physical and sexual abuse of a child I've ever seen. I'm scheduled to testify against the bastard next week. Judge Sheffield's not going to be real crazy about hearing what I have to say in *that* case if he finds out I'm considering him a homicide suspect in *this* one."

She blinked at him. "You...you think *Andrew* killed Tina?"

"I'd say this letter certainly puts him on my A-list of suspects."

"No! That's impossible!"

"Think about it, Elizabeth. If Tina was putting the squeeze on him over the kid, he had plenty of motive to shut her up."

"But in the letter he...he sounds thrilled about it, about Alex!"

To her horror, her throat closed with emotion, and tears began to burn behind her eyes. She couldn't believe it of Andrew. She couldn't! It was like asking a child to imagine a benevolent, loving Santa Claus as Jack the Ripper. Andrew had never been anything but kind to her, more paternal than her own father. The idea of him killing Tina to hide their love child would have been completely ludicrous without the evidence inside the safe-deposit box.

Andrew had always been her champion, interceding on her behalf with her father, even to the point of convincing Jonathan before his death that she could handle the responsibility of managing his charitable activities through the Quinn Foundation.

She had an acute childhood memory of Andrew's reaction after he overheard a particularly cruel taunt from Leigh once when they had come to Harbor View for dinner. Both she and Leigh had probably been around ten. At the time she had stammered terribly. Worse, she had tangled her words often, using wholly inappropriate ones, and Leigh had taken great delight in mocking her mercilessly for it.

After sharply reprimanding his daughter with fury in his voice, Andrew had taken Elizabeth for a long walk along the shore. They had walked in silence for a long time and then Andrew had stopped her, pulled her into an embrace, then settled her onto a fallen log.

"You are a beautiful, smart young lady, Elizabeth," she remembered him saying in that commanding, articulate voice. "Don't ever let anyone convince you otherwise. Your words might not always come out the way you would like them but that doesn't make what you have to say any less important than the words of anyone else."

He paused again for a long time, looking out at the water and the gulls diving and crying overhead, then he squeezed her hand, sorrow in his eyes.

"Some people find pleasure in others' pain. I regret deeply that my daughter is sometimes one of them. I pray you will one day be able to see the courage and strength inside you that I can see shining through."

She had treasured those words. Held them close to her heart through all the years she had tried so desperately to please her father.

Dear heaven. She could never believe him capable of killing Tina.

"You okay?" Beau asked softly. The quiet concern in his voice devastated her. Despite every effort she made to contain them, the tears burning behind her eyes spilled free.

Under other circumstances she might have laughed at the sudden panic flaring in Beau's eyes. He looked as if he would rather be anyplace on earth than trapped in a bank vault with a crying woman.

When he pulled her into his arms and patted her head in an awkward, clumsy attempt to comfort, more tears welled up in her eyes and she thought she could almost feel the long, slow slide of her heart falling a little in love with him.

"Don't cry, Elizabeth. Please. We could be way off base here."

But they weren't. Somehow, she knew they weren't and she wasn't sure if she could bear it.

They stood that way for several moments with his arms around her while she wept softly. When she finally managed to rein in her emotions, she stepped away from him, chagrined at herself for losing control.

"I'm sorry. You must think I'm nothing but a…a stupid baby. And I am."

"Of course I don't think that. You're not. You've had a shock. One thing I've learned after ten years on the job is that people react in different ways to hard news. Nothing wrong with crying."

He paused, then added gruffly, "Although to be real honest here, I have to admit I'd prefer if you wouldn't do it again when I'm around."

She smiled a little at his tone, then glanced up to find him watching her with a strange expression. She caught her breath and for several seconds she couldn't breathe. He wanted to kiss her. She could see it glittering in his green eyes like sunlight on the water and, oh, she wanted him to.

Maybe if she gave in to the hunger for just a moment,

his kiss would take away the bitter taste of betrayal in her mouth.

Before she could think it through—before she could let common sense prevail and listen to the warning voice in her head—she leaned forward slightly until their mouths were only inches apart and parted her lips, the slow heat of anticipation uncurling in her stomach.

That panicked look returned to his eyes, then he muttered a curse and captured her mouth with his.

She sighed and settled against him. The kiss was soft and sweet, like taffy on a hot summer day. His skin was warm and smelled of his cologne, a rain-soaked forest of pine and spruce, and she inhaled it deeply into her lungs while his mouth caressed hers.

The kiss deepened and she clutched at his jacket, hanging on tightly while the world began to whirl and tilt. A part of her mind knew this was wholly inappropriate. They were in a bank vault, for heaven's sake, being closely monitored by what she was sure was all manner of state-of-the-art surveillance equipment.

Under other circumstances she would rather have her derriere tattooed with a snake than be caught in the middle of an embrace like this where any stranger might see them.

But how could she step away when she had thought about being in his arms like this, secretly yearned for it, since that evening on the Dugans' deck months ago? When she had imagined his kiss so many times—and was discovering the reality of it far, far exceeded any fantasy.

She would have to go back to her dull, insular existence soon enough. For now she wanted to savor every second of his kiss.

He was dumber than a bagful of rocks. What was he thinking kissing Elizabeth Quinn—Elizabeth Quinn, for

Pete's sake!—in the safe-deposit vault of the First Federal Bank?

What an idiot. What a complete and total moron he was to kiss a woman who had made it abundantly clear she wanted a personal relationship with him about as badly as she wanted a poke in the eye with a sharp pencil.

Not that she was fighting him or anything. In fact, if he didn't know better he would have thought she was as tangled up in their kiss as he was. Her eyes were closed, her breathing was quick and uneven and her hands clutched the lapels of his jacket as if they had both been tossed into the Sound and he was the only thing keeping her afloat.

A momentary insanity, he was sure. Any second now she'd go back to freezing him out.

But she didn't. She just sighed and pulled him closer, nestling against him as though she wanted to crawl right inside his skin. Beau knew he should pull away from her. He could think of a million reasons he should *not* be doing this. Besides the fact that he was here in a relatively official capacity and the security cameras were recording every detail, the damn clerk could walk in on them any second.

He had to stop. Somehow he had to find the strength to put an end to what was turning into the most erotic kiss of his life.

Elizabeth sighed his name against his mouth, her fingers clenching and unclenching in the material of his jacket. He kissed her one last time, scrunched his eyes shut and wrenched away from her.

"Well," he murmured, after he finally caught his breath. "That was surprising."

She blinked rapidly, as if awakening from a particularly good dream, then color soaked her pale, delicate cheekbones in a fiery rush.

"Oh. I'm sorry. I don't...I don't know what came over me."

"I'm the one who kissed you. If an apology is called for here, I'm the one who should be making it." But he wasn't ready to apologize. Not when his blood still thrummed through his veins and his heartbeat was racing like a Thoroughbred heading for the finish line at Emerald Downs.

"I allowed you to kiss me, though. No, more than that. I…I encouraged it. I shouldn't have." She colored even more fiercely, her gaze on the marble floor inside the vault.

"Elizabeth, you couldn't have stopped me. I've been wanting to do that for a while now. If I have half a chance I'll probably do it again."

A complex mix of emotions flitted across her expressive features—dismay, denial and, if he wasn't mistaken, a fair degree of intrigue.

Before she could come up with some objection, he headed her off. "We need to sign these things and get out of here. I have to be back in court this afternoon, and Griff's got to be wondering where we are."

After a moment she nodded and gathered her attaché then carefully pushed the chair back under the table. Just as he was reaching for the door handle, she laid her fingers on his arm. "Beau, I need to say…that is, I…thank you," she finally murmured.

He grinned and couldn't resist. "For the kiss? Anytime, sweetheart. Just say the word."

The color that had begun to fade from her face flared back. "No. For comforting me back there. Being so understanding of my…ambivalence. I *do* want to know what happened to Tina but…I'm still terrified I'm not going to like the answers we come up with. You've been very kind to put up with me through everything."

"I'm not kind, Elizabeth. Not by a long shot." He didn't know why he felt so compelled to warn her, but he couldn't let her think he was one of her smooth society escort types.

He worked damn hard at being rough and abrasive and he didn't expect that to change anytime soon.

"I'm not kind," he repeated. "I'm rude and bad-tempered and I don't do anything unless it serves my own purposes. Remember that, and we'll get along fine."

She looked startled, but before she could answer, he thrust open the door and walked back out into the bank.

Chapter 8

Beau and Elizabeth had been inside the safe-deposit vault for longer than thirty minutes but when they walked outside the bank after signing out the contents of the box, they found Griff waiting in front of the building like some kind of eager, faithful retriever.

His partner spotted them and stood up, lobbing his empty lunch container into a trash can nearby. "It's about time. I was just about to send for backup and storm the place."

"Oh. I didn't realize we had taken so long." Elizabeth looked upset. "I'm sorry to monopolize your partner's time."

Beau was disgruntled to see Griff's irritation vanish in a heartbeat. The kid gave Elizabeth an infatuated smile. "Don't worry about it. It's a beautiful day, perfect for people watching. While I was sitting here, I saw six babies in strollers, twenty dogs on leashes and a class full of what looked like kindergartners out for a field trip."

Beau glowered. He didn't doubt that J.J. was exactly the

kind of man Elizabeth preferred. For some strange reason women went crazy for that pretty-boy face and smooth charm. Elizabeth didn't seem to be any different from the other hordes of females who constantly crowded around Griff. Her answering smile was about twenty degrees warmer than anything she had ever given *him*.

He didn't want to stop and analyze why that bugged the hell out of him. How could she lock lips with him one minute then smile so pretty at his partner while she barely even looked at him?

"People watching is one of my favorite things," Elizabeth said with another smile. "Especially with the weather so mild for Seattle in October."

"I think if I spend enough time out here, I could see the whole human condition walking past."

Beau rolled his eyes. Human condition, his left butt cheek. What did a kid like Griff know about the human condition? "This is all very interesting, but we need to get back to work," he muttered.

"Mind if I ask what was inside the safe-deposit box?" Griff asked.

Before he could tell his partner—again—to stay out of things that didn't concern him, Elizabeth answered. "My friend was a single mother and items in her box referred to her son's paternity."

"Is the father a suspect?"

Elizabeth was silent, her features distressed again at the reminder that her godfather might have been involved in murder. He'd seen it before. It was always a bitter pill for people to swallow when they first realized someone they cared about and trusted might have committed a terrible crime.

For one crazy second he almost grabbed her hand to give it a comforting squeeze but he checked the motion. He couldn't show that kind of mushy softness. Not here, not with his rookie partner looking on with such undisguised interest.

"It's complicated," Beau finally said. "But, yeah, he's a suspect."

"What do we do now?" Elizabeth asked. "I'm assuming you'll want to speak with Andrew. Take him down to the station for an interview or something, right?"

Wasn't that a lovely image? Him marching into Judge Sheffield's office at the justice building and hauling him down to grill him in one of the interview rooms at the precinct?

He grimaced, imagining his lieutenant's reaction if he informed him the direction the investigation was taking—the investigation he'd been told was a waste of time.

Charlie, I think I'll haul in Andrew Sheffield—yeah, that Andrew Sheffield, the well-respected juror—and interrogate him about the illegitimate kid he fathered on a murdered stripper.

That was sure to go over real well. He rubbed at the headache beginning to form behind his eyelids. How was he supposed to even bring up Tina Hidalgo and her son to Sheffield and still hope for any degree of judicial impartiality in the Benelli trial?

He had worked so damn hard to build a strong case against Joseph Benelli. To find justice for little Laura Benelli who had endured unspeakable horror in her eight years on the earth. He couldn't blow it now, not when they were so close to putting Laura's son-of-a-bitch father behind bars for the rest of his life.

"This is complicated, Elizabeth," he finally said. "We need to figure out a strategy here."

Griff gave him an odd look. "What's the complication? We just go to his house and ask him about his relationship to the deceased. We don't need a warrant just to talk to the man."

Had he ever been that relentlessly idealistic? If he had, he sure couldn't remember it. Maybe when he was five or six, before his parents' death. "It's not that easy. We're not assigned to work this case, remember?"

"So we take our evidence to the lieutenant and get assigned to it. How hard can it be?"

A whole lot harder than you think. Beau sighed, wishing fiercely for Gracie. She had always been the one in their partnership who handled the political side of things. Gracie treated everyone with the same patience and respect, from the commissioner to the dirtiest street bum. She had a real knack for finding her way through sticky situations like this one.

But Gracie wasn't here. He was on his own. He was hopeless at diplomacy, but he was just going to have to do his best on this one.

"Why don't you go get the car?" He cut off his partner before he could push any harder. "Just come pick me up here."

Griff's eyes widened. "You're really going to let me drive? You sick or something?"

"Just get the damn car."

The kid bounded away, reminding Beau forcefully of Maddie chasing her ball into the water.

"Beau, tell me the truth," Elizabeth said after he left. "Is there a problem with you helping me?"

He thought of Charlie's resistance to reopening the case. He would not be thrilled about this latest development. "Don't worry about it, Elizabeth. I'll deal with it."

"Are you sure?"

He shrugged. "My lieutenant is not real crazy about me digging into a closed case when I have a backlog of open cases on my desk. And I'll be honest, getting a conviction in the case Sheffield is hearing right now is important to me and to a little girl whose father made her short life hell on earth. I can't do anything to jeopardize that right now, at least not until after I've had a chance to testify.''

"What if I talk to Andrew? We…we've always been close. I can ask him about Tina. About Alex. At least that way we'd know for sure that he was the one who wrote the letter.''

"You don't know the right buttons to push, Elizabeth. And any answers he gave you would be hearsay. Not admissible in court.''

"We could go together to talk to him.''

"What difference would that make?''

"What if we made it seem casual, if I just spoke with him at a social function or something where he would assume you were there just as my…my date. Not as a police officer.''

He saw a million flaws in the idea. "I don't exactly move in the same social circles as the judge.''

"I do.'' He watched with fascination as her face lit up a little, as her brow furrowed with concentration while she tried to come up with a plan. "It's Andrew's birthday Sunday. Leigh—his daughter—is throwing a big formal party. I've been invited—Andrew insisted on it, of course. I already sent my regrets but I can ring Leigh and tell her I've changed my mind and I'm bringing a…a date.''

That was twice now she'd stumbled over that particular word. Did she really have such a hard time imagining him as her escort?

He almost agreed just to be contrary but he couldn't see what they would accomplish in the middle of a high-society affair. "I don't think it's such a good idea.''

"I do.'' She set her jaw with unexpected stubbornness. "I think it's a wonderful idea. I want to talk to Andrew about this. I *have* to talk to him. If he really is the one who wrote that letter, I'm raising his son.''

She paused, sending him a beseeching look. "Beau, I

need to know if Alex is his child. And to…to be honest, I would be more comfortable talking to him if you were there.''

Beau hissed an oath. How the hell was he supposed to resist her when she implored him with those blasted blue eyes of hers and asked him so sweetly? ''And then what?'' he muttered, grimly aware that once more he wasn't going to be able to say no to her. ''We accost the man at his own birthday party and throw his affair with Tina in his face?''

''No. You can…coach me in the questions I should ask and how to ask them. I can take him aside sometime during the party or…or afterward and show him the letter. Ask him if he wrote it. If nothing else, we could possibly learn a few more details about why Tina asked him for the money and who else might have known about it.''

She had a point there. ''I suppose this is a formal party,'' he said glumly.

''Yes, I think so,'' she answered just as Griff pulled up to the curb in the department-issue navy-blue sedan.

That meant he was going to have to dig out the tuxedo he bought for Gracie's wedding two years ago and hadn't taken out of the dry cleaning bag since. He sighed. He really hated wearing a tuxedo. ''Where and what time is this little soiree?'' he asked.

''They live on Mercer. I'll have to check the invitation but if I remember correctly, the party begins at eight.''

''I'll pick you up around six-thirty, then.''

''That would be silly for you to come all the way to Bainbridge on the ferry and then have to drive back to the city. It would make more sense for me to use the car service. We'll pick you up.''

If he needed any more reminders that kissing her earlier had been a major mistake, she'd just handed him a big fat juicy one. She used a car service and he drove a beat-up pickup truck with a kick-butt stereo system. How much more different could they be?

"Right. Then I'll see you Sunday evening."

"Wait," she said just before he climbed into the sedan.

He stopped, his arm resting on the door. "Yeah?"

"What about…about helping me figure out the kinds of questions to ask Andrew? Do you want to meet beforehand?"

He considered his schedule for the week. Between the trial he was testifying in now, the one next week, his regular caseload and the work he was doing in his off hours on this investigation, he was swamped. Just about the only free day he had was Saturday, which he'd planned to spend on his sadly neglected boat.

Guess he'd have to kiss those plans goodbye. Unless…

He shut the door on his partner's all-too-obvious interest in their conversation. "I don't suppose you like boating, do you?"

"Wh-what?" She looked disoriented, as if he'd asked her if she favored snacking on garden snakes.

He was already wishing he'd just kept his big mouth shut, but it was too late to turn back. "I was going to take my cabin cruiser out Saturday morning. I just had it in for service and I need to check it out. Make sure everything's in working order before storing it for the winter. If I took you and Alex with me, I'm sure we could find a minute to talk out on the water."

Another complex mix of emotions flitted across her features. "Oh. Alex would love that," she finally said.

What about you? he wondered, but didn't ask. "Just don't expect anything fancy," he muttered, positive he would spend the rest of the week calling himself a dozen kinds of fool.

Elizabeth wasn't sure which of them was more excited about their outing with Beau—Alex or her. Saturday morn-

ing they sat at her favorite bench near the water waiting for
him to collect them for their boating expedition.

All week she had been uncomfortably aware of the low
thrum of anticipation beating through her on butterfly wings
whenever she thought about spending an entire day with
him.

Anticipation was a sweet and powerful thing, she had
discovered, like that last, endless moment before diving into
a cool swimming pool on a hot summer's day. She hadn't
realized how constant and overwhelming her grief over
Tina's death had become until Beau had given her the promise of something else to distract her from it.

If she was excited, Alex was positively giddy. He
couldn't sit still for longer than ten seconds and bounced
around the lawn like a hyperactive kangaroo, Maddie
bounding at his heels.

When will Beau get here? he signed for at least the twen-
tieth time.

I'm not sure, she replied. *He said around ten. Look at my
watch. We still have fifteen minutes before then.*

He held out her arm and peered at the face of her watch.
I want to go now, he signed.

*We can't go anywhere without a boat, silly. You're not a
fish, you're a boy, remember?*

He giggled and made a fish face, smacking his puckered
lips together. She laughed at him and kissed the fish lips,
then yanked down the bill of the baseball cap she'd insisted
he wear for sun protection.

Just a little longer then Beau will be here, she signed,
and handed him the set of binoculars she'd purchased for
him the day before. *Pretend you're a sea captain looking
for…* Pirate. How did she say pirate? She remembered it
suddenly and finished the sign with the fingers of her right
hand covering her eye like an eyepatch. *Watch for pirates.*

Alex snatched the binoculars from her and climbed onto the adjacent bench for a better view, leaving Elizabeth to her anticipation once more. Anticipation mingled with no small amount of apprehension.

Despite her excitement, she had no doubt going out on the water with Beau would likely prove to be a disastrous mistake. How could it be anything else? She was fiercely attracted to him already. Each moment she spent with him only increased that awareness. If she possessed a smidgen of sense, she would stay as far as possible from the man who could evoke such a powerful, compelling response from her.

How could there ever be anything between them? Beau was vibrant, forceful, intense. And she was boring, tongue-tied Elizabeth Quinn. The ice princess.

She didn't feel very cold when she thought about Beau Riley, about those incredible moments in his arms. Her stomach spun, and a slow, seductive heat wound sinuously through her.

What would it be like to be normal, without the crushing onus of her speech difficulties? To be able to play and laugh and be able to relax around him. If only she could be free to be funny and glib and flirtatious. Would he like her then?

He was physically attracted to her. He'd made that clear, both the day he had come down to the water to play with Alex and Maddie and the other day in the bank vault. Maybe she should just let that be enough, just go on trying to hide her stammering inadequacies as best she could.

No. It was too draining on her to have to concentrate so fiercely around him when he made her so flustered. Eventually she would slip and he would figure it out.

She couldn't bear to watch the desire she'd seen in those green eyes change to disgust.

Stupid cow. Stupid, tongue-tied cow.

A cool gust of wind blew off the Sound, rattling the

leaves of the Japanese maples next to the bench, and she shivered just as a watercraft approached Harbor View's private deep-water dock.

Alex leaped to his feet suddenly, his dark eyes snapping with elation. *Beau's here! Beau's here! Beau's here!* he signed, his hands moving furiously, then he whipped off his cap and tossed it into the air.

She laughed at his joy even as her heart began to race. *I see him,* she signed back, then plopped the hat back on the boy's head with a kiss on his nose.

She grabbed his hand and walked down the dock to greet Beau. She and Alex waited while he moored the boat then climbed out, wearing cotton Dockers and a pine-green golf shirt.

The first thing he did was bend to Alex's level and make the sign for hello. He followed by asking in ASL if Alex was ready to go.

The boy giggled and started into a series of complicated signs about how excited he was to go on the boat and could he catch a fish and would they see a whale?

Beau laughed with a slightly bemused look on his dark features. "Whoa, partner," he said aloud. "Slow down. I'm still learning."

Elizabeth stepped forward, her stomach twitching, and set a hand on Alex's shoulder. She quietly translated what the boy signed, then told Alex he needed to remember Beau didn't know sign language.

"Thanks," Beau murmured to her. "I bought an ASL dictionary and a video but I'm still working on the alphabet and a few basic signs."

Her heart jerked and fluttered as she gazed at that rueful grin. This big, tough cop who spent his days in the dark, ugly world of crime fighting had purchased an American Sign Language dictionary so he could communicate with a little boy he barely knew.

It was just about the sweetest thing she'd ever heard.

She was moved beyond words and couldn't think of a single thing to say in response. They stood in silence for a moment, then Beau finally spoke. "So are you two ready to go?"

No. She was suddenly scared to death to spend even another moment with the man. Panic fluttered through her like an angry bird. She couldn't do this. She wasn't strong enough to stop these growing feelings inside her. Unless she did, she knew she was in for nothing but heartache and grief.

But how could she tell him she'd changed her mind when he'd gone to all the trouble to come out to Bainbridge Island for them?

She drew in a sharp breath then let it out again with a grim sense of inevitability. "Just a moment, please. I need to tell Luisa we're leaving."

He smiled. "Okay. That will give me time to show Alex around."

It took every ounce of hard-earned poise she possessed not to wring her hands and bolt back to the house like the scared little rabbit she was. She forced herself to walk slowly, with studied casualness, and by the time she reached the kitchen, she could at least breathe again. Still, she didn't know how she would survive the afternoon with him.

In the kitchen she found Luisa closing the lid to a large wicker basket. "I fix you a lunch," the housekeeper murmured in her musical voice.

Elizabeth made a strangled sound and hurried to the sink for a glass of water.

"Is everything okay?" Luisa asked.

"Yes. Fine," she replied, though it was about as blatant a lie as she'd ever uttered. "Thank you for fixing a basket for us."

"I would not let you starve out on that boat."

Despite her emotional trauma, Elizabeth had to smile. Luisa might disapprove of Beau and the investigation he was conducting into Tina's death. But she would rather have her hair yanked out strand by strand than let someone under her care go hungry.

"Here. Take it." Luisa handed her the basket, then surprised her by pressing a hand to her cheek. "Be careful, *hija.*"

Somehow Elizabeth didn't think Luisa was referring to the basics of water safety. She nodded and looked away for fear Luisa's sharp eyes would discover the warning came far too late.

When she returned to the dock, Beau and Alex were both standing on the deck of the cabin cruiser and Beau was putting a life jacket on the little boy. She hadn't paid much attention to the boat when Beau first arrived but now she saw it was a good-size blue-and-white cabin cruiser with the name the *Mari* on the side in curling script.

Who was Mari? she wondered. Probably someone glib and funny and flirtatious, she thought bitterly, then was ashamed of herself for the hot jealousy spearing through her. It wasn't any of her business what Beau named his boat—or whom he named it after. She'd do well to remember that.

Beau snapped the last buckle on Alex's bright-orange life jacket, then hurried to the gangway and reached for the basket so she could board. "Here. Let me take that. What have you got here?"

"Lunch. Luisa packed a basket for us."

His masculine features lit up in a devastating smile, and she could swear the anchored dock just shook under her feet. "If Luisa fixed it, I can't wait to eat it. That woman is one seriously good cook."

Elizabeth still felt wobbly as he reached out a hand to help her board but somehow she found the courage to place her hand in his. His fingers were warm and solid around hers, and as he pulled her toward him and onto the boat, she smelled sunscreen and hot, sexy male.

Oh, she was in trouble.

"I was just showing Alex around. Why don't you come with me to put lunch down in the galley and you can take the grand tour?"

She nodded and followed him below deck.

The boat was well maintained with a small salon-galley and two staterooms below deck and an efficient, enclosed pilothouse up top.

He was right, it wasn't luxurious—certainly not in the same league as the succession of yachts her father had owned—but it looked comfortable and well maintained.

"She's beautiful," Elizabeth said when they returned to the pilothouse. "Do you spend much time on her?"

"Not as much as I'd like. Unfortunately, the bad guys are pretty inconsiderate that way—the job doesn't give me much free time for things like fishing on my boat."

He settled them into deck chairs, then powered up the cruiser and prepared to cast off from the dock. Alex's eyes were huge at the deep throb of the twin engines, and Elizabeth smiled at his enthusiasm.

"With a nice deep-water dock like that, you probably have spent plenty of time out on the water yourself." Beau raised his voice over the sound of the engines.

She gazed out at the water. "My father had several sailing yachts in his lifetime."

"Then you must be an old salty-dog sailor."

His comment poked at old, half-scabbed wounds. If he only knew how desperately she had always longed to go with her father on one of those damn boats, but he never once took her aboard.

Her bedroom had always overlooked the water. On the mornings when Jonathan would take his yacht out, she would wait in vain for him to just once come for her and ask her to go along.

With a sick, hollow feeling in her stomach she would watch his preparations as his crew arrived and he readied the yacht, then lifted anchor and sailed out of sight. She could remember sitting at her window all day—and sometimes long into the night—waiting for his return.

Wishing with all her might that her father loved her.

Hating him for always, always leaving her behind.

"No. My father didn't take me with him." She tried to make her voice terse, matter-of-fact, with no trace of the self-pity she so abhorred.

She must not have been completely successful because Beau frowned and sent her a searching look. He opened his mouth as if to probe. *No,* she thought. *Don't ask me.* Hot relief flowed through her when he closed it again and let the matter drop, and returned to piloting the boat through the busy channel.

Chapter 9

He was a goner.

From his spot at the controls of the *Mari,* Beau watched as Elizabeth lifted her face to the October sun shining in through the clear roof of the cabin. Her eyes were closed and a soft smile of pure delight tipped the corners of her mouth.

He found it unbearably sexy to watch a woman who was usually so tightly wound unravel in front of his eyes with every passing minute.

The sharp sea breeze coming in through the open portholes whipped bright, vibrant color into her cheeks, and under her wide-brimmed hat, strands of her blond hair had pulled loose from the clip she contained it with and now fluttered wildly in the wind.

She looked young and sweet and vibrant.

He'd been attracted to her before. He wasn't particularly pleased by that admission but he couldn't lie to himself about it. What he was feeling now as he watched her couldn't ever be classified as something as mild as attraction. He figured it was safe to say he was completely entranced.

The boy said something to her in sign language and she laughed, her smile gleaming white in the sunlight, and pulled him to her into a hug then kissed his forehead.

Beau quickly jerked his gaze back to the water cutting away in front of the boat. He did *not* need this. What the hell had he been thinking to invite her and the kid out on the *Mari* today? He still couldn't believe he'd actually asked her—it had been one of those crazy, irrational impulses. The kind he couldn't ignore even though he knew damn well he was going to live to regret it later.

He didn't like this at all. This constant desire was like walking around all day with sand in his shoes—he felt itchy and uncomfortable and couldn't think about anything else.

A commercial fishing trawler approached starboard and Beau gave the trawler its right-of-way under international steering and sailing rules, then started them up again and headed north through the Sound, toward Point No Point.

Before Marisa was killed, he and Grace used to take this route often. A budding marine biologist, Marisa used to love looking for orcas, harbor seals and other sea life that inhabited the fertile waters of Puget Sound and the San Juan islands.

After her death, he had to admit much of the joy he used to find out on the water eluded him. He wasn't sure why. He still fished once in a while and he still enjoyed exploring remote islands when he had a chance. He had even replaced his old junk heap with this fifteen-year-old Grand Banks the year before.

Someday he wanted to cruise all the way to Alaska then down to Mexico, but he wasn't sure if he would ever have that much time. And even if he had the time, he wasn't sure he wanted to do it without somebody he enjoyed being with enough to take along.

He liked his solitude, probably because he'd spent so much of his childhood alone. But he had to admit the salt air seemed more crisp, the sun warmer, the water more brilliant when he had someone to share it with.

He glanced at his companions—at the slim, elegant blonde as enthralled by the water as the little solemn-eyed boy—and realized he was enjoying himself out here more than he had in a long time, even with the relentless tug of desire yanking him toward Elizabeth.

She turned and caught him staring at her—or maybe she didn't realize he'd been staring, because she gave him a quick smile.

"I thought we'd head over to Port Ludlow and have lunch," he said over the growling diesel motors. "I've seen a stray pod of orcas near there a few times, and I thought Alex might enjoy seeing them."

She smiled again and nodded. "Anywhere is fine. This is wonderful, Beau. Thank you so much for inviting us."

Yep. He was a goner.

"Care to take the controls?"

Her jaw sagged at the suggestion. "You want me to…to drive the boat?"

He laughed at her horror-stricken look. "Sure. It's easy, I promise."

"Oh, no. I couldn't. What if I hit something? Or ran us aground."

"You think I'm going to let you hurt my baby? Trust me. I'd take over well before you could do any serious damage. Everything will be fine. Come on. Give it a try."

Although she still looked as if he'd just asked her to eat raw salmon eggs out of his tackle box, she stood and eased closer toward the helm—and toward him, a pretty decent side benefit.

She was close enough that he could smell the peach scent of her shampoo and feel the heat of their shoulders brushing slightly as the *Mari* rode the waves.

For the next hour he showed her the basics of piloting the cruiser—how to check the depth sounder, how to read the GPS, how to use the VHF radio, even how to use the EPIRB—emergency position indicating radio beacon—to summon help if the need ever arose.

She was a fast learner and soon she was handling the *Mari* like a seasoned trawler pilot.

"You want something to drink?" Beau asked when he was confident she was comfortable enough at the controls that he could walk down to the galley. "I've got pop in the fridge and bottled water. Sorry I don't have anything stronger but I don't like to drink on the boat. I've seen too many drunk idiots who have no business behind the wheel of anything."

"Don't leave!"

He laughed. "I'm only walking down to the galley. Just yell if you hit a shoal."

"That's not funny." She made a face but never took her gaze off the horizon.

"Relax and enjoy yourself. You're doing great."

She looked skeptical. "Really?"

"I promise. If I didn't have confidence that you can handle it, I would have taken over a long time ago. You're a natural out here."

This time she *did* glance at him. She looked shocked at first, then she offered him a brilliant, radiant smile that just about jerked his sea legs out from under him.

Man, oh, man.

"What do you want to drink?" he growled.

"I wouldn't mind a bottled water," she said.

He tapped Alex on the shoulder and pantomimed taking a drink with a question in his eyes. He was pleased when

Alex nodded. He didn't know much sign language yet, but he had discovered he could make basic things understood.

He gestured for the boy to follow him down into the galley, then showed him the selection in the fridge. With another of those quicksilver smiles, Alex selected a root beer and Beau pulled out a water for himself and one for Elizabeth then returned topside.

"How do I say 'watch for whales'?" he asked Elizabeth after he tucked her water in the holder on the captain's chair.

She gazed helplessly at the wheel. "I can't show you right now! My hands are a little tied up here."

He laughed. "It's not like a car. You do have to be alert but you don't have to keep your hands busy every second." His intention was innocent—to reach around her and engage the automatic pilot but as soon as he touched her he wanted more. She was warm and smelled fresh and sweet, and all he could think about was tasting those luscious lips again.

Bad idea. He tried to remind himself of all the reasons why kissing her would be about as smart as sticking his hand down into the prop. She was everything he *wasn't* looking for in a woman—refined and elegant and snotty.

But the more time he spent with her, the more that argument rang hollow.

Elizabeth Quinn the multigazillionaire heiress might be cool and distant. But Elizabeth Quinn the woman was like these waters, with hundreds of tantalizing inlets and shoreline he hadn't even begun to explore.

Not that he planned to start. He was a simple man who liked the women in his life to be as easy and uncomplicated as he considered himself.

He cleared sudden roughness out of his throat and quickly engaged the automatic pilot. "There. Now she'll just follow the chart I've set for a minute, and you can show me the sign for whale."

He had to admit he found her sudden blush dangerously

appealing. So he wasn't the only one affected by their nearness. Was it his imagination or did her breathing speed up a notch when he brushed against her? If he gave in to impulse and kissed her, would she push him away or pull him closer as she had in the bank vault?

Damn. He had to stop thinking about that. He yanked his mind away and practiced the signs she showed him a few times to make sure he had them right, then repeated them to Alex, touching the binoculars that hadn't left the boy's neck.

While Alex applied himself diligently to this important task, Beau turned back to Elizabeth. "Do you want me to take over again?"

"Not unless you want to. I'm enjoying it."

"With a great deep-water dock like you've got at your place, you ought to get a boat of your own."

"Oh, I couldn't!"

"Why not? You're loaded. You can probably afford the best."

It probably wasn't too tactful to mention her fortune but she didn't look offended. "Oh, no. I couldn't," she said again. "I'd be too nervous to…to pilot my own boat."

"There's nothing to it once you get the hang of it. It's all a matter of putting in the time to learn. You can practice on the *Mari* any time you want until you feel comfortable enough for your own cruiser."

Now why the hell would he make an offer like that? He needed to stay away from the woman, not make up flimsy excuses for them to spend more time together.

Still, he was glad he had when she gave him another of those stunning smiles. "Thank you. I'll…think about it. It's a very sweet offer."

He wanted to warn her again that he was not sweet. He was rude and abrupt and surly. Everybody said so.

Even as a kid, he'd been a rotten little cuss who took

every chance he could to break all the rules and restrictions his grandmother could think up for him. He hated living in that damn museum, isolated from other boys his age, head-butting constantly against Marie's unrealistic expectations for her only grandson.

The only time he'd been free—the only time he had escaped the weight of his grandmother's cold disapproval—had been fixing up his dead grandfather's battered old woodside yacht and then sailing out on the freshwater lake near his grandmother's house.

Maybe that's why he still loved the water so much. It reminded him of another lifetime ago, when he'd been young and wild and carefree.

Before he managed to unravel the tangle of lies and half-truths Marie had fed him all his life. He'd been sixteen before he learned the bitter truth about his parents, the scandal his grandmother had carefully hidden from everyone.

When his safe but stifling world was blown apart.

He grimaced, thinking of those grim days after he learned how his parents had died. If that lake hadn't been land-locked, he would have climbed into that old yacht and sailed out to sea and never looked back. Instead, he'd turned so wild that Marie had finally, out of desperation, sent him to a military academy to finish his last two years of high school.

As long as he was away from her and Big Piney, he didn't care where he was.

He was wrenched out of the grim memories when Alex ran to Elizabeth and tugged on her windbreaker. "What do you see?" She signed and spoke at the same time for his benefit. Beau picked out the sign for whales in Alex's excited answer but that was about it.

He glanced to where Alex pointed. Sure enough, a small pod of killer whales, three adults and one juvenile, was swimming about five hundred yards to starboard.

"Why don't you let me take her now while you watch the orcas. I'll move a little closer for a better view."

Beau brought the *Mari* two hundred yards from the pod— the protective distance required by law—and cut her engines, then led them to the flybridge, for a better view.

The whales seemed to enjoy the company and weren't in any hurry to move away. For a good ten minutes they stayed close, splashing their fins and leaping out of the water in pirouettes a ballet troupe would envy.

He stood near the aft railing keeping a protective eye on Alex while they watched the whales.

After a few moments Elizabeth sighed. "They're... magnificent! I don't have words."

It took everything in him not to reach for her, to kiss that bright, elated face.

"Yeah, they make me pretty speechless, too," he said gruffly and turned back to the whales.

At last the pod moved away, diving below the surface as they raced each other through the strait. Alex didn't tear his gaze off the whales as they swam out of sight, shoving his binoculars tightly to his eyes so he could catch every last glimpse, but Elizabeth turned to Beau, her own eyes shining with excitement.

"Oh, Beau. That was incredible. Thank you so much for showing us!"

He couldn't help himself. A man could only be so strong. He had to kiss her.

Don't be an idiot, Riley. The thought registered briefly, like a kingfisher touching water just long enough to snap up a meal, but he ignored it and touched his mouth to hers.

She froze, eyes wide, then she sighed and her lashes fluttered down. He would have stopped right then—what was a friendly kiss between shipmates, after all?—but she leaned into him, her hands climbing up to tuck against his jacket, and he deepened the kiss.

She tasted of mint and smelled of peach and she had the most incredible way of sighing against his mouth.

He was *such* a goner.

The kiss probably didn't last longer than thirty seconds. He would have gone on kissing her forever, but reason intruded. They were adrift on open water with a five-year-old boy on board. He had absolutely no business stealing a kiss under any circumstances but especially not under these.

When he pulled away, she gazed at him in stunned disbelief, then cast a quick look to Alex. Beau followed her gaze and saw to his vast relief that the kid wasn't paying them any mind at all, still enthralled by the whales, now only black-and-white specks against the horizon.

Elizabeth didn't say anything, just continued watching him out of wide blue eyes, but Beau would be damned before he apologized. He wasn't sorry he'd kissed her, except it would be that much harder to keep his distance if he couldn't close his eyes without remembering the taste of her.

"We should be reaching Port Ludlow within the hour."

She nodded, her color high. "Okay."

He'd be *damned* before he apologized.

The *Mari* roared to life with his vicious twist of the control and cut powerfully through the waves once more.

They stayed on the flybridge while Beau guided the cruiser with the second control station up top, through places whose names he tersely related—Skunk Bay, Foulweather Bluff, Hood Canal.

Elizabeth was glad they were outside instead of in the close confines of the cabin. With Alex tucked against her, she turned her face to the sunshine and the cool, wet wind as she tried to make sense of that stunning kiss.

It would be so easy—so temptingly easy—to surrender to the hot current of need pulsing through her. Beau was a powerfully attractive man who by all indications was as drawn to her as she was to him.

They were two unattached adults—at least she assumed he was unattached. Terrible thought. She suddenly couldn't bear the idea of him with another woman, kissing someone else, tasting her skin, holding her in those strong hands.

He couldn't be, she assured herself. Beau would never have kissed her with such intensity if he was involved with someone else.

So they were both unattached. Why couldn't they engage in a purely physical relationship? Tangled sheets and sweat-soaked bodies might be just what she needed.

Her stomach fluttered at even considering the idea of making love with him. No. She couldn't afford to be that crazy, that irresponsible with her heart. She was already half in love with him, far too vulnerable to protect herself from slipping all the way there if they made love.

She couldn't fall in love with him. She *couldn't*. It would be nothing short of disastrous when she knew with bitter certainty that all she would get out of an affair with a man like Beau Riley would be a broken heart. How could it be otherwise? Even though he might desire her physically, he could never possibly return her feelings.

She had spent her entire pathetic life offering her heart to men who didn't want it, first her father, then Stephen, both of whom had been unable to find anything in her worth loving. She didn't know if she could survive such ravaging pain again.

Besides that, the timing couldn't be worse. She had to focus on finding Tina's killer, and beyond that Alex needed her full attention right now. He had lost his mother only a few short weeks ago and would need nurturing and stability for a long time.

She sighed and leaned against the metal railing. She wouldn't have thought he could hear the small sound over the thrum of the motors, but Beau glanced over at her, his expression remote.

"There's Ludlow. You think that will suit you for lunch?"

She hated the cool distance in his voice, even though she knew it was far better for him to freeze her out than to offer her more of that beguiling heat. When she answered, she tried to match his cool tone, though her vocal cords felt tight and achy. "Yes. I believe so."

"Good. Would you tell Alex I have to moor to the buoy and then he can help me row the dinghy to shore?"

She translated the message to Alex, who was thrilled to have another task. She had to admit she found it a little surprising that Beau had such dead-on instincts with Alex. He treated him just like any other child, giving him jobs and responsibilities.

Some people assumed Alex's hearing impairment made him somehow incapable of anything challenging. She found that about as frustrating as the people who seemed to think he should be able to hear them if they only yelled a little louder.

She thought of Beau taking the time to buy ASL tutorials, of him trying so earnestly to communicate with Alex. Not many men she knew would have gone to so much trouble for a child they knew on only a casual basis. It would be far too easy to develop feelings for a man like that.

If it wasn't too late.

She watched while Beau dropped anchor and moored to the buoy a few hundred yards offshore. He lowered the dinghy into the water, then helped them in, along with the basket Luisa had fixed.

When they were settled, he handed her a long, rectangular package wrapped in black plastic but didn't offer any explanation. He climbed in after them, showed Alex how to wield the second set of oars, then started rowing the hundred yards or so to shore, muscles rippling beneath the knit shirt he wore.

She tried fiercely not to gawk, focusing on the seagulls wheeling and diving overhead and on Alex manfully attempting to help propel the dinghy through the water with both hands clenched together on one oar.

She was tempted to help him, then remembered what she'd been thinking earlier. She needed to let him try for himself.

Still, she didn't comment when Alex stopped rowing after a few moments, panting hard.

What's in the bag? Alex signed.

She related the question to Beau, who shed his prickly hide long enough to give the boy a grin. "A secret. I'm not telling."

Pirate treasure? Alex asked.

Beau smiled again when she related the question. "Something like that. Tell him if he wants to find out, he'll have to row. I need his muscle—I'm too weak to get us there by myself."

Those muscles of his would probably row them clear to Vancouver if he wanted, she thought, then cursed herself for staring again, and relayed the message to Alex.

Chapter 10

Elizabeth hadn't been to Port Ludlow before but she quickly fell in love with the picturesque area, enchanted by its neat, orderly houses and unspoiled views.

When they landed the dinghy, Beau and his little shadow spread a blanket on the beach and they quickly ate the lunch Luisa had fixed. Alex ate everything Beau did—though in much smaller quantities. Beau obviously enjoyed Luisa's cooking. He had two helpings of her crispy-fried chicken and a second slice of chocolate cake.

After they finished and packed what little food remained back in the basket, Beau retrieved the mysterious package he had handed her earlier.

"Are you ready to see what's inside?"

She translated for him, and both of them smiled as Alex nodded so vigorously his hat flopped off.

Beau stuck it back on again and then made a big show of setting the package on the blanket and preparing to un-wrap it.

She had to admit she was as curious as Alex. She leaned forward as he pulled down the last package, then laughed at Alex's indrawn breath of excitement.

Kite! Kite. Alex signed.

"Show me that one again," Beau said.

Alex demonstrated, making an ASL *K* with his fingers then wiggling them upward like a kite dancing on the wind.

Beau tried it, then grinned at Alex's nod of approval. The two of them bent their heads back to the colorful nylon kite in the shape of a fish.

Elizabeth sat back, content to watch them. She wanted to treasure every last moment of this day in her memory, collect it like a beachcomber after water-smoothed driftwood.

She wanted to stay forever, even as part of her wanted to leave immediately so she didn't have to endure any more of the sweet torture, watching Alex lap up Beau's attention like Maddie at her water dish after a hard run.

Okay, Beau signed. *Ready.*

"Did I do that right?" he asked her.

She nodded. "Perfect."

For the next half hour the two of them raced up and down the beach with the kite dancing in the cool October breeze. After a while Beau turned control of the kite over to Alex and flopped down beside her.

"It's hard work chasing that kid up and down the beach," he said after taking a long swig from his water bottle.

She was intensely conscious of his long length stretched out beside her, the hard muscles relaxed but ready, the lock of dark hair flipping across his forehead.

"He does have a lot of energy," she agreed. "You've been wonderful with him, Beau. Thank you for being willing to play with him."

"It hasn't been a hardship. He's a great kid."

They drifted into a not-uncomfortable silence, accompanied by the gulls and the waves licking the sand and by Alex's giggling efforts to hold the kite against the wind.

"Who's Mari?" The question she'd been wondering all day slipped out of her subconscious before she had time to consider the wisdom of asking it.

To her chagrin, he froze and she saw raw pain flicker through his green eyes.

"I'm sorry, Beau," she said quickly. "Forget I asked. It's…none of my business."

He was quiet for a long time, until she began to wish for a nice strong undertow to carry her out to sea. She was so stupid. Stupid and jealous over someone she had no right to even care about.

When he finally spoke, his voice was low. "Mari was short for Marisa. She was Grace's daughter."

Elizabeth gazed at him, stunned. "Grace Dugan?"

He nodded and she sat back, trying to process the information. Grace had another child. She had never once mentioned her. Although Elizabeth did remember seeing a picture of a dark-eyed girl hanging in the Dugan home, she had somehow always assumed she was a sister or niece of Grace's. But a daughter?

"Was she…yours?" she couldn't resist asking.

He stared at her. "No! Of course not!"

He sounded so astonished by the very idea that she had no doubt whatsoever he was telling the truth. "She wasn't mine biologically, anyway," he continued in a milder voice. "But she might as well have been. We were pretty close."

A dozen questions raced through her mind, but she was afraid to ask any of them.

"She was the funniest little kid," Beau finally continued. "She was curious about everything and had this little brain that I swear went a million miles an hour. She loved the water, and the three of us used to take my old cruiser out just about every weekend to explore the islands around here. Mari always appointed herself first mate.''

Any other person might have missed the low undercurrent of grief in his voice. But she was used to watching for shades and nuances of speech, for body language that often conveyed more meaning than the words people said. Beau's tone of voice was casual enough but his shoulders had tightened and his face had a distant look to it.

Her throat swelled with empathy, and she wanted to tell him to stop, that he didn't need to go on. She started to open her mouth to say just that, then she closed it again, sensing perhaps he needed to talk about Grace Dugan's child whom he had loved enough to name his boat after.

They sat in silence for several moments while the waves licked at the shore and the afternoon sunlight glistened on the water, creating a vast blue blanket of diamonds.

Finally she drew up her courage and asked, although her heart was already breaking for both him and for Grace at what she knew his answer would be. ''What…what happened?''

He gazed at Whidbey Island in the distance, his features stony and his voice flat, emotionless. ''She was killed three years ago when she was only eleven. Drive-by shooting.''

She had expected something grim but not that horrible. She wanted to rub her hand across the twinge in her chest, but she knew it wouldn't take away the heartache.

Grace had never told her. She imagined it wasn't one of those things that was easy to bring up in their casual conversation, but she wished she had known.

And Beau. As a cop, how he must have suffered to lose someone he loved in one of the very acts of violence he fought against.

As usual, she couldn't find any words of comfort—were there any?—so she did the only thing she could think of.

She reached across the space of blanket between them and covered his fingers with hers.

A look of surprise flickered across his strong features, then a tiny smile lifted the corners of his mouth. He turned his hand over and clasped hers and they sat that way for a long time, their fingers entwined while the gulls cried out overhead and the rainbow-colored fish kite dipped and swayed in the wind.

Funny thing about some women. They were like barnacles—once one of them managed to wrap her sneaky way around a man's softer side, he had a devil of a time shaking her off.

Elizabeth probably wouldn't appreciate being compared to a barnacle, but Beau had a feeling when this case was over he'd have to dry dock his heart for a while just to pry her loose.

He did his best to restore a nice safe emotional distance between him and Elizabeth through the rest of their little outing. He made jokes and practiced sign language with Alex and taught her more about piloting a large motorcraft.

Through it all, he fought like hell to pretend he didn't notice the low thrum of desire pulsing through him.

He did his best to ignore it. But every once in a while an errant sea breeze would pick up the scent of peaches and carry it over to tease and tantalize him, and his mouth would begin to water.

He could handle even that, but this new emotional tug between them was far more insidious. He should never have told her about Mari. The soft sympathy in those blue eyes had just about undone him. When she had reached out to do something as mundane as simply holding his hand, he'd been stunned into speechlessness.

Thick emotion flowed through him like warm, sticky

syrup, and he couldn't remember the last time he'd been so touched.

They sat there for a while, hands entwined, until Alex tripped over a rock and let go of the kite and Beau had to jump up to retrieve the string.

They stayed on the beach flying the kite for an hour or so until Alex grew bored. He should have loaded them back onto the *Mari* and headed back to Seattle but he had to admit he was loath for the day to end. He suggested a hike, and Elizabeth was so enthusiastic about the idea he wondered if she might also want to stretch out their time together.

He took them up one of the twisting paths through thick evergreen forests. While they walked, with Alex racing a few yards ahead of their more sedate pace, he figured he ought to at least bring up the reason he'd invited her along.

"Do you want to talk about the party tomorrow and the questions you plan to ask Andrew?"

She grimaced. "Not really. But I suppose we'd better."

"The way I see it, all we're looking to do is verify he wrote the letter and gauge his reaction to being confronted with it. If he was involved in killing her, he's obviously not going to come right out and admit anything. But he might reveal something that could be helpful."

He plucked a pinecone from an overhanging branch and twirled it with his fingers while he talked. "Remember to let him do the talking. Just pause a lot, let him fill in the silence. It all comes down to listening to him. You're good at that."

He didn't understand the sidelong look she sent him or the glint of humor in her eyes.

"I'll do my best," she promised.

"You'll be fine. If nothing comes of it, we can go at him another way after the prosecutors get a conviction on the Benelli case."

"Is it a big case?"

He thought of little Laura Benelli and how her photograph still haunted his dreams. "Big enough. A little girl was tortured and murdered. By her sick bastard of a father, no less."

She took a quick indrawn breath, and he regretted telling her that. Ugly things certainly happened in her world of upscale shops and black-tie parties. The difference—one he knew entirely too well—was that money could make even the ugliest of secrets disappear.

He crushed the scales on the pinecone. "Our case is weak by evidentiary standards but I know he did it. I can't take the risk of screwing the trial up until he's convicted."

"Beau, I understand. You don't have to explain."

If Andrew Sheffield had been a construction worker or a bus driver instead of a wealthy, well-respected justice, he probably would have been down at the station house answering questions right now. The thought didn't sit well with his democratic principles.

"I've got a friend who's a private investigator. He's got all kinds of cool little gadgets. I'll see if he can set me up with a hidden microphone and a receiver so I can listen in on your chat with Andrew."

"Do you really think that's…necessary?"

"Maybe not. But in this case four ears might be better than two. I might pick out something in the conversation you missed."

"That shouldn't be too difficult," she muttered.

"Why not?"

But she had already hurried away from him to keep Alex from wandering too far ahead on his own.

They hiked for an hour, until they were all hot and tired. But soon he knew he couldn't delay their return any longer if he wanted to get them home at a decent time. These were dangerous waters to navigate in the dark, with plenty of floating logs and other debris that could wreak havoc with an unsuspecting watercraft.

It was late afternoon by the time they hiked back down to the beach. This time he used the outboard motor on the dinghy and they boarded the *Mari* quickly.

Once on the cruiser again, Alex had at first been full of chatter, signing like crazy for the first hour about everything they'd done that day. As Beau cut back up Admiralty Inlet, he noticed Alex's eyelids gradually starting to droop. A few moments later the kid was down for the count, curled up on one of the deck cushions in the pilothouse.

"I think he'd probably be more comfortable down on one of the beds. Why don't you take over at the helm for a minute, and I'll carry him down to one of the staterooms?"

When he returned, Elizabeth seemed more quiet than usual. Beau gazed out at the dying light of the sun painting the water a pale lavender and wished he could figure out what was running around that brain of hers as she watched the *Mari* cut through the water.

He had always considered himself fairly good at reading people. In his line of work it was a useful skill to cultivate, just as important as working a crime scene or practicing at the firing range.

But somehow Elizabeth managed to slip under his radar and confound all his best efforts to figure her out. One minute she was soft and compassionate, sweetly shy. The next she retreated into that cool politeness he found so damn frustrating.

He wanted to pierce that chilly reserve of hers into a thousand icy pieces. Somehow he managed to ignore the impulse until they passed Port Madison and headed south toward Harbor View.

"Why didn't your father take you out on the water with him?"

She blinked at the blunt question that had been teasing at

him all day. She loved being out on the water—any idiot could see that. She glowed out here from more than just a sunburned nose. So what the hell kind of father deprived his only child of that kind of joy?

Still, he was sorry he asked when her features froze into tight lines.

"My father and I weren't very close. He was a very… exacting man." She paused for several moments then she gave a smile that didn't quite make it to her eyes. "I didn't…measure up in many ways, I suppose you could say. I was a grave disappointment to him because I wasn't a son and because of…because of other things."

"And your mother?"

"I never knew her. She had a difficult delivery with me. There were problems and she died a few weeks after I was born from an infection she contracted." She was silent, her gaze on the city lights of Bainbridge on one side and Seattle on the other.

"I used to imagine perhaps that was the reason for the…distance between my father and me. Maybe he was so heartbroken at my mother's death that he couldn't bear the reminder of her."

Her laugh sounded raw. "That was a young girl's foolishness, of course. The truth was far less romantic, I'm afraid. My father simply had little time for a daughter he…he didn't understand and didn't like very much."

So they had that much in common, at least. Throughout most of his life, his only family had been a coldhearted woman obsessed with false dignity and maintaining her precarious social position.

For one crazy moment he was tempted to tell her about Marie but he yanked in the impulse before it could get out of control. "I'm sorry. Old family scars never quite heal, do they?"

They were both silent for a moment, with only the growling engines.

"My turn to ask you a question," she asked. "What brought you to the Northwest?"

He raised an eyebrow. "How do you know I'm not a born-and-bred Seattle-ite?"

She smiled a little and he was relieved to see her expression lose some of that haunting sadness. "Your accent gives you away. Georgia, right?"

"Nobody figures that out! How did you know?"

"It's hardly noticeable. I just…listen closely when people speak."

"I'm from a town about a hundred miles from Atlanta." Big Piney was large in nothing but its name. Everything else—from the downtown business district to the collective mind of its snobby society—had been decidedly small.

"That's a long way from Seattle."

"I was stationed here in the Navy for a couple years and fell in love with the area. The water and the trees and the mountains. I loved all of it. So when my tour ended, I just stayed."

"Do you miss Georgia?"

"Not really. Every once in a while I get a hankering for a good pecan pie but that's about it."

He had no family to go back to. Any chance he might have had to mend fences with his grandmother—if he had ever had any desire to do so—had ended with her death five years earlier.

"And you've been with the police department ever since you left the Navy?"

"Yep."

"You're a good cop, from what Grace tells me."

"Grace is a little biased. We've known each other since the Academy. When we worked together on the job, she

Play the
Lucky
Hea

and get...
2 FREE BOO
and a **FREE MYST**

yes! YOURS

I have scratched off th
Please send me my *2 FREE*
FREE Mystery GIFT. I underst
under no obligation to purchase
explained on the back of this card

345 SDL DUZX

FIRST NAME	LA

ADDRESS

APT.#	CITY

STATE/PROV.	ZIP/POSTAL

Twenty-one gets you
2 FREE BOOKS
and a *FREE MYSTERY GIFT!*

Twenty gets y
2 FREE BOO

Offer limited to one per household and n
subscribers. All orders subject to approva

▼ **DETACH AND MAIL CARD TODAY!** ▼

Silhouette®
Where love comes alive™

Visit us online at
www.eHarlequin.com

BUSINESS REPLY MAIL

FIRST-CLASS MAIL   PERMIT NO. 717-003   BUFFALO, NY

POSTAGE WILL BE PAID BY ADDRESSEE

SILHOUETTE READER SERVICE
3010 WALDEN AVE
PO BOX 1867
BUFFALO NY 14240-9952

NO POSTAGE
NECESSARY
IF MAILED
IN THE
UNITED STATES

used to finish my sentences for me half the time. Drove me nuts at the time but I kind of miss it now.''

''Everyone should have a friend like that. Someone who knows all about you and…loves you anyway.''

She was talking about Tina, he realized, and his heart squeezed with sympathy. What if he'd lost Gracie?

He didn't like thinking about how she had considered killing herself during those dark months after Marisa died. She had never told him but Dugan had.

He would have been devastated to lose her, and it would have been so much worse if she died amid a tangle of unanswered questions.

He had to help Elizabeth. Somehow in the last week, investigating the death of Tina Hidalgo had become far more than a favor to Grace. It was important to Elizabeth so it was important to him.

Now there was a scary thought. When did her happiness become such a blasted matter of concern?

They were approaching Harbor View, he saw by the landmarks. ''Do you want to try docking?''

''Oh, no. I couldn't!''

''That's what you said about navigating her and you did great. Come on. I'll walk you through it.''

How did she still manage to smell so heavenly after all day on the water? he wondered. He wanted to stand here all night and just sniff her hair.

Hell, if he were honest with himself, what he really wanted to do was take over the controls and head out to open water and just cruise with her for the next month or two or six.

''That's it. Just a little closer. There. You've got her.'' He jumped to the dock and quickly hitched up the bow and stern lines, then returned to the cabin.

''Perfect landing.'' He grinned at her. ''I couldn't have done a better job myself.''

"Really?" Her face lit up with pleasure, her eyes gleaming in the dusky light. She smelled so heavenly and he realized grimly that he had absolutely no self-control when it came to Elizabeth Quinn.

What else could he do? He kissed her.

She sighed and leaned into him as if she'd been waiting for exactly this moment.

Talk about perfect landings. She fit just right against him, her willowy body soft and supple. The need he'd been suppressing the whole damn day burst free and he growled and licked at the corners of her mouth, needing to taste her, to feast.

She parted her lips on a gasp and he slipped inside, his fingers entwined in her hair.

Ah, heaven.

She moaned and wrapped her arms tightly around his neck, holding him fast.

"You still taste like chocolate cake," he murmured. "Did I mention I'm crazy about chocolate cake?"

Her laugh sounded ragged. "I think I figured that out around the third slice."

He decided he loved her teasing. She unbent enough to do it so rarely it was like that first precious glimpse of sunlight after a long, cold winter.

He returned to kissing her, and she participated with such sweet enthusiasm his body naturally craved more. Without thinking anything beyond getting closer to her, he backed her up a few feet to the cushioned bench along the bulkhead of the pilothouse and lowered her down. There wasn't a whole lot of room here, but then, that wasn't necessarily such a bad thing.

When he slid down to her, she made a soft, erotic sound in her throat and arched against him. Her hands fluttered like hummingbirds at sugar water, dancing to his shoulders, then his back, then his hair, then back to his shoulders.

The sun finally slipped behind the horizon, and the interior of the cabin dimmed but he could still make out the pale, fragile beauty of her features.

He touched her then, just lightly through her cotton shirt on the curve of one small, perfect breast, but she jumped as if he'd shot her with ten thousand watts of power.

Her eyes were wide, unfocused. Unbearably aroused. He'd never affected a woman with such a mild caress. After that, he lost whatever slim hold he might have possessed over his control. He couldn't kiss her enough, couldn't touch her enough.

He wanted to take her right here, while the *Mari* rocked and swayed on the surf and the stars popped into the sky one by one.

Hard, fast, urgent.

Any way he could.

He was trying frantically to remember whether he might by some miracle have any condoms onboard when she drew in a ragged breath and wrenched her mouth away.

"Beau, you've…we've got to stop this."

Maybe in the medicine cabinet in the aft head. There might be one left at the bottom of the box. He nibbled her lip, trying to calculate how long it would take him to go down and check.

"Beau, stop."

This time she pushed against him and her message finally pierced the haze of desire enveloping him. When a woman said stop, he stopped.

But nobody ever said he had to like it.

"Why?"

"A-Alex."

Damn. He hadn't even given the kid a thought. "He's down for the count, and I don't think he'll be coming up anytime soon. Anyway, we can take this down to the other stateroom and lock the door."

"Not just Alex. Other things."

She drew a shaky breath and moved to the other end of the pilothouse, then lifted trembling hands to her ponytail in an effort to restore what his fingers had tugged free.

"What other things? Why are you running away?"

She was silent, her gaze out on the water. "I need… space. I can't think when you're so close."

"What's wrong with not being able to think once in a while? With just letting yourself feel? We both wanted the same thing back there. You can't tell me we didn't."

"I can't," she agreed, her voice small. "Beau, we have this…heat between us. I would be foolish to deny that. But that's all it is. All it could ever be. A…a momentary passion."

He didn't know why her words hurt him and wasn't sure he wanted to dig any deeper into his psyche to find out.

"I don't have flings," she went on. "I just…don't. And there are too many…differences between us for anything else."

"Differences between us? What the hell is that supposed to mean?"

She had restored her hair, and her face in the dim light was once more that cool, distant mask. "We might have heat between us but that's all. We have very little in common. We're two very different people from two very… different worlds."

He listened to her but he could hardly believe what he was hearing. So there it was. Different worlds, hell. That was just a polite way of saying she was an heiress and he was a good-ol'-boy cop with a fifteen-year-old boat and a hick Southern drawl.

With a jerk of his thumb, Beau flicked on the inside lights. He gave her a hard stare across the width of the cabin. How could she stand there looking so soft and innocent and heartbreakingly—deceptively—sweet?

She was just like Marie, ridiculously class conscious in a country where class dividing lines had supposedly been erased hundreds of years ago.

Did he need a stinking tree to fall on his head? How could he have been stupid enough to forget that the woman had ice water flowing through her veins?

Even as he thought it, he knew he couldn't use such a sweeping generality to describe a woman as complicated as Elizabeth. She wasn't cold all the time. What about the kid? With Alex she was loving and gentle. She couldn't be faking that.

So what was the act and what was real?

Or was it just him? Was she just grabbing on to any excuse to push him away?

Whatever the reason, she'd done a good job, striking out the one way that was guaranteed to cool his desire faster than shoving an iceberg down his jeans.

Three times she had bluntly and abruptly rejected him. Not again. He would be damned before he let her play him for the fool once more.

Chapter 11

Hold it together. Just a few moments more.

Elizabeth chanted the mantra to herself as she followed Beau up the stairs, Alex in his arms. Her voice sounded amazingly cool as she directed him to Alex's room, then slipped the half-asleep little boy out of his sandy clothes and into clean pajamas.

Bath, Alex signed, his eye drooping drowsily.

Not tonight, she signed back. *You're too tired. You can bathe in the morning.*

He nodded and offered them a sleepy smile, then gave up the battle to stay awake the moment he hit the pillow.

They stood by the bedside together for a few seconds, tension thick and heavy between them, then Elizabeth led the way out of the room.

Just a few more moments. Then he would leave and she could examine her battered emotions in solitude.

"I...thank you for a wonderful day, Beau. It was...almost perfect. I'm only sorry for the way things ended."

He would never know how very sorry she was that she had stopped. She had never wanted anything in her life more than she had wanted to take him up on his offer and go below deck to the other stateroom, lock the door and lose herself in his arms.

Lose herself was exactly the right choice of words, and there was the problem. She couldn't afford to make love with Beau Riley. She *couldn't*.

"It's over," he muttered. "Let's just forget it. Believe me, it won't happen again."

She thought of the wonderful day they had shared, and her heart broke a little at the realization that it was a once-in-a-lifetime experience, never to be repeated.

Just as well. As she'd tried to explain to him in her usual clumsy fashion, they came from different worlds. He was smart and clever, commanding and confident. He made his living with his brain, piecing together clues to solve crimes and catch criminals.

She, on the other hand, was tongue-tied and awkward. Insecure. Stupid.

She had tried to explain it, but she had a feeling her meaning hadn't come across right. He had been offended, although she wasn't exactly sure what she had said that had turned those eyes a storm-tossed green like the Sound on a winter day.

How could she have explained without telling him the truth about her impairment? She couldn't! So far she thought she had done a fair job of concealing it. She would never be exactly glib, but she hadn't made too many horrible gaffes around him.

She had been lucky, she knew. But she couldn't keep it hidden forever. Eventually he would use that clever brain of his to figure out something was wrong with her. Then he would be disgusted. She had to do everything she could to maintain as much distance as possible between them to make certain that didn't happen.

When her emotions were involved, she was far more prone to making mistakes. So all she had to do was keep her emotions detached, to maintain a nice, safe distance between them.

And maybe one day she could sail around the globe by herself, too.

She sighed. "Anyway, thank you for a…a lovely day."

"You're welcome. Tell me again the plan for tomorrow."

She frowned, not sure for a moment what he meant, then it hit her. Andrew's birthday party. How could she have become so wrapped up in her own angst over that shattering kiss that she'd forgotten?

It took her a moment to remember the details. "The party begins at eight. As we said before, it makes more sense for me to use the car service and have the driver pick you up at your house in town."

His mouth tightened as if the suggestion annoyed him, then he nodded. "Fine. Give me a piece of paper and I'll write down the directions to my house."

She quickly found one in a drawer near the front door, and he wrote in a slashing, bold hand. She found herself watching those strong fingers move across the paper, thinking about them stroking with such tantalizing heat across her skin. Her nipples budded to life at the memory, at the yearning to feel not only his fingers but his mouth, as well.

He glanced up and caught her watching his hands. Color soaked her skin. Oh, she hoped her expression didn't reveal the racy things she had been thinking.

Beau cleared his throat. "Come early enough that we can test out the electronics."

"All right," she murmured. "We'll see you about quarter after seven, then."

She walked him to the back door, then stood on the patio and watched him ready the *Mari* for departure.

The clouds that had threatened since the sunset finally delivered a soft, hesitant rain. She stood with the mist pearling against her face and watched him cast off from the dock and enter the channel.

It took her several moments to realize the heavy ache in her chest was painfully similar to the sense of forlorn abandonment that used to lodge there every time she watched her father head out to sea.

"Yes, Mr. Parker. This is the correct neighborhood. I have the address right here."

Despite the nerves waltzing through her the next evening, Elizabeth summoned a smile for the man in the front seat of the limousine.

Anthony Parker was one of her favorite drivers at the car service she used. In his early sixties with salt-and-pepper hair, a thick chest and an eternally cheerful attitude, Tony never failed to charm a smile out of her, no matter how badly her day was going.

"You said 3560 was the address, right?"

"Yes. That's what Detective Riley said."

"That should be right at the end of this street, then."

Elizabeth looked out the window, trying to focus on something besides her stomach twirling with nerves. She wouldn't have expected this kind of neighborhood to appeal to a hard-edged detective. She supposed if she had to guess, she would have pictured him living in a bachelor apartment somewhere without much furniture.

This was a family neighborhood of modest, well-kept homes with basketball standards mounted above garage doors and minivans in the driveways.

Tony pulled in front of a house matching the address Beau had given her, and she gazed at the small redbrick dwelling. Black shutters flanked the windows and the branches of a climbing rose, bare now, curved over the door. A thin blanket of leaves from a red maple covered a small circle in the front grass but the rest of the yard seemed immaculate.

The house was charming and warm, far more welcoming than her home, with its imposing iron gates and sophisticated security system.

She drew in a deep breath, wishing she could stay here admiring his house for the rest of the evening. She did *not* want to do this.

"Would you like me to go ring the doorbell?"

She drew a deep breath. "What's the usual protocol for these situations, Mr. Parker? Should I go to the door in person or send you to do my dirty work for me?"

An amused smile creased his dark features. "You do whatever feels right, I guess."

What felt right was for her to ask him to turn around right now and take her home where she was safe. But she didn't suppose that was what the driver meant.

She dithered for another twenty seconds. "I'd better go to the door," she decided. She thought Beau had said something the night before about testing the microphone and receiver before they left, and it would probably be easier to do that inside than in the limousine on the way to the party.

Anthony immediately stepped from the car and spread open a wide black umbrella against the soft rain. She knew it was foolish, even cowardly of her, but she couldn't help being comforted by his presence. She felt as awkward and unsure of herself as a silly teenage girl on her first date.

This wasn't a date, she reminded herself sternly. Beau Riley was escorting her to the party only for moral and investigative support while she talked with Andrew.

Still, wouldn't it be heavenly if she and Beau weren't going to a crowded society party to interrogate a possible suspect? If instead they were going on a real date, somewhere dark and romantic, where they could laugh and kiss and share a meal, then end the evening wrapped in each other's arms?

She blew out her breath, trying to ignore the silly fantasy while Mr. Parker rang the doorbell.

After a few moments Beau yanked it open. He was only half-dressed, which spawned a whole new crop of fantasies, in just black slacks, a white shirt, with a crooked tie and a scowl.

"Sorry you had to walk up in the rain. I would have come out, but I was still trying to fix this damn tie. Help me, here, will you?"

She gazed at him helplessly. She didn't know the first thing about tying a bow tie. How could she? It wasn't exactly a skill she'd ever had reason to learn. Under other circumstances she might have helped with her father occasionally but Jonathan always had an old-fashioned manservant to help him.

"I'm sorry. I don't..."

To her vast relief, Anthony stepped forward. "If you don't mind, sir, I might be able to help."

Beau gave him a distracted look. "Who are you?"

Elizabeth cringed at her poor manners. "I'm sorry. Beau, this is Anthony Parker. He'll be driving us to the..." Her mind went completely blank, a vast vacant field of nothing. How was she supposed to think with Beau standing in front of her, looking gorgeous and wild and grumpy with his dark hair slightly mussed and that crisp white shirt showing every ripple of his hard-muscled chest?

"It's my pleasure to be taking you to your social engagement this evening," Anthony interjected smoothly into the breach. "And if you don't mind my saying, I'm considered quite an expert at the fine art of knotting bowties."

"Fine. Whatever. Just help me here."

Elizabeth watched while Anthony quickly and competently knotted the tie then stepped back to admire his handiwork.

"Thanks," Beau muttered. "I was just about to forget this whole thing and change back into a regular jacket and tie."

He pivoted and disappeared into another room, leaving behind just an enormous tomcat who watched them from the doorway with an unblinking gaze, exactly as if they were two juicy mice.

She never would have figured Beau for a cat person. He struck her as the kind of man who would have a big, athletic dog like Maddie. The cat sauntered over and began to rub against her leg, purring like a freight train. She bent to pet his ginger-colored fur just as Beau returned.

"Gordo, cut it out," he muttered. "He'll get hair all over you."

"He's fine."

"I can't seem to break him of the belief that the whole world exists just to keep him happy."

She gave the cat one last stroke, then straightened and caught her first full glance at Beau in all his finery—black tuxedo jacket on and his hair combed again. "Wow. You look...beautiful."

As soon as the word escaped her mouth, she knew it was the wrong one. Horribly wrong. Mortifyingly wrong. She flinched, but before she could come up with a better one, Beau offered a devastating smile.

"I think that's my line, isn't it? And let me just say, that's one hell of a dress."

Elizabeth felt herself flush pink, more pleased than she should be by the frank approval in his eyes. So her frenzied morning of shopping hadn't been completely in vain. She had never been one to spend hours shopping but she had started at first light, searching every boutique in Seattle until she finally discovered this deceptively simple long black sheath and off-the-shoulder wrap at a tiny boutique near the market. With it she wore only her mother's slim diamond chain and matching earrings.

They stood gazing at each other for a moment, then Beau cleared his throat and held out a diamond stickpin that looked incongruously tiny in his large dark hands. "It's a great dress but I'm not sure where you're going to put this. It's the microphone."

Elizabeth jerked her attention away from the splendor of Beau in evening attire. She needed that reminder of her purpose tonight. This wasn't a date, she reminded herself forcefully. Even if she had spent six hours looking for a dress.

"I'll find a place to pin it," she murmured. There was no way on earth she could let him attach it to her dress— let his fingers graze her skin—without melting all over his hardwood floor.

She took the pin from him, trying to ignore the snap of electricity when their hands touched. The most convenient spot happened to be right at the vee neck of her dress. It looked discreet and elegant, she thought.

"Does that work?"

He nodded. "I'm already wearing the receiver. It's made up of two parts, an ear piece that's invisible unless somebody gets real close and personal and a small credit-card-size control unit in my pocket. I'll go in the other room so we can test it. Just say a few words so I can tell if I need to adjust the volume or anything."

After he walked out of the room, she discovered she had no idea what to say. She thought of a Browning poem she'd read in college, about the gray sea and the long black land and the yellow half-moon large and low. She was afraid she would sound corny if she said it so she settled on the highly unoriginal. "Beau? Can you hear me? Testing. Testing."

He returned to the room. "Sounds good. Make sure you speak in your normal voice, though. Sometimes you get so quiet I can hardly hear you."

That was usually the idea, another bad habit she'd developed in childhood and worked hard to break as an adult. If people couldn't hear her, they couldn't mock her. Simple protective mechanism. The downside was, if people couldn't hear her, she faded to near invisibility.

"I think I'm ready. Shall we hit the road?"

She nodded, and Anthony magically produced a second umbrella and had the deviousness to hand it to Beau. With a sly wink to her that she fervently hoped Beau didn't notice, he walked out into the rainy evening with the other one, arranging things so she and Beau had no choice but to share an umbrella.

As they walked out of his charming little house, she was intensely aware of him. He smelled incredibly sexy, with the evergreen scent of his cologne accented by the clean, honest smell of the rain.

She wanted to close her eyes and freeze everything about this moment, imprint it all into her synapses, but she was afraid she would stumble on the rain-slicked bricks of his sidewalk if she did.

They leaned close, heads together under the umbrella, as they hurried to the limousine. Anthony was waiting with the door open. She glared at him for his dirty trick but he only smiled benignly and helped her slide in. After he closed the door behind Beau and climbed into the driver's seat, he pulled smoothly back onto the road.

For several moments the only sound inside the limousine was the low murmur of strings from the Vivaldi concerto playing through the speakers, the steady swish of the windshield wipers and the tires humming along the wet road.

If she hadn't already been a bundle of nerves, the protracted silence would have done it. All she could think about were those heavenly moments in Beau's arms the evening before. The heat and magic and excitement that still echoed through her whenever she thought of it.

"Would you like something to drink?" she finally managed to squeak out. "I believe there's champagne and a nice wine selection."

"No. Not when I'm on duty."

"How about bottled water or a soda?"

"I'm good. Thanks."

The silence lengthened like twilight shadows and she tried once more. "I hope the evening is not too…unbearable for you."

Beau's shoulders stretched the black silk of his jacket. "I've been on worse assignments, believe me. At least they should have some fancy food tonight. I once spent two weeks in a surveillance van with nothing but convenience store hotdogs and stale corn chips."

She had nothing to say to that—what in her life experience possibly compared to stakeouts?—so she just nodded and fell silent again.

After another awkward pause, he tilted his head and studied her. "You sure you're up to talking to the judge?"

She caught herself before she could chew all her lipstick off again. She knew she had to confront Andrew with that letter, but she was dreading the moment when she actually had to do it.

"I'll speak to him but I don't know…I don't know what we'll find out. I still can't believe Andrew might be capable of killing Tina."

"Right now he's all we've got. We'll shake his tree tonight first and see what else might fall out."

She felt sick just thinking about it. She wanted to find Tina's killer but, oh, she didn't want it to be Andrew.

"I'm going to be sticking close to you throughout the

evening," Beau said after a moment. "You sure you can deal with that?"

She thought it would be both heaven and hell to have him close to her for an entire evening. "Yes. I think so."

"Good. Even if we get separated, I'll still be watching you. You don't have to worry."

She stared at him. "You say that as if I might be in some sort of danger. Surely I'm not."

"We don't know that. Even if he didn't kill her, I doubt Sheffield will be real thrilled when he finds out you know about the kid's paternity."

"He would never hurt me. Never!"

"If he killed your friend—the mother of his son—to keep her mouth shut, you really think he would balk at giving you similar treatment?"

She drew in a sharp breath as the butterflies in her stomach started fluttering harder.

"I don't mean to scare you, but you're going to have to be careful."

"I will be," she murmured. She was always careful, except when it came to green-eyed detectives.

"An alert investigator is always on the lookout for opportunities," he went on. "Find an excuse to pull Sheffield aside and talk to him. I'll be watching, and as soon as I see you leave together I'll try to follow. Remember, all you're going to do is show him the copy of the letter we found and ask him about it. That's it. Don't do anything crazy, okay?"

She nodded, nerves scrambling.

"I won't let anything happen to you, Elizabeth. I may not be much for high-society formal shindigs but I'm a damn good cop. I'll be watching, I promise."

The concern in his eyes warmed her more than she cared to admit, even when it came tempered by a reserve that hadn't been there the day before, after she had pushed him away.

Chapter 12

He had to be out of his ever-loving mind.

At the Sheffield mansion—he couldn't call such a grand, imposing structure anything but that—Beau helped Elizabeth out of the limousine, trying like hell not to goggle at the endless length of sleek, shapely leg revealed by the slit in her dress.

She was beautiful, elegant and cool and sleek, and he felt like a peasant farmer in medieval England somewhere, yanked out of his fields to escort a princess to the ball.

This had to be the most lamebrain thing he'd ever done. He should have ignored his worries over the Benelli case and just hauled the judge to the precinct for questioning. It would have been far easier than this.

He didn't even want to be in the same room with Elizabeth. Not after the night before, not when he still craved her like a kid running after the ice cream truck on a hot summer's day.

Beau wasn't sure exactly what he expected Elizabeth to

accomplish. Even a trained detective probably wouldn't be able to get much useful information out of a suspect in the middle of a dinner party. Besides, even if Sheffield was overcome by some guilt-induced fit and confessed all to her, not a single damn word would hold up in court.

He ought to just call the whole thing off, just tell Elizabeth not to say anything to the judge yet until he had more of a chance to build a case against him.

He started to do just that, but the words died in his throat. This was important to Elizabeth. She deserved to know the truth about Alex's paternity, at least.

Besides, they had made it this far. Might as well play it out. He'd already gone to all the trouble to get dressed in the monkey suit. Might as well escort Princess Elizabeth inside.

The place was bedecked with millions of little lights sparkling throughout the elaborate landscaping and strung along the walkway, and he could hear a string quartet playing somewhere inside, along with tinkling glasses and muted laughter.

He wanted to go inside about as badly as he wanted his eyebrows singed off. But he had to.

Remembering all those blasted etiquette lessons forced on him by Marie when he was too young to object too loudly, he took Elizabeth's hand, intending to tuck it into the crook of his arm. He was surprised to find her fingers ice-cold.

He clasped her hand tightly and took a good, hard look at her fine-boned features under the fairy lights. Her delicate skin looked pale in contrast to her black dress, and her eyes were wide and slightly unfocused.

She looked terrified, suddenly. Scared out of her wits.

"Elizabeth, we don't have to do this. We can leave right now."

She'd pulled most of her hair into an upstyle-type thing, but a few loose strands brushed the diamonds around her neck as she shook her head. "No. I'm okay. I'm not leaving."

What had her so scared? Did she think he wouldn't be able to protect her if Sheffield turned nasty? The thought hurt more than it should. Yeah, she was right, they were from different worlds. But *his* world was tough, mean. Ugly. He'd handled much worse than anything they were likely to encounter at a dinner party.

"I'm ready. Let's go inside," she murmured, pinning a polite smile on those elegant features. She tilted her chin defiantly, exposing that long, slender neck he still ached to kiss, damn his hide.

If she could put on a good show of enjoying herself, he sure as hell could, too. He wrapped his other hand around her fingers resting on his arm and escorted her inside.

The party was in full swing, he noted, and immediately started casing the scene. Men in black tie and women in designer party wear mingled through numerous rooms of the house amid what he was sure were priceless antiques and furniture most people probably couldn't even afford to look at.

Waiters in black bow ties and cummerbunds moved smoothly through the crowd with platters of gleaming champagne flutes and canapés. A towering birthday cake stood on a little table in the corner that looked like a twin to his grandmother's prized Duncan Phyfe.

Several prominent Seattle personalities circulated among the guests. He picked out the mayor, a couple of congressional representatives, a consulate general or two. Quite a guest list.

They had only been in the door for a minute or two when a woman about Elizabeth's age with hennaed hair, a barely there emerald gown and matching gems approached them. Her green-eyed gaze narrowed as she caught sight of them.

"Elizabeth Quinn! The recluse herself. This is certainly a surprise."

And not a pleasant one, Beau thought, if the thinly veiled dislike in the redhead's eyes was anything to go by.

"I phoned a few days ago to RSVP and spoke with Mrs. Wong. I apologize for the...the late notice."

"No doubt it slipped your mind."

Beau formed an instant dislike to the woman for that subtly derisive look in her cat eyes.

"Not at all," Elizabeth said coolly. "I would never forget Andrew's birthday. I simply wasn't sure of my plans for the evening until the last moment."

"Well, how lovely to see you. You must try the champagne. It's guaranteed to loosen the tongue."

Now why would that make Elizabeth flush so pink? he wondered. A strange, powerful undercurrent ebbed and flowed around the two women like the riptides in the Rosario Strait. Like any sane man, it made him want to pack up for higher, safer ground. Before he could lead Elizabeth away, the redhead turned her attention to him.

"And who is your friend?"

"I'm sorry. Beau, this is Leigh Sheffield. Judge Sheffield's daughter. Leigh, this is my very good friend Beau Riley."

To his surprise Elizabeth smiled up at him with more warmth than she had shown him all evening and leaned against his arm as if they'd been longtime lovers, her blue eyes bright. Ah. So that's the way she wanted to play it. He could do lovesick.

Just as long as he wasn't tempted to forget he was only pretending.

He easily manufactured a private smile for Elizabeth before he turned to the other woman.

"Pleased to meet you," he lied smoothly. "You and your father have a beautiful home."

She touched his arm with long red-tipped nails. "Thank you. I'd be thrilled to death to give you a private tour. Just grab me anytime tonight and I'll be happy to show you all kinds of secret little nooks and crannies."

I'll just bet you will, Beau thought. Under other circumstances, he might have been flattered by the blatant invitation in her eyes—she was a beautiful woman, after all, and he was, well, a man. But he had a funny feeling she wouldn't have given him a second glance if he had come to the party with anyone else.

Before he could respond, one of the servers stopped near Leigh and murmured something to her about a problem in the kitchen. Annoyance tightened her expression, then Leigh smiled at them. To be precise, she smiled at him. Elizabeth, she ignored.

"Will you excuse me? I've got to go deal with an incompetent caterer. I'm sure I'll run into you later."

Not if he could help it. Beau waited until she'd hurried away, heels clicking on the polished marble floor, before he turned his attention back to Elizabeth.

"You want to tell me about all that animosity?"

Elizabeth blinked and offered up another one of those long pauses of hers. "I don't know what you mean," she finally said.

"You and Ms. Sheffield. It was colder than a meat locker in here."

"You're imagining things, I'm sure. Leigh and I have known each other all our lives."

He noticed her choice of words and had a feeling it was intentional. She didn't say they'd been *friends,* just that they knew each other. He wanted to push her about the relationship but she cut him off before he could.

"There's Andrew," she said quietly, gazing through a doorway into an adjoining room.

The judge stood out from the half dozen people surrounding him, not only because he towered about half a foot higher than everyone else around him but because of his shock of pure-white hair.

He was an imposing figure of a man, tall and commanding. A man Beau had always respected prior to this investigation.

He studied the group around him, picking out a few familiar faces, then his gaze narrowed at the man hovering just outside their circle, watching the room just as alertly as Beau was doing. Something about him—maybe the hard glint in his eyes or the unsmiling mouth—looked out of place among the lighthearted chatter.

"Who's that with him?"

Elizabeth craned her neck. "Oh, that's sweet Mrs. Partridge. Her family owns a dry-cleaning chain based in Tacoma."

"No. The other one. The guy who looks like a hired gun in a rented tux."

Her gaze narrowed as she tried to identify the object of his scrutiny. "That's Andrew's bodyguard, Mikhail something or other. I think he's from one of the Baltic states."

"Why does Sheffield need a bodyguard at a party like this in his own home, with a hand-selected guest list?"

She frowned. "I don't know. Andrew doesn't go anywhere without him, I can tell you that. A year or so ago Andrew received several death threats because of a case he presided over with ties to Asian gangs. I assume Mikhail's presence has something to do with that. He's very loyal and protective of Andrew."

Loyal and protective enough to take care of a nuisance like Tina Hidalgo if she threatened his boss's nice, secure, comfortable life? The man sure looked like trouble on toast.

Beau made a mental note to check into the man's background. It shouldn't be too tough to find out a last name and have Griff run a check through the various criminal databanks available, to see if anything popped up.

He didn't find it so hard to envision Sheffield having someone else do his dirty work. And who better than a bodyguard with hard eyes, who looked like he might be capable of anything?

This wasn't so terrible.

Elizabeth smiled at Barre Wellington and asked another question about the older woman's favorite topic, her small stable of Thoroughbreds.

Barre immediately launched into a soliloquy about her newest purchase, a yearling out of a previous Belmont Stakes winner fated to follow in his sire's grand footsteps.

Elizabeth had always liked Barre, even though she was consumed with her horses to the point of obsession. At one point she thought the still-lovely divorcee and her father might make a match of it, then Jonathan had been diagnosed with lymphoma and his priorities changed.

She pushed away the thought of her father and tuned back in to listen to Barre.

She could do this. She just had to keep in mind that most people at society parties like this one weren't looking for a sparkling conversationalist so much as a listening post. If she could smile and nod and ask a few cogent questions at appropriate moments, she would get along just fine.

Barre was telling her about the struggles she had finding competent trainers when Elizabeth spotted Andrew out of her peripheral vision, heading directly toward them.

She wasn't ready to talk to him yet. Panic shot through her like the rich scotch he liked to drink. He reached them and kissed Barre on the cheek. "Two of the loveliest ladies here, and I have them all to myself."

Barre gave her low, musical laugh. "I was just talking

dear Elizabeth's ear off about my newest prize. You must come to the stable and see him soon."

"I'll do that," he murmured.

"Will you excuse me?" Barre said. "I haven't seen Liza Ellison in ages. I simply must speak to her."

"Of course," Andrew said, then turned to her, pleasure in his gray eyes.

"Elizabeth, my dear. What a wonderful surprise to see you. I wasn't expecting you! I know how little you enjoy these things."

He smiled at her with a genuine warmth that scorched her conscience. How could she do this? Smile and chat and act as if she didn't know about Alex? About Andrew and Tina?

But she had to. This wasn't the right time or place to bring it all up. She forced herself to lean on tiptoes and kissed his cheek, then looked away quickly before she could search his features for some resemblance to Tina's son. "Happy birthday," she murmured.

Andrew made a face. "I tried to tell Leigh I wasn't particularly interested in celebrating six and a half decades but she insisted. I'm very much afraid my daughter is always looking for any excuse to throw a party."

"Leigh does enjoy entertaining, doesn't she?"

"Yes, more's the pity. You know I'd rather be out on the yacht than have to make small talk with people I don't know. And speaking of strangers, who is the man I saw you come in with before? The one who's standing over there scowling at us?"

She glanced over at Beau and found him only ten or so feet away with a group of men, one of whom she thought might be a senator. Though he looked to be engrossed in the conversation, he was indeed scowling at them. Probably angry because he didn't have his ear piece in, which was yet another reason she couldn't bring up Tina yet.

''He's my d-date.'' Oh, she hated herself for her inability to utter the lie casually.

''He looks familiar. Would I know him?''

''Yes, I believe so. His name is Beau Riley and he's a detective with the Seattle Police Department. He told me he has testified in your courtroom a few times.''

''Oh, of course, of course. I should have recognized him immediately.'' Andrew paused and gave her his paternal, standing-in-for-your-father look, and she braced herself for the inquisition. Jonathan wouldn't have even noticed any man she dated—except for Stephen, his hand-picked choice—but Andrew had always been a different story.

''And how did the two of you meet?''

She scrambled to come up with an appropriate lie but the truth seemed much easier. ''We have mutual friends. Jack and Grace Dugan.''

''Oh, yes. Lovely people. Tell me, have you been seeing this Detective Riley long?''

Her palms began to sweat at having to expand on her dishonesty. ''A few weeks.''

She did *not* want to get into this with him so she blurted out the speech she'd been rehearsing all afternoon. ''Andrew, if it's possible, I'd like to talk to you before the evening is over. Privately, please.''

He looked surprised. ''Of course, Elizabeth. You know I'll always have time for one of my favorite people.''

She managed to summon a smile and was deeply grateful when someone else demanded his attention. While he was occupied speaking with someone else, she slipped away and had to fight hard against the sudden harsh sting of tears.

Oh, she couldn't bear this. Why did Andrew have to be involved in this whole ugly mess? He had always been such a steady source of love and support in her life, and the prospect of losing that close relationship left her aching, bereft.

All the people she loved were slipping away from her, one by one. First Tina, now Andrew. Who was next?

It was all too much for her suddenly. The cloying, expensive perfumes and press of bodies sent greasy nausea spinning through her. She needed air, she thought frantically.

She pushed through the French doors leading to the expansive terrace that overlooked Lake Washington. The night air was cool, moist, and she breathed it deeply into her lungs, one hand pressed to her stomach. She leaned a hip against the railing and gazed at a few flickering, boat running lights out on the water.

The sight inevitably reminded her of the day before, of the purgatory and the paradise of spending an entire day with Beau, on his boat, by his side.

In his arms.

She pressed her hand harder to her stomach, wishing she could rub away the vast, empty ache there.

A few seconds later the French doors flung open and Beau stalked out onto the terrace. "There you are. Don't run away like that!"

"I'm s-sorry. I just needed air."

"I was having trouble with the receiver and didn't catch most of it. Next thing I knew, you disappeared. What did the bastard say to you?"

"He didn't say anything. Not about Tina, anyway. I didn't show him the letter yet. We're meeting later in…private."

"Then why are you so upset?"

She sighed. She would sound maudlin and melodramatic if she told him she felt as if she were about to lose one of her few close friends in the world.

"I don't want to do this," she finally said.

"You don't have to. This was a crazy idea, anyway. I told you I'll go at him another way."

"No. I might not *want* to talk to him about Tina but I need to. I...have to know."

He studied her for a moment, then he nodded and dropped the subject. They stayed out on the terrace in silence with the cool, wet breeze a soft caress and the sweet, pure notes of the string quartet murmuring through the lovely evening.

Gradually her shoulders began to relax and she closed her eyes, savoring the music and the night, enjoying herself for the first time all evening, probably because she was out here alone with Beau.

"You're not big on parties, are you?" he said.

She jerked her eyes open and gazed at him. Was she that pitifully obvious?

"No," she finally admitted. "I'm not really...comfortable with big crowds."

"So it wasn't personal?"

"What?"

He sent her a sidelong look. "That first time. At Gracie's benefit thingie. You walking away from me before I could even use the line I'd just spent a half hour polishing."

She hitched in a breath, wishing she could lie and agree with him. It would be so much easier than the truth. But it would also be cowardly.

"I wish I could say it wasn't personal but...it was."

In the twinkling lights, she could see a muscle jump in his jaw. "I see," he said after a pause. "That's sort of what I figured."

She wanted desperately to change the subject, but she knew she had to explain. She couldn't leave things unsettled between them. "Beau, crowds make me nervous." She took a deep breath. "You...terrify me."

He looked startled. "Why? What did I ever do to you?"

He deserved the truth about this, at least. "It's nothing you did. It's just me. You make me uncomfortable. I'm not very good at the whole man-woman thing. To be honest,

I'm attracted to you and I don't know how to handle all these feelings you...you arouse in me.''

She blushed, mortified both at her frankness and at her unintentional word choice. No, it wasn't the wrong word, she admitted. It was exactly the right one—he aroused her in every possible way.

She refused to look at him—how could she?—but even so, she couldn't miss the sudden thick tension radiating from him in hot, tight waves.

Had her words done that? Was he angry? She forced herself to finish this and then she prayed he would let the matter drop.

"You make me feel out of control and I...don't like it very much," she admitted in a small voice. "Control is important to me. I don't quite know how to respond when I feel it...slipping away."

"So you run."

She winced. Bluntly put but accurate. "Yes. Sometimes. So you see, it is about you but it's also about...me. I'm s-sorry if I hurt you."

She waited for his reply, but when nothing was forthcoming, she finally risked looking at him. He was watching her out of green eyes that seemed brighter, even more intense than usual, in the subtle lights.

The breath caught in her throat at the expression in them—desire and need and what she thought might even be tenderness.

"Beau," she whispered, not sure what else she wished to say.

His smile was soft as he grabbed her hands, holding her in place. "You don't have to be afraid of me, Elizabeth. Ever."

She did. Oh, she did.

Right now, for instance. Now would probably be an excellent time to run. But she could do nothing as he leaned forward, his breath warm and smelling sweetly of chocolate and raspberries. She was frozen into place, anticipation swirling through her.

As if to prove his words, his kiss was almost painfully gentle. His mouth settled over hers with the softest of touches, barely brushing his lips against hers, his arms held her as carefully as a small boy carrying his mother's favorite vase.

Her lashes fluttered down and she settled closer, her hands on the lapel of his jacket. Heaven. Oh, heaven. How could she have known a strong, powerful man like Beau could be so sweet?

He didn't deepen the kiss but kept it slow, easy, until she thought she would weep from the gentleness of it. And then he eased away from her, just enough to give one of those smiles she loved so much.

Her heart pounded as the truth slammed into her, just about knocking her to her knees. She didn't just love Beau Riley's smile. She loved *him.* She was head-over-heels, completely, thoroughly in love with a man she could barely talk to.

She was such an idiot. He would break her heart into a thousand tiny pieces and probably never even realize it.

Before she could say anything—or even put some desperately needed space between them—she heard the click of high heels on terra cotta tile. Over Beau's shoulder she saw Leigh Sheffield approaching, her mouth pursed as if she'd just taken a swallow of something nasty.

Elizabeth stepped away from Beau's arms quickly, steeling herself for another unpleasant encounter, but Leigh surprised her by straightening her expression into a warm smile instead.

For Beau's benefit, she realized suddenly. Leigh would never waste politeness on her. Her eyes widened as she watched the other woman smile up at him like a Siamese cat ready to pounce on a patch of catnip.

This was just like when they were children. Leigh had always been this way—if she wanted something of Elizabeth's as a child, she would find a way to take it for herself. Either she would tell Jonathan in her completely manipulative way how much she admired it—and more often than not he would simply give it to her because Elizabeth had never been able to voice an objection—or else Leigh would simply take whatever caught her fancy.

Whenever Elizabeth learned Leigh and her parents were coming over, she and Tina would go through her room ahead of time, gather up all Elizabeth's favorite things and hide them in Luisa's apartments.

Only this time Leigh wanted something a little larger than a Cabbage Patch doll.

"Sorry to interrupt," she purred to Beau, ignoring Elizabeth as if she were one of those marble statues scattered around the garden. "I just wanted to let everyone who might be out here on the terrace know we're serving dinner now."

"Um, thanks."

Beau's polite smile looked pained around the edges, and Elizabeth had to admit she relished his obvious discomfort at Leigh's flirtatiousness. Most men had a far different reaction to Leigh's sensual beauty. She'd seen her reduce an entire room of professionals to gibbering idiots.

Though Elizabeth had no idea why Beau seemed oblivious to the other woman's allure, she couldn't help but be grateful.

"We'll be right in," he told Leigh, his voice cool, distant.

"You don't want to miss it. The caterer is incompetent at organization but divine in the kitchen. I'm sure a big, strong man like you needs plenty of fuel to keep those muscles running in fine form."

That was a little over the top, even for Leigh. Beau, poor man, was even blushing a little.

Elizabeth decided she'd had enough. She'd come a long way from that little girl silently watching all her best toys disappear.

She tucked her hand into the crook of his elbow. "Yes, darling," she murmured, smiling up at him. "By all means, let's go inside for dinner. We must make certain you can keep your…energy up."

For once her pause was completely intentional. Beau gave her a startled look as if he couldn't quite believe she'd murmured such a double entendre, then with a strangled cough he turned and led her back into the party.

Chapter 13

The opportunity to speak with Andrew came shortly after dessert was removed by the black-clad army of waiters Leigh had hired. The guests began to mill about again, drinks in hand. She and Beau had been cornered by Colby Carr, a yacht-mad high-tech guru who had sailed with both her father and Andrew.

He and Beau were comparing the merits of various hull designs when Andrew approached, shadowed by Mikhail. He and Colby greeted each other warmly and he offered his opinion with the same gravity he pronounced a sentence in his courtroom.

He didn't give the men a chance to argue with him but turned to her. "Elizabeth, my dear, I must show you the new Jackson Pollock I purchased as a birthday gift to myself. I know how much you enjoy his work. Gentlemen, will you excuse us?"

This was it. He was providing her the perfect opening to talk to him about the entire reason they were here. She sent a slightly panicked look to Beau.

His expression didn't change but his eyes sent her a silent message, one she could read clearly. *You can do it. I know you can.*

She drew a shaky breath, heartened by that silent message, then followed Andrew through the crowd and down a hallway to his vast library lined with shelf after shelf of law books.

"Sit down, Elizabeth. You said you wanted to speak with me. How may I help you?"

Now that she was here, she didn't have the first idea how to begin. Embarrassment and uncertainty settled like thick mud in her throat. How could she possibly speak casually about sexual affairs and blackmail and murder with the man who had always been a kind and loving father figure in her life? It was impossible. She couldn't.

But she had to.

Andrew settled in one of the leather wing chairs in his library and gestured to the matching chair. She swallowed and perched on the edge, wishing she could see Beau. She knew he was nearby, that he must have switched on the receiver by now and should be able to hear the entire conversation.

The idea of Beau listening to her stuttering, clumsy attempts to converse with Andrew should have made her feel awkward, inept. Oddly, she found it comforting instead, and drew a strange kind of strength and courage just knowing he was nearby.

"What's all this about, Elizabeth?" Andrew asked, with just a hint of impatience coiling through his deep, modulated voice that had earned him such respect during his years as a trial attorney. "Are you in need of legal advice? Perhaps a problem with your father's estate?"

She couldn't delay further. "No. Nothing like that. I...I need to show you something and I'm just trying to figure out the best way to do it," she admitted.

"I hope you know there's nothing you can't talk about with me."

"Don't be so sure," she muttered, then felt heat soak her cheeks as she remembered Beau listening to even her private asides. She could do this. He believed in her, she reminded herself. It was just the push she needed to delve into her small velvet clutch and extract the copy of Tina's letter she'd brought along.

She unfolded it and held it out to him. "This. This is what I wanted to ask you about."

With a puzzled frown, Andrew took the letter from her. He scanned the first few lines, then dropped it against his leg. Other than sudden tight lines around his mouth, she could see little reaction.

"So you know." Like his features, his voice was flat, expressionless.

"I'm not sure *what* I know. Did you write that letter?"

"You must have known I did or you wouldn't have come here and shown it to me." Was that anger in his voice? He seemed much colder than usual—but perhaps he was only embarrassed.

"I suspected," she answered. "I recognized the…the type of stationery you used. But I wasn't sure until just this moment."

Questions flapped through her mind like silvery streamers in the wind, but she focused on her own hurt and anger.

"Why didn't you tell me?"

He raised one white eyebrow. "Because I didn't think it was any of your business."

"How could it not be my b-business? Your son is living in my house! I'm helping his grandmother to raise him!"

He had no answer to that, only a drawn-out sigh. He looked older, suddenly, she thought. Not as vibrant as when they walked into the library together.

"How long have you known?" Andrew asked.

"A few days. That's all."

"Then she didn't tell you before she—" He paused, and a spasm of some emotion she couldn't identify twisted his mouth. "Before she committed suicide?"

"No. She never said a word." A portion of her anger was directed at Tina for exactly that. Why would Tina have believed she needed to hide her son's parentage behind lies and secrecy?

"She always refused to reveal the name of Alex's father. I probably wouldn't have believed her if she *had* told me."

He nodded slowly, then rose to one of the four arched windows in the room overlooking the gardens and Lake Washington. He was silent, contemplating the night for several moments, then he turned back to her. "I didn't know about the boy until a month ago when Tina wrote me unexpectedly. I swear, I didn't know. If I'd had the first idea, you can be sure I would have taken care of her."

His words sent an ominous shiver rippling down her spine. *I would have taken care of her.* He could mean something benign, innocent. But they could also mean something far more sinister.

"Didn't you ever wonder about the…timing? You have an affair with her and nine months later she has a son. Didn't that ever strike you as extremely coincidental? I know you have to have seen Alex when you've come to Harbor View. He spent a great deal of his life there. Surely you had to…to wonder."

"I do remember seeing him a few times. I always thought he was a beautiful child but I never put the pieces together. I'll admit, the thought might have crossed my mind a time or two but the boy always seemed small to me. The time frame didn't fit. Foolish of me, I can see that now, but I didn't know how old he was. Besides, I always assumed Tina would have told me if he was my son."

Ah, and here was another big element of the picture that

simply didn't fit. "Tina was not a vindictive woman. That was never her way. I don't understand why she would keep you from your own son."

He faced the window again. In the reflection, she could see sadness and regret on his features. "I've wondered that same thing since learning about the boy. I'm afraid I am wholly to blame. We only saw each other for a few weeks. A few wonderful weeks."

The reflected Andrew pursed his mouth, then sighed heavily. "Then I'm afraid I ended things rather abruptly and with unnecessary cruelness, only because we ran into a colleague of mine at a little restaurant in the city."

"Why?"

"Pride. Stupidity. I worried too much about appearances. How would it look for a superior court justice to be running around with someone like Tina?"

"Someone like Tina?" She heard the coldness in her voice but couldn't help it. She would not sit in this richly appointed library and listen to him cast aspersions on a woman who worked hard at any job she could find to support her son.

He didn't appear to notice her chilly tone. "Yes. Someone like her. Someone beautiful and vivacious and the same age as my own daughter."

She relaxed her fingers. He didn't sound condescending. If she wasn't mistaken, she would almost think he had feelings for Tina. "Anyone with sense would think you were a lucky man."

"I was." He turned to face her, and she was stunned by the raw emotion in his blue eyes. "No man had ever been luckier than me. And I threw it away because of stupid, vainglorious pride. I couldn't bear thinking my colleagues might believe I had hit some midlife crisis, that I was searching for eternal youth with a woman like Tina, someone from an entirely different world. I was stupid and I've paid for it.''

''I'm sorry,'' she whispered.

He was silent for several moments, then turned to her again, and his features were once more the composed Andrew she had known all her life, not some agonized stranger. ''How is my son?''

It took her a few beats to realize he meant Alex. ''Fine. He misses his mother and doesn't quite understand that she won't be coming home again but he's…adjusting.''

''Tina said in her correspondence that he needed surgery. That's the only reason she finally told me the truth after all these years and asked for my help. Is he, that is, does the surgery have anything to do with his…hearing impairment?''

He didn't know? Could he actually have written out a six-figure check without any idea why?

''Before she…died, Tina apparently was making plans for him to get a cochlear implant.''

''A cochlear implant? Will that help him hear?''

''Somewhat. It's certainly not guaranteed to work, but it might.''

''Are you going to continue with the surgery?''

''Luisa and I haven't made a decision yet. We're still trying to…to adjust, as well.''

A terrible thought slammed into her, and she hitched in a breath at the impact. What if Andrew decided to fight for custody of the child? Tina had named her guardian of Alex but surely, as his father, Andrew would have some rights to him. He could be preparing legal action right now….

Andrew interrupted her thoughts. ''You love him, don't you?''

She thought of her feelings for Tina's sweet little boy with his bright smile and funny curiosity. Oh, yes, she loved him. If Andrew decided to take the child, it would utterly destroy her.

She wished she could find the right words to tell him all that was in her heart, but once more they slipped from her grasp like slick soap. "Yes," she finally whispered. "Fiercely."

He nodded with a small smile. "I know I don't deserve it, but I'd like some sort of relationship with him. It doesn't have to be father-son. I'm afraid I'm not one for playing catch in the backyard but I thought perhaps I could be a…a sort of honorary grandfather. If Luisa doesn't mind."

She gazed at him, almost dizzy with relief. That didn't sound like a man eager to take on a small child with a hearing impairment. "No. I'm…I'm sure we can work something out."

"Good. And of course I will make financial arrangements for him."

"That's not necessary," she said stiffly.

"To me it is." He paused and returned to the matching armchair next to her and rested a hand on her fingers gripping the armrest. "I'm terribly sorry about this, Elizabeth. I can tell you've been hurt by all of this."

"I only wish Tina hadn't kept so many secrets from me. We were friends. She should have told me."

"In her own way, I suppose, Tina had as much stiff pride as I did. I tried to reach her a few times after ending things but she wouldn't even consider forgiving me. I gave up after a while, once I realized it was probably for the best, that the differences between us were just too great. Now I wish I'd tried a little harder."

She thought of Beau and her words to him the evening before, on the *Mari*.

We might have heat between us but that's all. We have very little in common. We're two very different people from two very different worlds.

Was she wrong? Could she tell him the truth about herself without him despising her? He cared about her, she knew he did. If she doubted it, all she had to remember was that tender, soul-shattering kiss outside on the terrace earlier.

Her love for him flashed through her again, pure and rich and so bright it hurt to even think about it. Did she have the courage to act on her feelings?

She didn't want to end up like Andrew, alone with his regrets.

"So tell me about your young man."

How had he so accurately guessed what she was thinking? She felt color climb her cheeks.

Andrew laughed softly. "I believe you're blushing. Is that a good sign?"

"Beau is a…a friend."

Andrew smiled. "I sense he's more than that."

"No. Not really."

"But you would like him to be?"

She sighed at his persistence. When he set his mind to it, Andrew could meddle like a maiden aunt. "I…enjoy being with him, and he's wonderful with Alex. Let's leave it at that for now."

And he can hear every word we're saying, she thought, but of course she couldn't say it. The idea of Beau sitting somewhere close by, listening to Andrew probe into their relationship was beyond mortifying.

To her chagrin, Andrew didn't pick up her broad hint to drop the subject. "I watched the two of you at dinner," he said. "I'm sure you weren't aware, my dear, but you were glowing in a way I've never seen before, even during your engagement. For that alone, I like him. You deserve to be happy. You have had far too little love in your life."

She'd never been tempted before to tell her godfather to please—for the love of God and all that was holy—just shut up, but she nearly did now.

"Is that your new Pollock?" she asked instead, doggedly trying to redirect the conversation. "It's very striking."

He gave her a look that told her he was too sharp not to know what she was doing, but to her vast, eternal relief, he allowed himself to be distracted before Beau could hear any more about her pathetic love life.

He could listen to her talk all day.

Out on the terrace again, just outside the library doors where he could bust through if necessary, Beau adjusted his ear piece and let Elizabeth's low, musical voice wash over him.

In an odd, probably twisted way, he found it incredibly sexy to hear her talking in his head.

But then, he found everything about her sexy, from the way she tucked her hair behind her ear to the tiny birthmark just at her jawline to the way her smile transformed her cool beauty into someone sweet and winsome and enchanting.

He reeled in his wayward thoughts and tried to steer his attention back to the conversation.

They were talking about Alex now. He still had a hard time imagining that cute kid being sired by the stiff, formal judge, but if nothing else, at least they had established that fact by this little chat.

The judge hadn't tried to hide his relationship with Tina from Elizabeth. But then, what choice did he have when confronted with the letter?

Beau wished to heaven he could see the man's face, study his mannerisms. People had to be real cold-blooded bastards to lie without revealing it in some way by their body language. A twitch, a shift in position, a flatness to their eyes. Something almost always gave it away. He hated only having the man's muted voice in his ear to go by.

The conversation shifted again, and it took him a minute to realize they were talking about him now.

The judge was saying something about watching them at dinner. ''I'm sure you weren't aware, my dear,'' Beau heard him say, ''but you were glowing in a way I've never seen before, even during your engagement.''

Beau blinked at that one. Engagement? She'd been *engaged* and she'd never told him? What happened? And what the hell else had she kept from him?

He was still reeling when he realized someone else had joined him on the terrace.

''There you are. I've been looking for you. What are you doing out here by yourself?'' With excruciatingly lousy timing, Leigh Sheffield, drink in hand, spoke at the same time as Elizabeth. Try as he might, he didn't catch what she said.

He growled to himself but managed—barely—to keep from snapping at Leigh to leave him alone. Instead he pasted on a polite smile. ''I'm just enjoying the quiet for a few moments. I'm not much for big parties.''

''I'm not either. I prefer more—'' she paused delicately ''—intimate engagements.''

He didn't know how to respond to the blatant—and unwanted—invitation in her eyes without sounding rude so he chose not to answer.

After a few beats, she went on in a slightly cooler voice. ''Where's Elizabeth? She hasn't moved twelve inches from your side all night.''

''I like her there,'' he muttered, trying hard not to feel like a day-old fishhead caught in the middle of a catfight. ''But your father stole her away from me for a few moments. I'm sure she'll be back any minute now.''

He thought he saw anger flash in her green eyes for just a moment, but it was quickly veiled. ''She and Daddy are always going off for little chats. If not for the age difference between them, one might start to wonder exactly what they're always going off to chat about.''

For about half a second he thought maybe Leigh's implication had been inadvertent, then he realized grimly that she knew exactly what she was saying. She wanted him to jump to the conclusion that Andrew and Elizabeth shared more than a paternal relationship.

He swallowed disgust, both at the quick mental picture of Elizabeth in Andrew's arms and at the kind of warped mind the man's daughter must have to conjure up such an idea.

"I wouldn't know," he said, using his best hard-ass cop voice.

It didn't seem to faze Ms. Sheffield. She leaned in closer to him and answered in a low, conspiratorial voice. "I'm only saying our little Lizzie is not exactly the most scintillating conversationalist, as I'm sure you know. But she and Daddy somehow can always find something to talk about."

He couldn't think of a single thing to say in response, and he suddenly realized the voices in his head had stopped. While Leigh had been busy spreading her poison, either he had lost the transmission or Andrew and Elizabeth had parted ways.

Or were engaged in activities other than talking.

No. No chance in hell. Elizabeth wouldn't have kissed him with such aching sweetness and then turned around to kiss Andrew Sheffield the same way.

"Beau? Where are you?" Elizabeth's soft voice whispered through his earpiece, so erotic it was almost as if he could feel the warmth of her breath swirling around his ear. "I'm still in the library. Andrew just left. I'm not sure whether to…to come find you or wait here for you."

He was severely tempted to just turn on his heel and leave his hostess so he could find Elizabeth but he couldn't quite overcome a childhood spent having Southern manners drilled into him. "Will you excuse me, ma'am?" He gave another fake smile. "I just remembered I'm supposed to meet Elizabeth right about now."

He *did* walk away before she could question him further. He could have walked straight into the library from the outside doors but he didn't want her following him, so he walked around to a different door and quickly made his way to the library.

The carved oak door into the room was open and he found her inside gazing at the artificial fire in the grate while her fingers aimlessly twisted the copy of the letter they had found in Tina Hidalgo's safe-deposit box. The door squeaked slightly as he pushed it open and she looked up, her expression melting into relief. "You heard me, then."

"Yeah. I heard everything perfectly." Well, almost everything.

A sudden flush climbed her cheeks and he cursed Leigh Sheffield again for making him miss Elizabeth's response to the judge's questioning about him.

"Did I ask the…the right questions?"

"You did good, sweetheart."

She smiled a little, just as he'd hoped, then the smile slid away. "What do you think? Did he sound guilty to you?"

"I don't know," he answered truthfully. "I couldn't really tell. But we didn't expect a confession."

"I know. But I was hoping for something more… concrete, I guess. We don't know any more now than we did before I spoke with him."

She sounded so dejected that he gave in to his sudden compelling need to touch her by reaching for her hand and rubbing a thumb across her fingers, right down to her short fingernails. Despite the overly warm room, her skin was cool, as usual, and he wanted to bring some heat to it.

He had never considered himself a touchy-feely kind of guy. Sure, he was a red-blooded American male with all the normal needs, but he'd never been one who particularly cared for all that mushy stuff like hand holding and soft petting.

So why was it he couldn't get within ten feet of the woman without this compelling need for some kind of physical contact between them?

He didn't take the time to analyze it now and instead focused on answering her. "We do know more than we did before you talked to him. We know for sure he was the one who wrote the letter, that he and Tina had an affair and why it ended. We know Alex is his kid and that he didn't know until several weeks ago."

Under his fingers, Elizabeth curled her hand into a small fist. "I suppose you're right." She paused. "Beau, I think he genuinely cared for her. I think he's devastated by her death, and I just can't imagine it's at all possible that he would kill her. I think he loved her."

The conviction in her voice made him blink. "How did you get that from your conversation?"

"You didn't see him, you only heard abstract voices. When he talked about her he looked…shattered."

"I'll have to take your word for that."

"He did. You should have seen the look in his eyes, Beau. I have never seen him like that. If he had such strong feelings, why did he let so much come between them?"

"Like he said, Judge Andrew Sheffield and an exotic dancer like Tina didn't have all that much in common. Maybe he figured they were from two different planets whose orbits just happened to collide for a brief instant." Just like a cop and an heiress, he thought bitterly.

"What do we do now? Are we…are there any other leads to pursue?"

If he ruled the judge out because of one overheard conversation, he wouldn't be much of a detective. He wanted to take a run at Sheffield himself but that would have to wait for a few days.

"We don't have to figure it out right now. We're in the middle of a party and we can't hide out here all night."

As much as he might like to.

"I don't really want to stay now. Now that I've spoken with Andrew, we have no reason to stay. Can we...would you mind terribly if we left?"

"I'm sure I'll manage to survive my disappointment," he murmured dryly.

Chapter 14

The ride between the Sheffield mansion on Mercer Island and his own little house in the 'burbs seemed much shorter on the flip side.

Even though time passed quickly, Beau found himself edgy, uncomfortable. Maybe he was a control freak, but he decided he wasn't all that crazy about having someone else drive him around. He much preferred being the one behind the wheel.

"Thank you for...everything," Elizabeth murmured when the limo driver pulled up to his house. "Your help has meant so much to me. I...can't find the words."

He gazed at her soft mouth and sleek, elegant hair. He wanted to touch both of them. To rumple that hair a little, to smear that lipstick again. Too bad he wasn't particularly crazy about having an audience, even a driver who was trying his best to pretend he wasn't listening.

"You're welcome," Beau said gruffly. He started to open the door but paused, his fingers on the handle.

Something about the situation didn't sit right with him. Call him a redneck chauvinist pig—Gracie sure did often enough—but he decided he didn't at all enjoy being delivered to his door like some sixteen-year-old girl after the prom.

Forget this. He grabbed her elbow and gave a little yank. "Come on. I'll drive you home."

She looked puzzled. "Mr. Parker can take me."

"So can I. Come on."

"Don't be silly! It's at least an hour from your house to mine, by the time we catch the ferry."

"I've got time. Come on." He tugged again on her arm, enough that her slippery dress made her slither a little across the seat toward him.

She looked at him as if he'd just reached over and given her ear a wet willie. "Wh-why?"

He shrugged. "Okay, so I'm old-fashioned, but I figure a man should drive his own date home. It's one of those unwritten rules, like never burping in public and always wearing clean underwear just in case you're in an accident."

She gaped at him and Beau saw that Anthony had given up all pretense of ignoring their interplay and had turned around to follow it better. Beau met the man's gaze and Anthony grinned at him.

"This is not a date," she finally said, her voice strangled.

"Close enough. I want to drive you home, Elizabeth. Let me, okay? Look at it this way, if I take you home, you can give our friend Mr. Parker here an early night of it."

She gazed back at the driver, clearly torn. He smiled at her helpfully, and she drew a ragged-sounding breath and stepped out of the limo.

"I still think you're crazy, but all right. Thank you, Anthony. I hope you enjoy your evening."

The driver chortled. "Oh, I will. You can be sure of that. Good night, miss."

With a wave Beau shut the door, then he and Elizabeth both watched the limo pull back out into the deserted street. He had probably sounded like a complete jerk, insisting on taking her home like that, but he was suddenly fiercely glad their evening didn't have to end yet.

"Let's go inside," he said after a moment. "I think I'll change out of the monkey suit first. You mind?"

"No. Of course not."

The rain had stopped, but the night air still pressed in on them, moist and cool and scented with autumn.

"Your yard is lovely," Elizabeth said as they made their way up the wet brick sidewalk. "You must have a wonderful gardening service."

"No gardeners. Just me."

In the moonlight he could see the surprise in her eyes. "You did all this?"

"I'm strictly about maintenance. Most of the fancy stuff was here when I bought the place and it comes back every year. I just mow and try to keep the weeds out of the flowers."

She gazed at the beds, at the late-blooming lilies and asters and Michaelmas daisies. She had been too nervous when she and Tony arrived earlier to pay much attention but now she saw the neat rows of flowers, the carefully pruned shrubs, the whimsical little stone toad she was suddenly sure had been a gift. Beau Riley wasn't the sort of man to pick out stone lawn ornaments, no matter how charming they might be.

"It's lovely. Truly lovely."

"I enjoy it. Helps with the stress, you know? Yanking weeds is better than busting heads at work. It helps me keep my job."

What an interesting mix of contrasts he was. He worked at a tough, demoralizing, often violent job, then came home and nurtured such beauty here.

They reached the door and he quickly unlocked it and ushered her inside. As she moved past him into the little entryway, she could feel the heat radiating from him, smell the outdoors scent of his aftershave. Her stomach fluttered and she had to force herself to step away and keep walking in the direction he pointed, through a doorway into a living area dominated by a large TV and stereo system.

Beau cleared his throat. "It shouldn't take me long to change. Would you like a drink?"

"No, thank you."

"Make yourself comfortable, then. I'll be back in a minute." He headed down a hallway leading to what she assumed was a bedroom. Alone in the room, she studied her surroundings, trying to gather more clues as to what made Beau Riley tick.

The room was neat, comfortable, with a plump, tweedy couch and a massive forest-green recliner. This must be the room he preferred, judging by the sparse furnishings she'd noticed earlier in the living room.

Too unsettled to sit, she wandered around the room studying his space. He had a large CD collection, mostly classic rock and country music with some jazz thrown in. His DVD collection seemed to run to the shoot-'em-up action flick but she was surprised to see a healthy mix of classics—several Alfred Hitchcock movies, some old Humphrey Bogart and even a couple Cary Grant romantic comedies.

On a bookshelf dominated by mysteries, she found two framed pictures—a candid that looked fairly recent of Grace Dugan, her new baby and her stepdaughter Emma. They were sitting on a beach somewhere, Emma leaning across her lap, all of them mugging for the camera. They all looked so happy together it made her chest ache.

The second picture was of a dark-eyed girl with long, glossy braids and a bright smile. Marisa. It had to be. Something sad and painful tugged at her heart for a life snuffed out too soon. Beau must have truly loved her, to name his boat after her and keep this reminder close.

Why didn't he have any other pictures? Nieces, nephews, siblings? He never talked about his family, she realized suddenly. She knew he grew up in a small town in Georgia but the rest of his past was a mystery. Why was he so private? Was he hiding something or did he simply prefer not to talk about himself?

He came back into the room just as she was setting the framed photograph back on the shelf. Beau in worn Levi's and a navy cotton golf shirt was even more devastating than Beau in formalwear.

He noticed her fingers lingering on the framed picture, and she thought she saw a spasm of emotion twist his features.

"You miss her, don't you?"

He was quiet for a moment, then nodded. "Yeah. It probably sounds strange to you. I mean, she wasn't even my kid. But we were close. The three of us did a lot together."

He crossed the room and picked up the photograph. "Kids are great, you know?" he said after a moment with a wistful smile that made her want to cry. "They love you no matter what. There's something addictive about having a kid in your life, someone who thinks you're the greatest thing since juice boxes. That's what I miss."

I think you're the greatest. She couldn't say the words, so she just smiled in response.

After a pause she gathered the nerve to ask the question she'd wondered about earlier. "Beau, why don't you have any family pictures?"

His smile slipped away and his eyes turned wintry as he carefully set Marisa's picture back on the shelf. "I don't have any family."

"Oh. I'm sorry I p-pried." Her face burned at his short

answer and at the stammer that slipped out, but Beau didn't seem to notice.

"I don't have a lot of real good childhood memories. I was an only child and my parents both died the year I turned six. After that, I went to live with my grandmother. She wasn't a real warm person and I left as soon as I could. We didn't stay in touch."

What kind of trauma and grief had he left out of that casual summation?

"I'm sorry," she murmured, and touched his hand.

He shrugged. "It's no big deal. I always had plenty of good food and a clean bed to sleep in. That's a hell of a lot more than many of the kids I see on the job, so I have nothing to complain about."

Children needed so much more than food and a clean bed. She thought of her own childhood, of the love and nurturing care she received from Luisa. She had to pray he had a Luisa of his own.

"How did your parents die?" The instant she asked the question, she knew it was a terrible mistake. His mouth hardened into a tight line and his eyes were shuttered once more.

He didn't answer for a long, drawn-out moment, until she felt heat scorch her cheeks and she wanted to crawl under his couch cushions.

"I'm s-sorry," she whispered. "I shouldn't have asked. It's really none of my business."

He studied her for several more seconds, then he sighed. "It's not you. I just don't like to talk about my parents. They're a touchy subject."

"I'm sorry," she said again and focused on the berber weave of his carpet, unable to meet his gaze. When would she ever learn to keep her blasted mouth shut? Anyone with common sense would have figured out this was a topic he wasn't interested in discussing. But not her. She pushed and pushed, even when all the signs clearly said Back Off.

All she could do now was pray the evening would end soon before she could do anything else idiotic.

"Will you take me home now?"

He tilted his head. "Is that what you really want?"

"Yes." More than she wanted to take another breath.

He leaned against the bookshelf and crossed his arms. "Too bad," he murmured. In the last minute or so his green eyes had warmed considerably and she wasn't completely sure whether that fact should make her relieved or apprehensive.

"Why is it…too bad?"

"Because what *I* really want is to kiss you again."

His words seemed to hover between them like a swarm of stirred-up honeybees. She stared at him in shock, heat curling through her, replacing her embarrassment.

How did he do that? Switch gears on her so fast he left her head spinning? "I don't think that's, um, such a great idea."

"Yeah, you're probably right." He paused, then grinned at her. "Let's do it, anyway."

Before she could protest, he stepped forward and kissed her, his mouth hard and hot on hers. Their kiss earlier on the terrace had been slow, sweet, gentle. This was anything but. This one was wild, passionate. Urgent.

While he seared her with his mouth, his hands held her tightly, pressing her against the length of his body.

Any lingering embarrassment shriveled up and blew away. She didn't have room for embarrassment, not when she could barely breathe under the overwhelming weight of her emotions.

Oh, she loved this man. The fierceness of it still shook her. She loved him no matter what his secrets. She wanted to kiss him and hold him and take the burden of his pain.

She threw herself with enthusiasm into the kiss, wrapping her arms around his neck, curving into his heat.

He made a raw, aroused sound in his throat and leaned closer, pressing her back until she bumped against the wall. He caged her in with his arms and his body, looming over her until her world became only him, only his scent and his taste and his strength.

He kissed her until she thought her bones would dissolve, until her brain turned to mush and her body became only a pulsing, sighing, quivering mass of need.

They were both gasping for air when he finally lifted his head. She managed to pry open her eyes and found him gazing at her, raw hunger in his green eyes.

"I'd better stop and take you home while I still can."

She gazed at him, her aching nipples brushing against his chest through their clothes with each tortured breath. Yes. That would be the smart thing, for him to take her home.

But for once in her life she was tired of trying so blasted hard to be smart. She wanted to burn away, to stay wrapped up in this heat that didn't need words from her.

A clock somewhere in the room ticked on as she gazed at his strong masculine features for another moment, then she gathered her courage and leaned forward the few inches that separated them.

She took the lead this time, kissing him fiercely, tangling the fingers of one hand in his hair while her other hand pressed against his chest.

His heart raced against her fingers, his breathing was ragged and shallow, and she reveled in it. He was close to the edge, she could feel it, and she wanted to push and push until he toppled over, taking her with him.

Finally he yanked his mouth away. "Whoa. I don't think my eyes will ever uncross again."

She laughed, empowered by his response and happier than she ever remembered feeling.

"Good. If your eyes are crossed it won't be safe for you to drive me home and I'll have no choice but to stay."

He stilled, those eyes turning watchful. "Is that really what you want? To stay?"

Okay. Decision time here. No more fooling around. All the reasons she should leave rushed through her mind, all those scaredy-cat things like playing it safe and protecting her heart. They were nothing, though—less than nothing—compared to the giant tidal wave of need crashing over her.

She wanted this, wanted him. And for once she decided she would follow Leigh Sheffield's example and take what she wanted. She smiled at him, a come-on-baby-light-my-fire kind of smile, then stepped forward and kissed him again.

She kept her eyes open this time, as Beau did, and she saw surprise flit across his gaze, then a fierce desire that made her insides tremble with anticipation.

He gave another of those low, growly sounds, and the next thing she knew, he was lifting her in his arms, formal gown and all, and carrying her through the house.

His bedroom was large, masculine, with dark oak furniture, a skylight letting in moonbeams and a huge bed covered in a patchwork quilt of black and deep purple. She caught only a glimpse of the vibrant colors before he laid her down on it.

"I don't think I can be gentle. Not the first time," he warned, sending her stomach fluttering at the idea that they might actually do this more than once!

"I'll try," he went on, "but I want you too damn much."

She had no idea how to respond to such a statement, and she wasn't sure she could find any words anyway, so she gripped his knit shirt and pulled him down to her.

She kept hold of his shirt while he kissed her for long, drugging moments, until all she could think about was finding a way to get closer. With one quick movement, she pulled the shirt over his head. After a startled moment he helped her get it off and tossed the thing on the floor. She swallowed at all those rippling muscles bared to her view.

Tina would have been impressed. A definite hottie.

"Your turn," he growled.

She stood to take off her gown then realized she had a slight problem. "I, um, need a little help getting out of this. I can't reach the...the thingy." For a terrible moment she couldn't think of the right word.

"The zipper?" he supplied helpfully.

She nodded and hoped he would blame her inarticulate state on flustered desire, which wasn't exactly far off the mark.

He grinned. "You're in luck. I have to admit, I'm considered something of a zipper expert. Big ones, little ones, stuck ones. I can do them all. Want to see?"

"Yes, please," she said.

She wasn't exactly sure what she'd said that made him laugh, but the sound of it rolled over her, around her. She was startled to realize she found his laughter every bit as arousing as his kiss.

He reached behind her and quickly unzipped the gown. The slick material slithered past her hips and pooled at her feet, leaving her in only her mother's diamond necklace and her unmentionables.

He muttered a strangled oath, and she turned around and found him gazing at her like he was dying of thirst and she was a long, tall glass of lemonade.

"Do you have any idea how incredible you look right now?"

She shook her head, heat flaring in her cheeks.

"Come here," he commanded. He led her to a bureau that was topped by a large rectangular mirror.

He stood behind her and pointed to the reflection. "Look

at that," he murmured, his voice rough. "You, Elizabeth Quinn, are the sexiest thing I have ever seen."

She blushed at his words but peeked at her reflected image. She didn't see anything all that spectacular. She was too skinny, she didn't have much in the chest department and she had bony knees.

Still, the black strapless bra and matching panties and garters were nice. She had a secret weakness for frothy, feminine lingerie, even though nobody ever saw it but her.

What she did find erotic was the reflected image of Beau looming behind her looking completely, darkly male, his chest bare and his jeans riding low on his hips.

She licked her lips, heat curling through her insides, and met his gaze in the mirror. With their gazes still locked, he reached around their bodies with one hand and cupped her breast through the lace of her bra then flicked his thumb over her nipple. It instantly hardened into a tight, aching bud. He glanced down as his thumb caressed her slowly.

Before she even realized it, he had unclasped the front catch of her bra, freeing her to his gaze and to his touch. For several agonizing, intense moments they stood that way, the solid strength of his body at her back while his hands teased and explored.

Her lips parted and she forgot to breathe as wet heat soaked through her. Now *that* was the sexiest thing she'd ever seen, his big hand cupping her, caressing her nipples while his eyes watched her like a hungry predator.

The fierceness of her response to him was exquisitely painful. She arched her head back and he lowered his mouth, his gaze locked again with hers in the mirror, and nuzzled her neck.

Finally she couldn't stand the slow torment another instant. She turned in his arms and kissed him deeply, her hands clasped around his neck and their naked skin brushing together. With a groan, he lowered her to the bed, then quickly removed the rest of their clothing.

She swallowed hard, wishing she had the words to tell him how beautiful he was, all hard muscles and broad strength. Her body ached to touch him, to feel him moving inside her.

They spent long moments exploring each other, until both of them were shaking with desire.

Finally, just before she was about to resort to begging, he reached for a condom. She watched him put it on, grateful she wouldn't have to ask about protection since she hadn't exactly had reason to use birth control pills for the past few years.

He kissed her fiercely while he entered her. That's all it took, just that first hard thrust, and she completely shattered, coming apart in a thousand brilliant colors as she bowed up from the bed with the overwhelming power of her release.

When she could think again, she realized he had stilled inside her as the aftershocks rippled through her. He was watching her, an arrested look on his face. "Wow," was all he said.

"S-sorry."

He gave a ragged laugh. "Why? You're making me feel like the world's greatest lover here and I haven't even done anything."

"The…the warm-up was pretty incredible."

"Wait until you catch the rest of my act." He grinned again and moved inside her.

Unbelievably, her body instantly rose to meet him again. She gasped as that glorious, aching pressure began to build again, until she was arching into him with each shattering press of his body. His kiss was fierce, possessive, and she cried out against his mouth, sensation after sensation rocking through her, as she found release again.

With a low groan he followed her to the stars.

"Remind me to thank Leigh," she gasped when she could manage to convince her lungs to work again.

He looked startled. "For what?"

"Well, to thank her caterer, anyway. For, uh, helping you keep up your strength."

He gave a ragged laugh. "I don't think you have anything to worry about in that department, Miss Quinn. I've been in a perpetual state of arousal since we met."

"Really?"

"Yeah, really," he mimicked.

"Oh," she breathed. She wasn't used to the idea that she could have such power over a man. She had to admit, she liked it.

They lay snuggled together in the bed while rain sizzled against the skylight. He was so gorgeous, so male. She still couldn't believe she was here with him, wrapped in his arms like this. It seemed like a dream, like some amazingly realistic secret fantasy.

She traced the hard planes of his chest, memorizing him with her fingertips. He stretched under her touch like a cat sprawled out in a sunbeam. He was even purring, a low, rumbly sound deep in his chest.

She explored him for a long time until her fingers touched something unusual, a dime-size section of raised tissue different from the rest of his skin. She propped up on an elbow for a better look and for the first time noticed a small, jagged starburst-shaped scar gleaming white in the moonlight.

"What happened there?" she asked.

His gaze followed the tracing of her finger. "Nothing. I got shot a couple years ago. It was no big deal."

She froze, horrified. "No big deal? You were shot and you say it was no big deal?"

The hard muscle under her fingers rippled as he shrugged. "It sounds worse than it was, believe me. If I had been paying attention like I should have been doing, it never would have happened.''

She couldn't begin to understand the breed of man who could speak so casually of such a traumatic thing as a gunshot wound. "Was it…did it happen in the line of duty?"

"Yeah."

She waited for him to elaborate but he said nothing more. He obviously didn't want to discuss the injury, but she couldn't leave the subject alone.

"What happened?"

He sighed. "You're not going to let up until I give all the gory details, are you?"

Her face burned at her own temerity but she shook her head, her hair brushing across his skin.

"Yeah, that's what I figured," he muttered glumly. He tangled his fingers in her hair. "Okay, here's the long and ugly story. I was working with a multijurisdictional task force investigating an assault weapons smuggling ring that eventually led us to Jack Dugan's company. Turns out a couple of his employees were trying to bring in a little money on the side. We were searching the company's airplane hangar when the suspects tried to hijack one of Dugan's jets and fly out of the country, taking along Emma and Grace for insurance."

He cleared his throat. "When I objected, one of them shot me."

He was quiet for a moment, his fingers stroking her hair like worry beads. "I ended up using deadly force on the person who shot me. A woman. I had to or she would have killed Grace and Em both and maybe Dugan, too. She, uh, died at the scene."

He had done his job but it hadn't been easy for him to kill a woman, Elizabeth realized. A tangle of emotions choked in her throat—love, pride and a vast, aching regret for his physical and emotional pain.

She wished desperately for some brilliant, healing words of comfort but could think of nothing that didn't sound trite. Finally, with tears burning behind her eyelids she leaned across his warm skin and pressed her mouth to the puckered scar just below his collarbone.

"I'm so sorry," she whispered.

When she met his gaze, his eyes were dark, stunned. He said nothing for several moments, his body still against her except for the slow rise and fall of his breathing.

She thought he might have drifted off to sleep but finally he spoke again, more shades of Georgia coloring his voice than she'd ever heard there.

"When I was a boy I always believed my parents died in a car accident."

It took her several beats to realize he was answering the question she had asked earlier in his living room.

She held her breath and listened to his heartbeat in her ear, afraid to speak for fear she would say something wrong.

"That's what my grandmama always told me. I found out the truth the year I turned sixteen. It wasn't a car accident like Marie always insisted. I don't know how she hushed it up so well, but that woman controlled everything in Big Piney. The police chief, the newspaper editor. Everyone. Somehow she managed to keep it a secret."

She risked a glance at him and saw his jaw tightly clenched. What was it costing him to tell her this? She wanted to tell him to stop, that she didn't need to know, but he went on before she could.

"For nine years she lived one nasty mother of a lie. I'd still probably be stupid enough to believe her if I hadn't met Harlan James, my father's best friend and the only other person alive who was willing to tell me the truth."

He paused, his fingers moving now to her shoulder. Premonition shivered down her spine with icy fingers as she waited for him to speak again.

"After a lifetime of being fed nothing but lies, I finally learned what really happened. My parents didn't die in a car accident. It was a murder-suicide."

A gasp escaped her before she could yank it back.

"Nothing new or original to it. My father caught my mother in bed with his best friend and shot them both. Killed my mother, wounded Harlan, then turned the gun on himself."

Her chest felt tight, achy. "Oh, Beau. I'm so sorry."

"It was tough enough finding out the truth. No kid needs to hear that kind of thing about his parents. But I could have handled that. What got to me was knowing my entire life had been based on one obscene lie after another."

"You were a child. I'm sure your grandmother was simply trying to protect you."

"She was trying to protect herself." His voice was harsh, tight, but she could hear pain threading through it. "Marie cared about protecting the Riley name and her place as the social leader of Big Piney. That was it. She didn't give a rat's rear end for the feelings of a scared little kid. Think of the scandal if all her snobby friends learned her son had done such a low-class kind of thing! She wouldn't have been able to bear it. So she paid everybody off to keep their mouths shut and they did."

"Is that what led you to become a police officer?" she asked after a moment. "Finding out the truth about your parents?"

His hand stilled its slow caress of her skin. "Yeah. I guess so. I never thought of it that way but you're probably right. Nothing makes me angrier than somebody trying to lie to me about who they are, what they've done. I hate being lied to, probably because of my grandmama."

A chill rippled down her spine at his words. She was the biggest liar of all. She had hidden the truth about herself behind a thin facade—created a wobbly mirage of a confident, self-assured woman, when her reality was far different.

I hate being lied to.

How would Beau react if he found out? He would be furious at her deception, would hate her for the grand lie of omission she had perpetrated on him.

Not *if* he found out. *When.* He was going to learn the truth. And when he did, she would lose everything. He wouldn't want to help a woman who had misrepresented herself so blatantly. And he certainly wouldn't want a woman he couldn't trust in his bed and his life.

Intellectually she knew she was being melodramatic. She had a speech impairment, not some hideous fatal disease. But while her mind might accept that her disorder didn't define her—that she was so much more than fumbling speech and missed words—it was hard to find comfort from that knowledge when she had so many emotional scars because of it. Her father's cold rejection, Stephen's mocking disdain, the cruelty of people like the Leigh Sheffields of the world.

Beau wouldn't be so unkind. She knew it—how could she love him otherwise?—but still she couldn't manage to battle through her fears enough to tell him.

"So now you know all my ugly secrets," Beau said. "This would probably be a good time for you to run away while you have the chance."

His ugly secrets had nothing on hers. She drew in a ragged breath, knowing she should do just that—leave while she still could. She couldn't, though. Not when his skin was warm and alive under her fingers and her senses were full of him.

She wanted one more memory to add to her precious trove.

With her heart pounding, she slid across his body. To her surprise, he was aroused again.

''Good thing I had that second helping of poached salmon at dinner,'' he said, smiling a little against her mouth. ''I think maybe I've still got a little strength left in me.''

She smiled in return. Framing his face with her hands, she kissed him deeply, pouring all her emotions into the kiss.

She would run away like the scared, stupid rabbit she was.

But not yet.

Chapter 15

It took him several moments after he awoke to realize something was wrong.

Beau came back to consciousness slowly stretching well-used muscles while rain softly clicked against the windows and the skylight. What a great night. A fabulous night. A wow-I-love-my-life kind of night.

He rolled to his side, reached for her, then crash-landed to full consciousness.

She was gone.

His eyes jerked open and he gazed around the empty bedroom. Nope. No Elizabeth. He must have dropped off like a rock, since he hadn't heard a damn thing.

Usually he was a restless sleeper, prone to waking up even if Gordo simply walked into the room, but he had apparently dozed through Elizabeth sneaking out of bed, getting dressed back in her formal clothes and walking out the door.

A whole herd of emotions thundered through him in just

a few seconds—most he couldn't identify. He was trying to sort them all out when he heard the low murmur of a woman's voice from some distant spot in the house and for the first time noticed the thin ribbon of light curling under the bedroom door.

Some detective he was. She hadn't deserted him yet, but she was on her way.

He tried to clamp down on the anger that exploded inside him. He'd told her to leave, right after he told her the truth about his parents. Why was he so bent out of shape when she took him up on it?

She had every right to creep away in the middle of the night if she wanted to. It was a free country.

That didn't keep him from simmering more than he knew he had a right to as he yanked on his jeans and shoved open the door then padded in his bare feet through the house.

His place was small enough that it didn't provide too many hiding places. He found her in the entryway, wearing her fancy dress and heels again, watching raindrops chase each other down the skinny window next to the front door.

At the sight of her, some of his anger escaped like steam from a teakettle. She looked fragile and a little lost with her hair loose and her wrap slipping off one elegant shoulder.

A rumpled princess waiting for her coach.

He leaned against the doorjamb. "Going somewhere?"

She jumped and whirled around, pressing a hand to the skin just above her neckline. "Beau! You startled me."

He crossed his arms across his bare chest and waited. It was a classic interrogation technique, one of those old saws based in grim, unalterable fact. Give a suspect enough rope and he—or she—will eventually be eager to knot his own noose.

Sure enough, color flared high on her cheeks and Elizabeth looked away from his gaze. "I-I'm sorry. It's late. I needed to return to Harbor View. You were, um…you were sleeping and I didn't want to disturb you.''

Too late, Princess. You've been disturbing me since the first time we met.

''I told you I would take you home.''

''I know. But I thought this would be…easier.''

''Easier?''

Of course she'd think that. Creeping out in the middle of the night without a word to him would have been a hell of a lot more enjoyable than this tense confrontation.

''Yes. It's a…long drive and it's late and I don't want to…to put you out. You've already been more than kind. I'd simply be more…comfortable with the car service taking me home.''

She still wouldn't look at him, as if those intense, profoundly, emotionally devastating hours they'd just spent wrapped around each other, inside each other, had been nothing more than a polite encounter between strangers.

Just like that, his initial fury returned. She was leaving, rejecting him again, and he wanted to pound his fist through that window she was staring through so intently.

What the hell was the matter with him? From the moment they met, the woman had rejected every single overture he'd ever made and yet he just came running back, begging her to kick him in the heart again.

Under other circumstances, he might have let her walk away—he'd experienced his own share of morning-after regrets—but he was too furious to think rationally. He wanted to lash out, hurt her like she'd hurt him.

Or at least force her to look at him one more time before she walked away.

''What is it about me that scares you so much?'' he growled.

Her gaze flitted to him then away. ''S-scares me?''

"Terrifies you. Isn't that what you said earlier? Crowds make you nervous but I terrify you."

He took a step closer to her and had the satisfaction of seeing her blink rapidly. She hitched in a little breath and would have moved away but she had nowhere left to go but the cold, hard door at her back.

"What is it about me that really scares you, Elizabeth? Is it because I'm a cop? Because I carry a gun and have used it on occasion? Or is it because of my parents and the sordid little story I told you earlier?"

He paused and loomed even closer, until he could feel her shallow breathing against his bare chest. "Or maybe it's something else. Maybe you just hate the idea of dirtying your elegant hands with somebody who's not part of your class and has absolutely no desire to be."

"Wh-what?" She lifted her gaze from the floor, her eyes wide and her color fading a little.

That astonished act might have been convincing to anyone else. But he was a cop, trained to figure out when a suspect's story didn't ring quite true. And Elizabeth Moneybags Quinn was doing her damnedest to hide something.

"I know I'm not country-club material, Princess. That's fine with me, believe me. I like driving an old pickup truck and eating in cheap diners. If you're such a snob you can't accept me the way I am, it's your problem, not mine."

She hitched in a little breath, her face as pale now as that lacy curtain Grace had put up on the window. She didn't say anything for a long time and then she finally met his gaze just for an instant, then looked away quickly. "I'm sorry, Beau. I…I don't know what you're talking about."

At the sound of her voice, small and forlorn and not at all convincing, some tiny, relentlessly hopeful corner of his heart shriveled and died. He wanted her to deny it in ringing terms, wanted her to yell at him. If she told him he was crazy, that she wasn't a rich elitist just like her beloved godfather, he would do his best to try believing her.

Instead, she could only manage to pretend she didn't know what he was talking about.

"Right."

"I don't!"

"You can play dumb if you want, but we both know I'm talking about the world of difference between us. Like you said, we don't have that much in common. We're like Tina and the judge, just not on the same page here. I don't see that changing any time soon."

"I…I see."

He gazed at her rumpled elegance, the hollows of her collarbone above her gown, the shadows under her eyes. Despite his anger, he wanted to tuck her against him, to cherish her.

To love her.

He had feelings for her, Beau realized. Big feelings, bigger than anything he'd known before, and they scared him worse than anything he'd ever faced on the job.

He heard the hum of tires on the wet road and saw headlights slicing through the rainy night then come to a stop in front of his house. Suddenly he wanted her gone, wanted to be alone to figure out what the hell had gone wrong here.

"There's your car service. You'd better go."

Her mouth tightened into a thin line. "Beau…"

Whatever she was going to say, he didn't want to hear. He'd survived just about all the damn rejection he could stand in one night. He took a lesson from her and pasted on a cool smile. "Hey, don't worry about me. I've got no complaints. If anybody asks, I'll tell them that for a cold-blooded ice princess, you can really burn up the sheets."

He wouldn't have thought it possible but her face paled even more, until she looked bloodless, ashen. She gazed at him out of blue eyes that looked far too big for her features, then she tilted her chin a little, opened the door and walked out into the rain.

As soon as she left he wanted to call her back, to apologize for being such a complete, unmitigated ass but he didn't. He stood at the door in only his Levi's and watched her climb into the limo with all her customary grace and style.

Before the driver shut the door, he saw her mouth move as she said something to the woman, but he couldn't tell what it was, then he saw Elizabeth lean against the seat and close her eyes, as if she wanted to block out the whole messy night from start to finish.

She refused to cry.

Elizabeth pushed the button to raise the privacy screen between her and the car service driver—a pretty young Asian woman she hadn't met. She leaned back against the leather upholstery of the limousine and closed her eyes, willing herself to hang on a little while longer.

Her chest ached as if she'd been punched by a prizefighter, her head pounded as if the monkeys in one of the books she signed to Alex had been pounding millions of drums in her head, and she wanted nothing more than to curl up on the seat and weep.

She was shivering, she realized. Profound, bone-deep shivers. She adjusted the limousine's heat but even that blast of warm air didn't seem to take the chill away.

What just happened in there? She hated that she wasn't exactly sure, that she had missed half of what Beau had said to her. When she was tired or stressed, her stupid brain was more likely to blitz out on her, and the strain of the party and then the emotional roller coaster afterward had left her exhausted.

His words hadn't made any sense to her. Had he said something about her being a snob? Where had that come from? Since his meaning wasn't clear to her, she had tried to focus on his expression. He'd been cold and remote, far different from the tender lover of a few hours earlier. The disdain in his eyes had slashed at her like a machete.

He despised her, had called her a cold-blooded ice princess. She'd caught that much, even if she didn't understand it. How could he think she was still cold after her passionate response in his arms?

She had completely unraveled in his arms, given him everything, had let him into every exposed corner of her soul.

And then she had left.

She frowned. Was that why he had been so angry? Of course, she realized. She had hurt him by leaving his bed without a word, by calling a driver to collect her instead of waking him to take her home, and he had lashed out by calling her a snob, a cold-blooded ice princess.

She wanted to laugh and was tempted to order the driver to turn around so she could tell Beau he couldn't have been further from the truth. She didn't care what kind of truck he drove or what might be in his bank statement.

Her father might have cared about silly things like that but she didn't. Beau was the most wonderful man she'd ever met, kind and smart and decent. That was all that mattered.

She couldn't tell him, though. It was far better for him to believe she was snobbish and cold than for him to ever suspect how stupid she was. For him to ever learn how she had lied to him, just as his grandmother had.

A Bach piano concerto played over the limousine's stereo system and she tried to let the soothing notes wash over her, but those stolen hours with Beau were too raw, too fresh, too consuming. She could think of nothing but him, of holding him, touching him, feeling him move inside her.

She had no regrets. She wouldn't allow them.

As she watched the city lights disappear in the limousine's back window, she only wished for a small amount of courage. Enough that she could find the strength—and the words—to tell Beau the truth.

Some days he really hated his job.

This wasn't one of them.

Beau grabbed a doughnut from the celebratory box being passed around the weekly briefing. It was one hell of a fine Friday morning.

"Good work, Riley," Dennis Speth said, then swore as a blob of raspberry jelly spurted out of the doughnut he was lifting to his mouth and plopped onto his tie.

"I wasn't too sure we'd really nailed this bastard," his lieutenant mumbled around a mouthful of bearclaw. "We had a few loose ends that still could have used a few more knots."

"The jury only needed an hour to come back with a guilty verdict last night so they must not have agreed. Benelli will have all the time he wants to try unraveling the state's case against him. Twenty-five to life."

He felt like celebrating, in more ways than one. Now that little Laura Benelli's torturer and executioner would spend the rest of his life in prison and the case against the bastard couldn't be jeopardized by his subsequent actions, he could accelerate his investigation against the not-so-honorable Judge Andrew Sheffield.

Maybe once he caught Tina Hidalgo's murderer, he could put Elizabeth Quinn behind him. Maybe the ripe peach scent of her would stop haunting his dreams. Maybe his life could get back to normal.

He had spent nearly a week of sleepless nights, tantalized by the sweet, summery scent of her that lingered in his house, in his bed—though how that damn aroma could still be hanging around defied logic. He'd spent the first sleepless night after she walked out on him doing laundry, washing all his sheets and bedding twice and using double fabric softener in every load. But still they smelled like Elizabeth, enticing and sweet and delectable.

If it was only a scent lingering in his house, he could handle it. Hell, he could always go down to the wharf and bring back a flounder to fry up to give his house a less pleasant aroma.

But thoughts of her were far more intrusive.

No matter how hard he tried—and he'd spent plenty of time since Sunday doing his best—he couldn't go more than a few moments without her elegant features sneaking into his mind, without remembering her heated response to his touch, the eager way she returned his kisses, as if she couldn't get enough.

When she came apart, her eyes went all unfocused and she made the most incredibly sexy sounds….

"Yo, Riley. You still with us?"

He jerked his attention back to the meeting and found a dozen people watching him expectantly. Hell. The meeting had begun and was in full swing while he was sitting here getting all turned on by a memory.

He cleared his throat. "Yeah. I'm here," he answered his lieutenant.

"What have you and Griffin got?"

He tried to focus on work. "We're still following up leads on the Martin hit-and-run and we're close to an arrest in the Chung stabbing. Oh, and I'd like to bring in a suspect for an interview in the Hidalgo case."

Banks frowned and checked the case files in front of him. "Hidalgo case. What Hidalgo case?"

"The exotic dancer who was shot a month ago at the LakeView apartment complex, remember?"

The frown deepened. "Would this be the same exotic dancer whose death the medical examiner and this department ruled a suicide?"

"Yeah. That would be the one."

"The same one I told you to drop?"

"Um, yeah."

"Damn it, we talked about this, Riley. Speth and Walker did clean work on the case. Why are you still wasting your energy and my department's resources?"

"You said I could do it on my own time, remember?"

"Why? It's a dead horse, Riley. Get the hell off."

He shrugged. "I'm still getting a vibe, Charlie. Tina Hidalgo was more than just a stripper. She had a deaf kid and was making plans for their future together, for a special surgical procedure that might have improved his hearing. Why would she do that if she was planning to kill herself?"

"I don't know. Why do jumpers make dinner plans for the next day even as they're heading to the bridge? They just do."

"I don't think Tina Hidalgo offed herself. I'm working on a couple of leads and, like I said, I'd like to interview a possible suspect and check out his alibi if that's okay with you."

"Obviously, a compelling need for my permission to do anything has never particularly bothered you before, Detective Riley."

Beau cleared his throat again. "It could, uh, have a few minor political ramifications for you."

"Oh, great. Just what I need. Who is it? The mayor?"

"No. Andrew Sheffield."

The lieutenant and every other detective in the room stared at him with the same stupefied expression. "Judge Andrew Sheffield?" Banks finally said in a strangled voice.

"Yeah. He and Hidalgo had a thing a few years ago. He was the kid's father and apparently didn't know until a couple weeks before her murder, about the same time he wrote out a check to the stripper. Not chump change, either. A hundred grand."

One of the other detectives whistled, but the lieutenant's

features began to turn an alarming shade of red. "Sheffield paid a stripper off over his illegitimate child to the tune of a hundred grand just days before she dies under suspicious circumstances. And you have known about this for how long?"

"A few weeks." Had it really only been two weeks since he'd kissed Elizabeth in that bank vault? With everything that had occurred between them since, he felt as if he'd known her forever.

"And you never thought to add me to the loop?"

"Obviously this was a delicate situation given the Benelli trial was still underway. We spent six months working the Benelli case, and I didn't want to jeopardize that. I thought it prudent to wait until the trial was over before moving forward."

"You don't know the meaning of the word prudent! Pay a visit to Sheffield and find out what he has to say. I'll try to brace myself for whatever's going to hit the fan."

Beau nodded, relieved at escaping so lightly. The meeting ended and he was on his way back to his desk before he realized his partner hadn't stopped glaring at him for the last twenty minutes.

He sighed and paused outside the door to the squad room. "What did I do now?"

"I'd like to know the same question the lieutenant asked back there. Why didn't you add me to the loop on the Hidalgo case? This is about the case you're working on for Elizabeth Quinn, isn't it?"

He hated the way his insides went all soft and mushy just at the mention of her name. "No," he growled. "This is about Tina Hidalgo. She deserves justice."

"If you had bothered to tell me what was going on in the case, maybe I could help you find it for her. I'm supposed to be your partner, remember? If you can ever manage to get your thick head past the fact that I'm not Grace Dugan."

He'd never seen Griff mad before, but steam was practically shooting out of the kid's ears. "Sorry. You're right, I should have told you."

"Why bother telling me anything? I'm just filling a slot here until you get a real partner, right? Well, here's a news flash for you, Riley. I was a good cop on the beat and I could be a damn good detective if I ever had the chance to do more than track down license numbers and all the rest of your scut work. Well, screw you. I'm putting in for a transfer to a place where maybe I can be more than somebody's errand boy."

Whoa. Where the hell did that come from? Beau gazed at the detective, trying to figure out how to respond. Before he could come up with anything, the phone rang.

He wanted to ignore it but knew he couldn't. Not when he was waiting for calls from a half dozen informants on the pending cases cluttering the top of his desk.

"Yeah," he snapped.

A long, protracted silence met his terse greeting and for a brief second he thought it might be Elizabeth. Before he could analyze his reaction, the caller spoke and extinguished an emotion Beau refused to admit was anything remotely resembling relief and joy.

"Is this Detective Riley?" a woman who most definitely was not Elizabeth asked.

"Yeah."

"This is Leigh Sheffield calling. We met the other night at a party at my home."

How could he forget? "Yes?"

She paused again, reminding him painfully of Elizabeth. "I hope you don't think I'm being too forward but I haven't been able to get you out of my mind."

Yeah, well, he hadn't given her another thought once he and Elizabeth walked out of the Sheffield mansion. Since he was fairly certain she probably wouldn't appreciate that little tidbit of information, he opted to keep his mouth shut.

"I'd like to see you again, Detective," Leigh went on. "I've got this thing for big, dark-haired men with intense eyes and powerful shoulders. I'm not usually so blunt, but I have a feeling the two of us would be phenomenal together."

Beau fought the urge to reach up and loosen his tie.

"I just bought a new yacht, a sweet thirty-six footer from Italy. I thought maybe the two of us could take an evening and sail somewhere private to watch the sunset and maybe not come back until morning. Anytime you want. In fact, I'm taking her out today if you would like to come. All you have to do is just say the word."

He'd rather be dragged buck naked behind a ferry full of his closest friends and co-workers.

"Um, it sounds great, really it does," he lied. "But I'm afraid I can't. I'm, uh, involved with someone right now."

Another long silence met his words, as if she couldn't actually believe someone would refuse her offer. "Don't tell me you and Elizabeth are actually serious."

The shock in her voice seriously annoyed him. While it wasn't technically true, he wasn't about to tell Leigh Sheffield that, not with the animosity between the two women.

"Why do you sound so surprised?"

"Come on, Detective. I figured the other night was a pity date or something. I mean, how could you possibly not be bored to tears after five minutes of conversation with Lizzie? A man like you couldn't seriously be interested in someone like her."

"Someone like her?"

"She's an idiot, Detective! A simpleton. Not quite right in the head, if you know what I mean."

He sat back in his chair, stupefied. What the hell was she

talking about? "Are you sure we're discussing the same person here?"

"Elizabeth Anne Quinn. Blond hair, blue eyes. Daughter to the late media mogul Jonathan Quinn. The Elizabeth Quinn whose IQ and dress size are roughly the same."

Even for Leigh Sheffield, that kind of remark seemed bitchy in the extreme.

"The Elizabeth Quinn I know is bright and funny," he said stiffly.

"She must really have you snowed." She didn't bother hiding her cruelty now. It was exposed in her voice, like a thin, jagged fissure bisecting limestone.

"Here's the way it is, Detective. Lizzie is a freak and she always has been. Believe me, I've known her all my life. She didn't even talk until she was six or seven and then she stuttered so badly you couldn't even understand her. When she did get a word out, it was usually the wrong one. It used to curdle my stomach at dinner parties to have to listen to Lizzie asking someone to pass the salt and p-p-p-puppy. Poor Jonathan. She was worse than a disappointment to him. She was a complete embarrassment. He could barely stand to be in the same room with her. She hasn't changed any over the years. She might be better at hiding it, but she's still the same babbling idiot she's always been."

It was a damn good thing he was already sitting down since all the air whooshed out of him as if he'd just taken a billy club to the gut.

Suddenly everything made sense. All the missing pieces of the Elizabeth Quinn puzzle came flying together and clicked into stunning place.

He thought of the way she hesitated before speaking, her dislike of crowds, the serious frown of concentration on her face whenever she was listening to him.

She wasn't cold or distant. She was struggling with a communicative disorder.

He was the idiot here. With grim clarity, he recalled his deliberate cruelty before she left his house Sunday night. How he had taunted her with her reputation as an ice princess, had called her cold.

His words must have seemed as cruel to Elizabeth as the venom the woman on the other end of the line was spewing.

Layered underneath his shock and self-disgust was another emotion, something tender and scary that he wasn't completely sure he wanted to identify.

"Now that you know about Elizabeth, are you ready to come out with me on my yacht?" Leigh Sheffield's purr in his ear grated down his spine like metal scraping on metal. "I can show you what it's like to be with a woman who not only knows what she wants but can string more than three words together at a time to tell you about it. What do you think?"

"I think I have far better things to do with my time than waste another minute of it talking to someone like you."

He slammed the phone back into the cradle and swore roundly.

Griffin had taken a seat at his own desk during Beau's phone conversation. Now he leaned back in his chair and watched him warily. "Everything okay?"

"No," Beau muttered. He wasn't sure anything would ever be okay again. His chest ached and he couldn't seem to catch his breath.

When he decided to tangle up his life, he did it with a holy vengeance. All those scary emotions floated to the surface, and he finally acknowledged what he'd been afraid to face for days.

He was in love with Elizabeth Quinn.

How the hell had that happened?

He thought of her on the *Mari*, her eyes shining and her slender hands flying as she talked with Alex. Of her laughing with Luisa the day he'd eaten dinner at Harbor View.

Of her gently kissing the scar tissue left over from his gun-shot wound.

He was such an idiot.

"Anything I can do to help?" Griff asked.

Yeah, take back the last two weeks, before Elizabeth walked into his life with her solemn eyes and her Grace Kelly hair and her lush mouth. "No. Unless you have any ideas about how to apologize to a woman when you've been a complete jackass."

Griffin raised an eyebrow. "I would have thought you've had plenty of practice with that in your lifetime, haven't you?"

He made a face. He hated to admit it, but Griffin was starting to grow on him. He was going to have to figure out how to keep the kid around. Right after he figured out how to convince the woman he loved to take a chance on a stubborn, ornery cuss of a cop.

Chapter 16

When can Beau come and play with us again?

In the vast, gleaming Harbor View kitchen, elbow-deep in dough, Elizabeth mentally groaned at what had become Alex's favorite question. In the week since their boat ride, the boy had mentioned Beau at least a few dozen times a day.

Beau said this. Beau did that. Beau is so strong he could row all the way to China.

She wasn't sure how much more she could take. Several times she had tried to gently explain to him that although Beau had been kind enough to take them out on his boat once, she wasn't sure when—or if—he would be able to do it again.

No matter how many times she explained it, though, Alex didn't seem to comprehend. He would nod as if he did, then bring up Beau's name again just a few moments later, asking the same question.

How could she tell him Beau would probably never be

coming again? Harbor View was likely the last place on earth Beau Riley wanted to see after the tension between them when she had left his house early Monday morning, but she didn't know how to tell Alex that.

As usual, no words came immediately to mind. Frustrated with herself—how hard could it be to speak to a five-year-old, for heaven's sake?—she glanced across the kitchen at Luisa, but the boy's grandmother wasn't any help at all. She simply raised one dark eyebrow, then went back to work at her cutting board.

"I'm not sure." Elizabeth finally repeated the same thing she'd been saying all week, signing the words as well as speaking them aloud. "Beau is very busy."

She tried to turn his attention back to the dough they were kneading for rolls, praying this time Alex would be content with the answer and stop asking.

Even the mention of his name scraped her raw heart. How could he have become so vital to her life in just a few short weeks? His smile, his laughter, his strong, sturdy shoulders. Without him, she felt bleak, hollow. Empty.

She missed him. Dear heaven, she missed him so much she wanted to weep with it.

She needed to call him, to ask the status of the investigation into Tina's murder—if there still indeed *was* an investigation. She knew she had to call him, but so far she hadn't been able to gather the courage.

Although she had picked up the phone several times since Sunday night when she had left his bed, each time her heart pounded so loudly in her ears she was afraid she wouldn't be able to hear herself think. She had hung up quickly before even dialing the last number.

She was such a baby. A big, stupid baby. She sighed and flipped the dough over, directing Alex to do the same with his smaller ball of dough. The little boy usually loved the tactile ritual of measuring ingredients, pouring, mixing, working the dough.

She could only hope it would keep his hands busy enough that he wouldn't be able to ask any more heartbreaking questions she didn't know how to answer.

Not this time. After another pause, Alex pulled his hands out of the dough and carefully wiped them on his white apron.

Is Beau mad at us? he signed the words with a forlorn little look.

Elizabeth's hands clenched in the dough. Because of Tina's lifestyle and his special needs, Alex had had so many transitory people in his little life. Baby-sitters, speech therapists, Tina's friends. She hated trying to make him understand that Beau—the man he so adored—would probably be another one.

Her heart heavy, she wiped her hands as well and signed back. *He's not mad at you. I promise.*

Just me, she added to herself.

Then why won't he come back?

I told you, honey. He's very busy. He works hard all day long to catch people who break the law. He doesn't have much time to go on his boat or to call us.

She paused and forced a smile. *Now let's stop talking about Beau and help your grandmother with the rolls.*

Alex's lower lip jutted out in ominous warning of an approaching tantrum. *I don't want to make rolls. I want to go on the boat again. I want to see the whales. I want to play with Beau!*

He signed this last so emphatically that his hands caught the side of the bowl containing the dough. It whirled around and then skated across the counter. Elizabeth reached for it but her hands were slick and messy and she couldn't grab hold. All she could do was gasp as it soared off the edge of the counter.

The dough went flying one way, the bowl another. The plop of the dough hitting the floor and the clang from the metal bowl doing the same seemed to echo on forever in the kitchen.

For one horrible moment Elizabeth was afraid she would burst into tears. Alex looked as stricken as she felt. He covered his mouth with sticky fingers, and his eyes welled up.

"Ah, niños. No es importante." Luisa bustled over and began cleaning up the mess. "I can make more dough."

I'm sorry, Alex signed with a sniffle, the tears now sliding down his little nose and pooling at the corners of his mouth.

"Oh, sweetheart. I know you are," Elizabeth replied.

"I will finish this," Luisa said. "Now that the rain has stopped, why don't you take that dog outside and enjoy the sunshine for a while? I will tell you when dinner is ready."

Shall we wash our hands and then take Maddie outside to play? she signed to Alex.

He nodded and swiped at his tears with his sleeve, then followed her to the sink to wash up.

By the time their hands were clean and they went to Maddie's crate in the family room where the puppy was taking a nap, his sniffles had stopped with the rapidfire mood swings of small children and he had tugged his hand from hers to sign rapidly to her about a game he had played at preschool that morning.

As she watched his pudgy little fingers signing so enthusiastically, she had to fight tears again. He was such a sweet, happy little child, brimming over with joy and love. How could anyone not adore him?

She wanted so many things for him—most of all for him to know without any doubt that he was loved. She and Luisa would give him that, now that his mother was gone. They already had through much of his life, but she wondered again if it would be enough.

He did have a parent left, she reminded herself. Her

thoughts immediately drifted to Andrew. Although he
hadn't called since the party Sunday night, he claimed he
wanted to be part of Alex's life. What part would he play?

She was so grateful he didn't appear in any hurry to make
a place for himself in his son's life. Alex needed time to
adjust to his new circumstances before he had to cope with
a father he didn't know.

Can we play in the water? Alex asked as they unhooked
the dog's crate and let her out to jump around them in
delight.

*It's probably too cold for us. But Maddie can swim if she
wants.* The dog was thrilled to be outside playing after several days of rain. With her tail pumping like crazy, she raced
around, sniffing at every rock and rain-soaked plant.

Alex giggled, content for now to chase after her around
the garden, so Elizabeth gravitated toward her favorite
bench overlooking the water and the city skyline where she
could keep a careful eye on them.

Traffic was light on the water today, probably because
the Sound was still choppy from a week of stormy weather.

She watched a few commercial ships for a while, trying
fiercely to keep her thoughts from straying toward Beau.
They had been outside for perhaps a half hour when she
spotted a blue-and-white craft veer away from the main
channel and head in her direction.

For one heart-stopping moment, she thought it might be
Beau. Joy burst through her and she caught her breath. As
the boat neared, she exhaled on a disappointed sigh. Not the
Mari, she could see now. Beau's cabin cruiser was comfortable and well-appointed but this yacht, though smaller,
screamed luxury, from the teak decks to the sophisticated
lines.

The yacht seemed to be heading right for Harbor View.
The captain brought her hard to starboard then maneuvered
against the dock. Elizabeth frowned again. She was going

to have to tell whoever was at the helm that this was a private moorage—the public landings were farther north in Eagle Harbor.

The yacht must have finally caught Alex's attention. He and the dog skidded to a stop near the bench, both panting hard. Alex gazed at the watercraft for a few seconds, then offered up a huge smile that lit up his little face.

"Beau!" he signed and spoke aloud. The word surprised her—although his therapists had been working on oral speech, Alex had stubbornly resisted using his voice.

"Beau! Beau! Beau!" Alex repeated. He gave three or four excited hops, then raced down the dock toward the boat.

"No, honey. It's not Beau," she began, but of course he couldn't tell what she was saying with his back turned. She hurried after him on the rain-slick dock, the dog racing around her legs.

Alex had a head start and his way wasn't hindered by fifty pounds of excited dog. He beat her to the yacht just as she saw someone throw a bowline to secure the craft to the dock.

She stopped in shock when she saw Leigh Sheffield step off the yacht "Leigh! This is a…surprise. What brings you to Harbor View?"

"I was visiting friends up north. As I was passing around the island and saw Harbor View, I realized I hadn't been here since your father died. I had a sudden whim to come out and show off my new Piazzo. I'm so excited about her, I'm showing everyone."

"She's beautiful. Truly b-beautiful." She cringed at the stutter, wondering why Leigh always seemed to bring out the worst in her. Probably because whenever she was with her, she was once more a lost, lonely little girl trapped in a world of silence, desperately eager to make herself understood.

To her relief, Leigh didn't make any of her usual sly, cutting comments. "Yes. She is," she murmured, then turned her attention to Alex. "And who's this?"

Elizabeth instinctively grabbed Alex's hand, even though she knew her sudden protective impulse was silly. Leigh wasn't going to hurt him.

Oh, dear heaven, she realized suddenly. Leigh was Alex's half sister. Why hadn't she made the connection before?

"This is Alex," she said after a moment, forcing a polite smile.

Leigh continued to study him with a strange expression on her face, one Elizabeth couldn't identify. Did she know about Andrew and Tina? That Alex was her father's child?

She couldn't possibly know. Elizabeth couldn't imagine Andrew taking his daughter into his confidence about something so awkward and complicated.

Still, she had to wonder, especially at Leigh's next question.

"Is this Tina's kid?" she asked, her voice taking on a hard, flat tone.

That didn't necessarily mean she knew Alex was Andrew's son, Elizabeth assured herself. Maybe it had more to do with Tina.

The two of them had always rubbed each other wrong. Leigh looked down her snobby nose at Tina for being the daughter of the hired help and Tina used to make Elizabeth rock with laughter at her dead-on imitations of Leigh at her most bitchy.

"Yes," she murmured just as Alex pulled his hand free and signed that he wanted to go onto the boat.

No, honey, she replied. *Not now.*

Leigh narrowed her gaze at the two of them. "What did you two just say?"

Elizabeth considered lying but she couldn't come up with

anything that sounded remotely credible so she stuck with the truth. "Alex wanted to see your yacht. I told him no."

Leigh's smile was several fathoms short of friendly. "I would love to show it to the cute little guy. Why don't the two of you come aboard and take a closer look?"

Elizabeth hesitated, uneasy for reasons she didn't quite understand. Every time she talked to Leigh she felt as if she was swimming through thick, confusing layers of meaning. Leigh probably did it on purpose to make her feel even more stupid.

She paused for too long, until Leigh began to frown with impatience. Still, Elizabeth couldn't come up with a single plausible excuse not to accept the invitation so she grabbed Alex's hand, ordered Maddie to stay and followed Leigh onto the yacht.

The craft was small, sleek. It wasn't as large as her father's yacht had been but was every bit as luxurious, from the glossy teak trim to the sparkling paint.

"It's lovely," Elizabeth murmured in the salon, with its plush cushions and efficient galley.

"Thank you. I had it custom-made in Italy for me. The Italians know their yachts, even though it took them long enough to finish the damn thing. I've been waiting nearly a year for it."

Of course Leigh would spare none of Andrew's money in pursuit of her own pleasure.

Elizabeth couldn't help comparing this grand craft to the *Mari*. Despite all the stately amenities of Leigh's yacht, she thought Beau's boat was far more comfortable.

Leigh paused at a doorway off the salon. "And this is the pièce de résistance. The stateroom." She opened the door and gestured for them to go inside ahead of her.

Elizabeth tightened her hold on Alex's hand, afraid he would accidentally break something, and stepped into the cabin.

The Italian designers had pulled out all the stops in here. If the rest of the yacht was luxurious, the stateroom was positively opulent, from the thick carpet to the glittering chandelier to a vast, plush-covered bed.

The only odd note was a huge mirror above the bed that gave the room the feel of a high-class floating bordello.

"Gorgeous, isn't it?" Leigh asked behind them.

"Um, yes," Elizabeth answered. Except for the mirror. She would absolutely hate staring at herself first thing in the morning before she had time to put on makeup or fix her hair. Leigh probably didn't need to worry about that, though. She likely woke up looking as gorgeous and polished as she did right now.

"Take a look at the marble tub in the head. I had it custom-made to my specification."

Elizabeth only wanted to get off the blasted boat and return to her comfort zone at Harbor View. Maybe if she humored Leigh, they could exit the yacht that much quicker. She opened the door to the bathroom and admired the creamy tub.

"It's beautiful," she started to murmur to Leigh just as she heard a door being closed.

What on earth? She turned to the now-empty stateroom just in time to hear the snick of a lock engaging.

"Leigh?" She hurried to the door and twisted the knob, but it wouldn't budge. "Leigh, what's going on?"

A harsh laugh on the other side of the door met her question. "Sorry about this, Lizzie. You'll be staying right where you are for a while. The three of us are going to have to take a little trip now and I'll be too busy up top to worry about you getting into trouble."

For the first time, panic began to replace her confusion. What was Leigh up to now? "We need to get off, Leigh. Luisa will be looking for us."

''Poor thing. She's going to have a long and fruitless search then, isn't she?''

Elizabeth stared at the teak door with its brass fittings, wishing she could see the other woman to read by her body language what in heaven's name was going on.

''Leigh, this isn't f-funny. Unlock the door.''

''F-f-fraid not, Lizzie.'' Leigh laughed again. ''You and the little deaf-mute are going to be staying right where you are.''

Elizabeth gazed down at Alex, grateful he couldn't hear Leigh's derision. He didn't seem to be paying any attention to them. He had settled on the wide bed and appeared to be having a grand time wielding the remote control to open and close the oak cabinet that held a sophisticated entertainment system.

''Leigh, please. Let us out.'' She hated the pleading note in her voice, especially when it was directed toward this woman who had always been so cruel to her, but for Alex she would endure any humiliation.

''Nope. Now I've got to run for a while. Don't you two go anywhere.''

Leigh laughed again and then all Elizabeth could hear was the sound of receding footsteps.

A few moments later she heard the yacht's diesel motors start up then the craft smoothly pulled away from the dock.

Alex grinned with excitement to be on the water again. *Are we going to see the whales?* he signed.

She gazed at him, panic a wild fluttering in her stomach. She had to stay calm for Alex's sake. *I'm not sure. Maybe.*

While Alex busied himself exploring the stateroom, Elizabeth sat on the edge of the luxurious bed, stunned into frozen inactivity. What could Leigh be thinking? Was this another of her cruel, taunting games? Would she circle around and drop them off at Harbor View in a few moments?

Somehow she didn't think so. This all had the feel of something carefully planned. But why? What could Leigh possibly have to gain by kidnapping them?

Ransom? If she had only taken Alex, Elizabeth might have reached that conclusion—she would pay *anything* to have the child back if someone kidnapped him. But Leigh certainly had no need of money. Andrew was as wealthy as her own father had been.

Besides, taking both her and Alex for ransom didn't make sense. Who would Leigh petition for the money? Certainly not Luisa. She wouldn't be able to access any of Elizabeth's accounts.

Alex stopped in front of her. He must have sensed her tension because he was suddenly subdued, watchful. *I wish Beau was here,* he signed.

Oh, me, too, honey. She managed a smile and pulled the child close to her.

I don't like that lady.

That makes two of us, she thought, then was suddenly struck by a horrible, hideous thought.

Alex.

Oh, dear Lord. Maybe this all had to do with Alex.

She could hear her pulse roaring like the sea in her ear, and the cabin suddenly seemed overwarm, airless. She started breathing in shallow, quick gulps and she felt light-headed, dizzy.

No. She couldn't panic, not when she had a child to protect.

Think about Beau, she urged herself. How would he handle this situation? He would be calm and level-headed, to start with. And he would figure out a way to escape.

She focused first on Alex. To her relief, the boy busied himself looking out the porthole for a while, then curled up on the bed and dozed off, rocked by the rough sea.

For the next hour Elizabeth tried to make sense of what

was happening. She was considering her very limited options when she heard a key being fitted to the lock and a moment later the door swung open. Her relief was short-lived. Leigh stood in the doorway holding an ugly black handgun.

That wild panic fluttered back. Leigh with a gun didn't strike her as a good combination.

"Why are we stopping?"

"We're not. We've just moved out of traffic enough that I can put her on autopilot. I just had to come down and make sure nobody's puked on my bed. Neither you or the kid is seasick, are you?"

She thought wildly about faking it and wondered if that would gain her any advantage but immediately discarded the idea. Though her stomach was queasy enough, she didn't think she could manage to convince Leigh she was *that* sick.

"No."

"Good. What do you think about my baby? She cuts through those waves like a bird riding the current."

How could she stand there with a gun in her hand and speak so casually about a damn boat? Elizabeth wasn't good at small talk under the best of circumstances. Since this obviously wasn't a social occasion, she wasn't even going to try.

"Leigh, what is this about? Have you gone completely crazy?"

The other woman's smile hardened. "No, I'm not crazy. I would have thought it was obvious what this is about. But maybe not to a half-wit like you."

"Yes. I'm stupid. We both know that. So spell it out for me in simple, easy to understand words. Why are you kidnapping us?"

Leigh glanced over at Alex sleeping on the bed then back at her, and the angry set to her features sent that panic fluttering through Elizabeth again. "Tina should have kept her big, greedy mouth shut. If she had never written that letter to my father, everything would have been fine. He never would have known about the brat.''

"This is about *Alex?*"

"Yeah. My dear baby brother.''

So Leigh knew about Tina's affair with Andrew. How long had she known? Before or after Tina's death?

Her freewheeling thoughts suddenly jerked to an abrupt halt. Tina. Oh, dear heaven.

"You killed Tina, didn't you?" She didn't know how she knew, but she had absolutely no doubt.

Leigh didn't bother to deny it. "Brilliant deduction, Sherlock. Yeah, I killed the whore. She deserved it. She would have ruined my father. Completely destroyed him! If word got out that he had a kid with a junkie stripper, his reputation would have been shredded. I refused to sit by and let that happen.''

Elizabeth barely heard her over the grief and shock rushing through her. She couldn't breathe again, could barely think to sort through the hundreds of questions crowding her brain.

"Why k-kill her?" she finally asked.

"To shut her up.''

"She wouldn't have told anyone! Alex is five years old and she never asked Andrew for…for anything in all those years!''

"She would have bled him dry eventually. I know she would have. Fifty-thousand here, a hundred thousand there. I'd be damned before I let some low-class slut of a stripper and her whiny brat take my share.''

"So you shot her.''

"What choice did I have? After she wrote to him, my father told me about his little indiscretion. He told me he planned to take full responsibility for the brat. My newfound little brother. It would be laughable if it wasn't so pathetic.

I argued with him—she knew exactly what she was doing when she chose to screw around, he didn't need to pay the price for her mistake—but he wouldn't listen.''

Why had she never noticed how cold Leigh's eyes could be? Elizabeth wondered.

"I like my father's fortune," she went on. "I've never made a secret of that. I like having money and I don't like having to share.''

"How did you…kill her?" She didn't want to hear the answer but she had to know.

"I thought I was being particularly clever, if I do say so myself. She wasn't expecting me to pay a little visit. It wasn't hard to take her by surprise at the door and inject her with enough heroin that she was feeling no pain. It took a few minutes for it to kick in but she was too stupid to realize what was going to happen. She didn't even put up a fight.''

"You forced her to…to write the suicide note?"

"Yeah. She was too dopey to do more than write those few words. I'm sorry. That's all, and believe me, by then she was. Then I just held her hand on the gun and pulled the trigger.''

Now she did think she would be sick, all over Leigh's luxuriously appointed stateroom. She forced down the slick nausea. Later. She could be sick later. Now she had to survive.

"What are you…" She drew several deep breaths, trying to gain control of her careening thoughts. "What are you planning for Alex and me?"

"Since there's nothing you can do about it, I may as well tell you. As soon as we get a little farther from civilization, you and the kid are going for a swim. Oh, did I mention you'll be unconscious at the time? Knock-out drugs can come in so handy. I'm sure you've heard that drowning is actually quite a pleasant way to die.''

Elizabeth stopped breathing. She wanted to curl up into a quivering ball of panic but couldn't.

"Someone will have…seen us come aboard."

"Who would have seen you? Luisa? Who's going to take the word of a barely literate housekeeper over me?"

"You won't get away with it. I have a…a friend who's a police detective. If Alex and I turn up missing, he's going to figure out why."

"Ah, yes. Your good friend Mr. Riley. I spoke with him today, did he tell you that?"

She gazed at Leigh, unable to answer. She couldn't very well tell her she hadn't spoken with Beau in nearly a week.

"Of course he didn't. Well, let me tell you, we had an interesting little chat. You've been a naughty girl, keeping secrets from your boyfriend, haven't you, Lizzie?"

The heat of her fear turned suddenly cold. "What do you…what do you mean?"

"Did you really think a man like that would be interested in someone like you?" She gave a mocking laugh. "I told him all about our poor bumble-tongued little Lizzie. He had quite a strong reaction, I can tell you that. Then the two of us had a good laugh over you and your pathetic attempts to appear normal."

Bile again rose in her throat. It shouldn't matter, not when she and Alex were about to die, but it did. Oh, it did.

And yet…

Her gaze narrowed as she studied the other woman.

"You're lying," she said calmly.

For an instant Leigh looked taken aback, as if the thick pile carpet under her feet had reached up and taken a chunk out of her big toe.

Elizabeth had absolutely no doubt she was lying. Beau never would have laughed at her. Never. The man she loved with all her soul was simply incapable of showing the kind of cruelty Leigh and others of her ilk seemed to revel in.

She'd been so stupid not to realize it before. Not to trust him enough to tell him the truth about her speech impairment.

Beau cared for her. She knew it, had known it in his arms, but she had been too frightened of rejection to trust her own instincts.

She had to get them through this so she could tell him how wrong she had been.

"You can believe what you want but your detective was as disgusted by you as your father always was. You're an idiot and you always have been," Leigh said with a sneer.

The words should have stung her like a thousand jellyfish but Elizabeth suddenly realized Leigh was right. She *had* been an idiot. She had given cruel, tiny-minded people like this woman and like her fiancé far too much power over her.

And her father. She couldn't forget her father. She had built her life around trying to gain his acceptance, trying to mold herself into becoming someone she was not.

But no matter how hard she tried, she could never be good enough for him—or for the Leigh Sheffields in her life—because she let them make her feel stupid and awkward.

She couldn't afford to be stupid now. She had to keep all her wits about her so she could figure out a way to get Alex to safety. She needed time and space to come up with a plan, and she could only think of one way to gain a little of both.

Praying her acting skills would be up to the challenge, she pressed a hand to her stomach and moaned. The sea helped her out by tossing the yacht just a little more than normal, until she was only half faking.

Leigh's eyes widened in consternation. "If you're going to hurl, do it in the head! That's a fifty-thousand-dollar antique Persian rug."

"Ohhh," she groaned.

"Hurry! If you throw up on my rug, I'll forget about the knockout drugs and just toss you overboard."

Elizabeth faked a gag and rushed to the bathroom. While she pretended to dry heave over the toilet, out of the corner of her gaze she saw Leigh give her a disgusted look for her weakness then leave the stateroom, locking the door behind her.

When she was sure Leigh was gone, Elizabeth sat up, wiping her mouth as if she really had been sick.

She had a little time now to come up with a plan but she didn't have the first clue where to start.

Chapter 17

The sun was just beginning its long, slow slide beneath the horizon when Beau maneuvered the *Mari* to the Harbor View dock.

He inhaled cool, moist air smelling of the sea and the sharp, citrusy scent of wet pine from the trees surrounding the estate.

Under ordinary circumstances, he would be enjoying such a beautifully crisp autumn evening after the constant rain they'd had for the past few days, but he was far too nervous.

He was nuts. He had to be. He had considered just driving out to Bainbridge on the ferry to talk to her. It would have been quicker and easier all around, but he was half-afraid Elizabeth wouldn't open the gates of Harbor View for him.

Coming in the back way from the water might be sneaky, but at least this way she couldn't turn him away.

He had some crazy idea of taking her out on the *Mari* to see the city lights, softening her up with wine and the dinner he'd picked up from his favorite restaurant before he left, then baring his heart to her. Nature hadn't cooperated very well, though. The Sound was probably too rough for an evening pleasure cruise anyway.

Beau glanced down at the items on the table next to him. He felt like a complete idiot. Did he really expect a bouquet of flowers—even if it was the largest one he could find— and a book of poems Griff promised would soften even the hardest hearts could make up for his cruelty?

She would probably refuse to even talk to him. And then what would he do? Slink back into the night, he guessed. Figure out a way to go on without her in his life.

He sat in the pilothouse for several more moments trying to figure out what to say to her. He wanted to stay right there where it was safe but knew he'd have to go inside soon. Someone inside the house must have seen the *Mari* dock, and they were probably in there wondering what the hell he was doing out here.

Feeling foolish and unsure of himself, he gripped the flowers in one hand, the book in the other and headed toward the house.

He heard Maddie inside as he approached the back door. She seemed to be just on the other side, barking up a storm. After he knocked, Luisa opened the door and the dog just about bowled him over in her frenzied rush toward the water.

"Whoa. What's your hurry, pup? Been inside a little too long?"

The dog raced to the dock, still barking. He turned back to Luisa and found her studying him, her expression puzzled.

"Detective." She looked over his shoulder. "Where are Miss Elizabeth and my Alex?"

"I don't know. Should I?"

Luisa's frown deepened, her eyes dark, uneasy. "They are not with you? On your boat?"

"No. I just arrived." Something didn't feel right here. His instincts suddenly started humming and sparking like a downed power line. "Why would you think they were with me?"

"I saw them from the window earlier. They were going onto a boat, a white-and-blue one like yours. I did not have a very good look at the person with them but I thought it must have been you and that you all went for a ride like before."

"Elizabeth didn't tell you where she and Alex were going and who they were with?"

"No. She said nothing."

That struck him as very strange. Out of character, not at all something Elizabeth would do. Luisa must have sensed the same thing. She began to look distressed, frightened. He had a feeling she was just a few seconds away from wringing her hands.

"What is happening? Where could they be?"

"I'm sure it's nothing. Maybe a friend stopped by and they went for a quick cruise around." A niggling little thought hovered at the edge of his consciousness but he couldn't quite put his finger on it.

"They left Maddie. I found her barking outside on the dock. It seemed strange but I did not worry because I thought they had gone with you. I thought you would bring them home soon."

"How long ago did you see them?"

She shrugged, her brown eyes wet now with unshed tears. "Maybe an hour, maybe more. I cannot say."

"What did the boat look like? Do you remember any identifying details at all?"

"I did not see very well. Like yours, that's all I remember. Blue and white."

"Did you happen to see a name on it?"

"No. I am sorry, Detective."

She looked so distressed he didn't want to push her but she was the only one who might have seen something so he had to keep at her. If he pushed hard enough, maybe she'd remember.

"Did Elizabeth know anyone else who had a boat that color?"

"No. No one. Just you. Her father, he had friends with boats but they do not come to see Miss Elizabeth. Something is wrong. I can feel it. She would not have left like that without telling me. I should have called the *policia* as soon as I knew they were gone."

He had to admit he was inclined to agree with her. The whole thing didn't smell right. "Let's not panic, Luisa. Since I have my own boat here, I'll go back out on the water and take a look around while I make a few phone calls to see what I can find out."

He didn't want to scare her further so he didn't add that he planned to alert the Coast Guard as soon as he could get to the radio.

"I'm sure they'll both be back any minute." He tried to give her a reassuring smile, but he had a feeling since she didn't react that he wasn't very convincing. "Why don't I give you my cell number, and you can call me when she shows up?"

She nodded and he quickly wrote down his number for her, then hurried back to the *Mari,* conscious of the tension rippling through him like relentless, storm-tossed waves.

The cruiser roared to life, her twin diesel engines throbbing, and he pulled away from the dock. He didn't have the first idea where to go. Puget Sound consisted of hundreds of tiny islands with two thousand miles of coastline. They could be anywhere.

He was probably making far too much of this. She and Alex were probably just fine, enjoying an evening cruise with a friend. But he couldn't help remembering how on the day she had sailed out with him, Elizabeth had made a point of returning to the house to tell Luisa before they headed out, even though Luisa had probably known all about their planned excursion.

Why would she break with routine this time and take off without a word to Alex's grandmother, leaving Maddie outside unattended in the process? It didn't make sense.

He frowned, wishing he could put a finger on the niggling little thought still hovering just out of reach.

He picked up the VHF and was tuning to the Coast Guard channel 16 when it struck him.

Andrew Sheffield had a yacht, and so did his daughter, a new Italian-built yacht she was all too eager to show off. Both of them would be well acquainted with the waters around Harbor View and would know all about the deep-water dock.

And Leigh had told him she planned to take her new yacht out that evening.

He frowned. Leigh would never take Elizabeth and Alex up for a pleasure cruise. Not with the enmity between the two women.

He carefully returned the handset to the radio back to the cradle, his mind racing. He stared at the horizon trying to make sense of his sudden suspicions as the moon began to rise above the shoreline.

If Andrew Sheffield killed Tina to keep her quiet, killing the kid would be a logical next step to make sure the whole deep, dark secret stayed buried forever. But Sheffield had to know that anybody who wanted the kid would have to go through Elizabeth first.

Damn it. He should have anticipated this.

He quickly hit the speed dial on his cell phone to reach the night shift at the precinct. To his surprise, Griffin answered the phone.

"What are you doing working so late?" he asked.

"I've been going over the Hidalgo case file, trying to see if I can find something here we're missing."

For a moment he didn't know what to say about Griff's diligence. Beau was passionate about his job but even he forced himself to take time off occasionally to protect against burnout.

"Well, good job," he finally said. "Listen, I need a favor. Can you get me Andrew Sheffield's private line? I don't have time to explain but I need it ASAP. Griff, it's important."

His partner didn't hesitate, and Beau realized again how unfair he'd been to the other detective. "Sure. Let me see what I can do."

He was passing Eagle Harbor when his cell phone rang just a few moments later. "I've got two numbers for you, his house on Mercer and his own office number. That cute new assistant district attorney says this is the emergency line they try to use when they need warrants in the middle of the night, so you should be able to reach him if he's home."

Beau wrote the numbers down on the edge of a chart. "Thanks."

"Anything else I can do?"

He thought about it and realized he would be stupid to play Lone Ranger on this one. Too much was at stake. "Yeah. I'm going to give you an address on Bainbridge Island. It's Elizabeth Quinn's place. I want you to go there and start interviewing neighbors, see if any of them saw Elizabeth and a little boy get onto a blue-and-white power yacht. I'm looking for anything that can identify the yacht. It might be a wasted trip for you but I could use your help."

"Right. Is this an official investigation?"

"Not yet, so play it low-key."

Griffin agreed, and Beau quickly gave him directions to Harbor View. It would take his partner an hour to get there but he had to admit it felt good to have someone watching his back.

He continued scanning for any other blue-and-white yachts on the water as he dialed Sheffield's private number. He didn't expect anyone to answer so he was surprise when the judge himself picked up after four rings.

"Yes?"

Beau paused, not sure what to do now. If the judge was at home to answer the phone then he hadn't taken Elizabeth and Alex.

That left Leigh—or someone else completely unknown.

What motive would the judge's daughter have to abduct Elizabeth and Alex? Did she know about her new half brother?

He cleared his throat. "This is Beau Riley."

There was a long pause on the other end where he guessed the judge was trying to figure out why he might be calling him at home.

"Yes, Detective Riley." Though puzzled, he sounded cordial enough, not like a person with something to hide. "How may I help you?"

"You can tell me if your daughter is home."

He could practically hear the temperature in the judge's voice plummet several degrees. "Leigh? What business do you have with my daughter?"

"It's, ah, personal."

Beau winced as soon as the words left his mouth. It would be entirely too easy for someone to misconstrue such a statement to mean he had a personal involvement with the barracuda. Last the judge knew, Beau and Elizabeth were hot and heavy. He probably wouldn't be too thrilled at the idea of Beau sniffing around his daughter now.

"I'm afraid Leigh is not at home right now." Sure enough, Sheffield's voice was positively frigid. "I shall certainly give her a message that you called."

He had never been less in the mood for diplomacy. "Where is she?"

The judge bristled. "I don't believe I like your tone, Detective. What business is it of yours?"

"Look, I need to know, did Leigh take her new yacht out this afternoon? It's important."

Sheffield paused for a moment. "Yes. At least that's what she told our housekeeper."

"What color and make is the yacht?" Beau asked urgently, his mind spinning with grim possibilities.

"Unless you explain to me what this is about, I don't think I need to give you that information."

He ground his teeth. Damn it, he did *not* have time for this. "It's about Elizabeth Quinn and your son."

"My…son?"

"Yes. Your kid, Alex Hidalgo. I have reason to believe he and Elizabeth might be in trouble. They've disappeared."

"And you think Leigh and her new yacht might have something to do with it?"

He hoped not. He sincerely hoped not. "I don't know." He paused then plowed ahead. "Can you tell me if your daughter knew about your affair with Tina?"

The judge said nothing for several seconds, then he sighed heavily. "Since you already appear to know so much about my personal business, I don't see any point in denying it. Yes. She knew. I told her as soon as I found out about Alex."

"I don't imagine she was too thrilled about it."

"Leigh can be…difficult. She was mortified about the whole mess, and with good reason. I'm sorry but I still don't understand how you think any of this might be linked to Elizabeth and Alex going missing."

Leigh had as much motive as her father to permanently silence Tina. How did he tell a man his daughter had just risen to the top of a pretty small list of murder suspects?

"Luisa Hidalgo saw them go onto a yacht this afternoon, then they vanished without a word to her about where they were going, very unusual for Elizabeth. I need you to give me the identifying detail of Leigh's yacht. Call numbers, color, make. Anything you know."

"You think they might be with Leigh?"

The judge's outrage was really starting to get on his nerves. "Look, Sheffield, Tina Hidalgo didn't commit suicide. She was murdered. Up until now, you've been the chief suspect but I'm beginning to think we may have been wrong. Elizabeth and Alex could be in danger."

"Are you saying you think Leigh killed Tina?" The judge's voice rose. "And that now she's planning to hurt Elizabeth and Alex? That's ridiculous! Completely ludicrous."

"Maybe so." Beau's voice hardened. "But if you don't help me and I find out your daughter is involved—if I find out she has managed to hurt Elizabeth or Alex in any way before I can get to them—I'm coming after you, Sheffield."

Silence met his harsh promise, then after several beats the judge spoke quietly, his tone subdued. "I think you're completely wrong but I don't see the harm in giving you the information you want. My daughter's yacht is a thirty-six-foot Piazzo. It's blue and white with a flybridge and a secondary mast. It goes by the name *Minx* and the call letters are alpha charlie four-niner-two."

He paused. "Find them, Detective. Please."

"I intend to," Beau vowed, and severed the connection.

I want to go home now, Alex signed, a petulant look on his face. *I'm hungry.*

I know, she answered. *We'll go home soon.*

Please, God. But first she had to figure out a way out of this. While the yacht's powerful motors carried them ever closer to what she feared would be their doom, Elizabeth continued her search of the stateroom, looking for any kind of weapon.

Oh, there were drawers full of skimpy lingerie and sex toys of all shapes and sizes. She wasn't sure she would ever be able to stop blushing from having to look through them all. But unless she could figure out some way to turn a bustier and a vibrator into a slingshot of some kind, they were in serious trouble.

She *had* found some handcuffs that might be useful if she could somehow figure out a way to distract Leigh while she took that deadly looking gun away from her.

She hated this! The only thing she wanted to do was climb into that bed and pull the covers over her head, pretend this was just some hideous dream. All her insecurities loomed huge and insurmountable in her mind. She couldn't possibly be smart enough to outwit Leigh.

Leigh was quick and bright and clever and she was awkward, tongue-tied Elizabeth.

But she had to be strong, had to think of something. Alex had no one else to help him but her, poor thing.

Fighting back her fear for the hundredth time, she continued searching through the stateroom, aware with each passing second that she was running out of time.

Perhaps an hour after she'd pretended to be sick, the yacht's motors suddenly, ominously, fell silent.

Oh, dear heaven.

This was it.

Panic threatened to crowd out any rational thought but she somehow managed to order herself to keep it together.

Alex, I need you to listen to me, she signed rapidly. *Go into the bathroom. Lock the door. Climb into the tub and lie down.*

She remembered reading that in a novel once, about a way to avoid bomb debris and flying bullets. If she failed and Leigh shot her, at least Alex would have that little extra protection. Maybe, by some miracle, that would give him enough time to be rescued.

She would be damned if she would make it easy for Leigh to get to the boy.

Don't come out for anything until I say it's okay, she signed. *It's a game, okay? Like hide and seek. You have to promise me.*

He nodded, and she suddenly remembered that he wouldn't be able to hear her tell him to unlock the door. *When I want you to come out, I'll pass my ring under the door,* she signed. *As soon as you see it, you can unlock the door. Come on, I'll show you how to lock it.*

She still didn't have more than a half-formed plan, but as she led him to the bathroom, she gathered the few paltry weapons she'd found earlier—the handcuffs, a can of aerosol hair spray from the bathroom, one of the heavy lamps she had spent twenty minutes trying to unbolt from a bedside table.

As weapons went, they weren't much but she didn't have too many other options here.

You can't do this, the nasty voice of self-doubt whispered in her ear. *She's smarter and stronger than you'll ever be.*

Elizabeth drew a shaky breath. Maybe Leigh was more clever but *she* had far more to lose. Alex was counting on her and she couldn't fail him. Besides, she had the element of surprise on her side. Judging by their past history together, Leigh probably expected her to sit meekly by and not even whisper a single objection while the bitch killed them both.

Adrenaline pumped through her as she helped Alex secure the head door. She gripped her paltry weapons and stood on the balls of her feet by the door leading into the salon.

She didn't have long to wait. A few moments later she

heard the sound of footsteps descending below deck, then a key turned with agonizing slowness in the lock.

You can do this. You can do this, she chanted to herself, her pulse as loud as a roaring waterfall in her ears. Finally, after what seemed an eternity where the entire world condensed to the twist of a key, the door opened, and Leigh peeked her head inside the room, that evil-looking gun in her hand and her features twisted into a smirk.

"Ready or not, here I come," she said.

Elizabeth took a deep breath and stepped out from behind the door, held out the hairspray just inches from Leigh's face and sprayed as hard as she could.

As a distraction, it worked perfectly. Taken off guard, Leigh shrieked and coughed and threw her hands—including the one holding the gun—up to her eyes. That gave Elizabeth a few extra seconds to drop the can of hairspray and use both hands to wield the heavy lamp high over her head. She brought it down as hard as she could, gasping as it connected with Leigh's head with a hollow, sickly thud.

An instant later the other woman crumpled to the ground like an inflatable punching bag with a big puncture, the gun loosely clutched in her outstretched hand.

Her breath came in hard, sharp huffs as Elizabeth gazed at Leigh's limp form in stunned disbelief. It worked! It actually worked!

They were safe!

Well, almost. She still had to figure out a way to get them off the water and onto solid ground.

With her knees wobbling and her stomach churning, she managed to take the gun away from Leigh and gingerly moved it out of reach, then she handcuffed a dazed, half-conscious Leigh to one of the bolted-down legs of the bed. It occurred to her that Leigh might know how to unlock the handcuffs without a key so she rooted through the X-rated drawers again and came up with several other useful restraint devices—ropes, velvet-lined ties and a handy leather whip.

And Leigh had called *her* naughty.

By the time she tied them around her hands and feet, Leigh was rendered completely immobile.

Elizabeth spent a few moments trying to catch her breath, her muscles aching now as her adrenaline level crashed, then she slipped her ring under the bathroom door to signal Alex to open it.

It took him a few tries but just as she was trying to figure out if she had any strength left to bust down the door, he managed to unlock it and stood in the doorway, a proud grin on his little face.

I waited, just like you told me, he signed.

Yes you did. You're such a good boy. With a strangled cry of relief, she scooped him into her arms and held him tight, pressing her mouth to the curve of his neck that smelled of sunshine and little-boy sweat.

They were safe! And she—stupid, stammering Elizabeth Quinn—had taken on her devil and won.

Chapter 18

"I don't care about your damn policy and procedure," Beau ground out into his cellular phone. "The lives of a woman and a child may be in jeopardy, and you want to sit there on your can."

"I'm sorry, Detective." The uptight Coast Guard lieutenant he had been transferred to after three underlings wouldn't budge. "We have to follow protocol, just as you are bound by constitutional protections in law enforcement."

She spoke patiently, like a parent talking to a particularly obtuse child. It was all he could do not to throw the phone overboard in frustration.

"We can't simply board a boat without some evidence that a crime has been committed or is about to be committed," the lieutenant went on. "If you can provide that, we will of course be happy to assist the metro police in any way we can."

"Can you at least try to raise the *Minx* on the radio again?"

"We've tried repeatedly. If the boat is indeed underway, anyone at the controls should have been monitoring Channel 16. They would have to have heard us by now and should have responded. I'm sorry, Detective. I don't think there's anything else we can do to help you. At this time, we are advising all recreational watercraft to find safe harbor as another storm is rapidly moving into the area."

Yeah, he kind of figured that out by the three-foot swells rocking the *Mari* like an amusement park ride on steroids. He shouldn't even be out on the Sound, not alone and not at night when he had no sure destination. He was breaking just about every single one of his personal standards of intelligent boating.

All he needed was to hit a log or some other piece of floating debris he couldn't see in the dark to jam his prop or even sink her.

He knew the dangers, but he couldn't leave. Not while Elizabeth and Alex were still out there facing those same dangers and much worse.

"Again, Detective, we strongly recommend that you find safe harbor as soon as possible."

"Thanks for the advice," he growled, and hung up the phone in frustration.

He was on his own out here and realized he had no clue what to do next. He didn't know the first place to look for them, had no idea how to even identify Leigh Sheffield's yacht, and as the Coast Guard officer pointed out, he really had no clear evidence they were even on her yacht with her.

For the first time, he wondered what he would do if he failed, if he wasn't able to find them. A hollow, painful fear like nothing he'd ever experienced burned in his gut. The idea of a world without Elizabeth's sweet smile and little Alex's eager giggle was unendurable.

He loved them both. The strength of it didn't scare him anymore. He was only scared he would never have a chance to tell Elizabeth. He had to find them. He wouldn't even consider the alternative.

He picked up the VHF microphone. "*Mari* to *Minx*. *Mari* to *Minx*," he said into the mike. "Come in, *Minx*."

Pick up, damn it.

He wasn't sure how long he kept on calling them while he battled the storm and the current. His valiant little cruiser had just crested a pretty big one and plunged down the other side when he heard something different on the channel, a woman's hesitant voice.

"Hello? M-mayday. Mayday."

He froze, his heart in his throat. That sure sounded a hell of a lot like Elizabeth.

The channel went instantly quiet as all watercraft within range waited to hear the distress call.

"Station calling, this is Coast Guard Group Seattle. What is your vessel location and the nature of your problem. Go ahead."

"I don't know the location. I'm alone out here and I don't…I don't know what to do."

"Roger. Station calling, this is Coast Guard Group Seattle. Identify yourself. Go ahead."

"I think the boat's name is the *Minx*. I know I'm supposed to give you the…" There was a long pause and then the woman's voice went on. "The c-call letters but I'm sorry. I don't know what they are."

Beau knew he should let the Coast Guard handle the situation. As a civilian boater, he wasn't supposed to do anything but monitor Channel 16 when another boat in the area was in crisis, but he couldn't stay silent. That was Elizabeth out there and she sounded frantic. He picked up the mike and spoke urgently into it.

"This is *Mari*. Elizabeth? Sweetheart, where are you? Over."

He heard only a crackle of static and his heart stopped,

afraid he'd lost her, then she spoke again. "B-Beau? Is that you?"

"This is *Mari*. Yeah, it's me. What's happening? Are you hurt?"

"No. I…I'm okay."

"What about Alex?"

"He's fine too. Scared and hungry but fine."

"Where are you?"

"I don't know. I can't see any landmarks I recognize. Everything is dark."

"What about the GPS? Remember when I showed you how to read it?"

"Coast Guard Group Seattle. *Mari*," a male voice spoke up tersely. "Cease transmissions immediately and let us handle this."

"Coast Guard, this is *Mari*. Detective Beau Riley speaking, Seattle police. This is a police matter. Call your Lieutenant Hershner and she can explain everything. *Mari* to *Minx,* Elizabeth, where's Leigh?"

He thought he heard something about her being handcuffed in the stateroom but he thought it must have been static. "Are you in danger? Go ahead."

"Not from Leigh but it's p-pretty rough out here. Beau, I don't think I can…can pilot the boat alone. I can't even find the GPS."

"Don't try to go anywhere. Just stay put. You need to find and activate the EPIRB. You remember what that is?"

"Yes. The…the emergency locator beacon you showed me on the *Mari*. I'm looking for it. Just a moment."

He waited through several moments of silence, fearing she might be washed overboard in the storm when she left the pilothouse to find the EPIRB unit. "There, I've found it. I pushed it. Now what?"

"Good girl. Now we wait a few moments until the satellite has time to relay your location. Coast Guard Group Seattle, this is *Mari*. Are you monitoring?''

"Yes, sir," the male radio operator said. A few moments later he piped up again. "Coast Guard Group Seattle, Coast Guard Group Seattle to *Minx*. We have your location and are sending out a rescue team. Stand by, please."

"Please hurry." She sounded breathless, at the edge of her control, and Beau wished more than anything that he could get to her.

"Coast Guard, this is *Mari*," he growled into the radio. "What are the coordinates of the *Minx*? Go ahead."

The radio operator gave him her latitude and longitude. Beau looked at his own GPS reading. He was at least ten miles south, and his fuel was running low. He wouldn't make it there for at least a half hour and even if he did, he'd only be in the way of the rescue operation. But, damn, he wanted to be there.

He picked up his cell phone and redialed the Coast Guard's land line. "I need to know where the SAR team will be taking the *Minx* passengers," he said abruptly to the lieutenant, who was all too eager to help him now.

"Just a moment, sir. I'll find out."

She returned a moment later. "The search and rescue team on the USCG cutter *Osprey* will be taking the rescued parties aboard the *Minx* to the rescue station at Edmonds. ETA twenty-two hundred hours."

If he pushed the Mari as hard as she would go in the rough waters, he could make it right after them. "Tell the SAR team I'll be there shortly."

"I'll relay that message, Detective."

He hung up then picked up the microphone. "*Mari* to the *Minx*. *Mari* to the *Minx*. Elizabeth, are you hanging in there? Go ahead."

It took her a minute or so to answer. "*M-Minx* to the *Mari*. Yes. I'm fine. Alex is a little seasick from all this tossing and turning. He just threw up all over the pilot-house.''

Leigh wouldn't be happy about that, but he couldn't work up much of a sweat over it. She wouldn't be enjoying too many cruises where she was going anyway and she'd probably have to sell the damn thing just to pay her legal expenses. ''Elizabeth, I'm heading to the rescue station where the cutter is taking you, okay? I should be there right after you.''

''R-Roger that,'' she said and he smiled at her use of radio lingo. ''There's a boat approaching. I think it's the rescue team. Yes, it is. They're here. Oh, thank heaven.''

''*Mari* to the *Minx*. You did good, Elizabeth. I'll see you in a little bit.''

He monitored Channel 16 all the way to the rescue station as he fought the approaching storm. The high winds and waves made docking a challenge, but he managed to do it without catastrophe.

Rain whipped his face and soaked his clothes even through his rain gear as he rushed into the small building. The moment he walked in, Alex spotted him and jumped into his arms.

''Beau. Beau. Beau,'' the boy chanted.

Hi. Beau signed through his stunned amazement at hearing the boy talk out loud. *Are you okay?*

The kid signed something back quickly that he didn't catch and rubbed his tummy like he was hungry. Beau looked around for Elizabeth to translate the signs.

He found both her and Leigh on benches against one wall, both wrapped in green military-issue wool blankets. Leigh looked dazed and out of it, but Elizabeth was gazing at him with so much raw joy in her eyes that emotion clogged his throat and just about spilled out.

Still carrying Alex, he hurried to her, thinking only about taking her in his arms. He stopped short when he reached her and realized why she hadn't risen to greet him or rushed into his arms. She was cuffed to her chair!

"What the hell is this? Get these handcuffs off her now!"

A young burly ensign whose name badge read Wosniski raised a thick eyebrow. "Which one?"

He pointed to Elizabeth. "This one!"

"You sure about that, Detective? We found the redhead down below. She was unconscious, wrapped up with enough restraints to tie up the entire USCG Seattle group. When she came to, she said the blonde attacked her and tried to hijack the boat. Since we couldn't get a clear story from either one of them about what was going on, we figured we'd better cuff them just to be safe."

"Why didn't you bother asking me, damn it? This one! Let this one free."

"What about the other one?"

"As soon as I can read her her rights, she's going to be under arrest for murder and kidnapping."

He waited impatiently while the man opened the cuffs. The instant she was free, Elizabeth leaped to her feet and into his arms with the same eager relief Alex had done a few moments earlier. She promptly burst into shuddering tears.

He held both her and Alex while she sniffled against him. This was all he wanted, he realized. Right here in his arms was his entire world, this woman and little boy he loved so fiercely.

"Oh, Beau. I'm so glad you're here. I was so f-frightened."

"Shh. I know. You're safe now."

"She k-killed Tina, Beau. She told me she did. All for…for money. She didn't want to share Andrew's fortune with Alex. She was going to kill us, too."

"I figured it was something like that."

"Can we go home now?"

"Not for a while. I'm sorry. You're going to have to give statements about what happened so we can keep her in custody. I'll try to expedite things as best I can so you and Alex can leave as soon as possible."

He wanted to tell her everything that was in his heart, but now wasn't the time. Not with a whole search and rescue team looking on.

Midnight was just a memory before Elizabeth finished giving her statement at the police station.

She was so tired her eyes were blurring with it. All she wanted to do was find a bed and collapse for a week. She was even willing to consider a cot in a cell somewhere, just as long as she could be horizontal.

"Are we nearly finished?" she asked Beau's young, friendly partner, Mr. Griffin, who had taken her statement.

"I think that should do it. We seem to have covered all the bases."

"Would it be possible for me to leave now?"

"I'll see what I can do," he promised, then left her alone in what she had learned was the detective's break room.

She closed her eyes, wishing with all her heart that Beau was here. She hadn't seen him since those moments at the Coast Guard rescue-station, when he had held her and Alex in his arms.

Soon after, he had taken charge of placing Leigh into custody, and he'd been busy processing her arrest ever since.

Even the best legal help Andrew could find wouldn't be enough to keep Leigh out of prison. In her dazed state she'd confessed everything to Beau, probably hoping for a little sympathy.

How had Leigh become so evil? she wondered. Andrew was a good, decent man. He had spoiled his daughter perhaps more than he should have, but she couldn't understand how Leigh could have committed such terrible crimes.

How did Beau deal with this day after day? She had only spent a few weeks brushing up against such ugliness and she could hardly bear it. He chose to make it his career.

She had to talk to him. Her stomach quivered but she knew she couldn't avoid it any longer. She had to tell him about her impairment. He deserved to know the truth, to know why she had run away that night.

Elizabeth yawned, grateful at least that Alex didn't have to endure this waiting. Luisa had come for him several hours ago and had taken him back to Harbor View with her. She hoped he was tucked into his bed, long asleep, and that he wouldn't carry any deep scars from the abduction.

He seemed to think the whole thing had been one big adventure. Ah, for the innocence of childhood. She was afraid she would have nightmares for months about what might have happened if she had failed.

Exhaustion weighed down her shoulders, made her head feel as if it weighed a hundred pounds. She hadn't slept well all week, not since the night she had spent in Beau's arms.

She would just rest here for a moment, until Mr. Griffin was able to find her a ride back to Harbor View....

Beau found her in the break room, her head resting on arms she'd folded on the dingy table. She was still wrapped in that Coast Guard blanket. Beneath it, the lines and angles of her slender body looked fragile, delicate.

He loved her so much he could barely breathe around it. He felt as if she'd been in his life forever, as if she was the missing piece of his heart he'd never realized was gone.

She looked so at peace he hated to disturb her but he didn't think he could manage to carry her out to his truck and find a bed for her without waking her up.

"Elizabeth? Princess? Let's go home."

She lifted her head and blinked at him blearily. "Oh. I must have dozed off."

"Looks like."

"Detective Griffin was…was finding me a ride."

"You're looking at it. Come on."

He helped her up and led her out into the rain to his pickup truck. She still seemed groggy so he picked her up and lifted her onto the seat so she didn't have to try climbing in.

"Where are we going?" she asked after he pulled away and headed east instead of west toward the Bainbridge ferry.

"My place. It's closer."

"I need to go home. Alex might need me."

"You need to sleep," he countered. "Alex has his grandmother for tonight."

She opened her mouth to object but he cut her off. "It's ten minutes to my house and at least an hour to Harbor View by the time we catch the ferry. Hate to break it to you, sweetheart, but I don't think you'll make it that long. You need a bed. Lucky for both of us, I have one."

She opened her mouth as if to object then closed it again. Too much of an effort, he figured. There was silence in the truck for several moments, until he thought she must have fallen asleep.

As much as he wanted to talk to her, he couldn't do it when she was wrung out with exhaustion. He would have to wait until the morning. Maybe by then he would have figured out what to say.

"Beau, I'm…sorry," she said suddenly into the silence.

Since he was stopped at a red light, he was able to look over at her in surprise. "For what?"

"Running away the other night. It was…cowardly. I see that now."

"You're not a coward, Princess."

"Yes I am."

"Look at what you did tonight. Singlehandedly knocked out a murderer and rescued yourself and Alex from a terrible fate, then kept a strange yacht afloat until help arrived. That was pretty darn brave."

"I meant before. That…that night with you, I was a coward then. I should have told you."

"Told me what?"

She was silent for several moments watching the bright parade of lights reflected on the wet streets as they cruised through the night. "I've been lying to you," she said in a small voice.

He glanced over and found her pale and still in the moonlight. She sounded so solemn. "About what?"

"I'm not who you…who you think I am," she said just as he pulled into his driveway.

"You don't have any idea who I think you are," he replied, suddenly realizing where this was going. "But before you say anything else, I'll tell you, just for the record. I think you're smart and sweet and the most beautiful woman I've ever known in person. You're amazingly brave, you're fiercely loyal to those you love and you're a wonderful, devoted caregiver to a little boy who needs you."

She lifted shocked eyes to him. He smiled at her tenderly and reached for her hand. "Oh, one more thing. I think you're also the woman I'm crazy in love with. No, scratch that. I know you are."

She gazed at him, and the raw yearning in her eyes told him everything he needed to know about her feelings. He started to reach for her but stopped in midmotion when she caught her breath on a sob.

"You can't love me," she whispered.

"Wanna bet?"

Her hand clenched in his, and she looked completely miserable. "Beau, I have to…to tell you something. I should have before but I was afraid. I'm not smart. I pretend but I'm not. I was born with an injury in one of the…the language areas of my b-brain. It makes me stutter and use wrong words, sometimes terribly.''

''Yeah, I know.''

''You…know?''

''Not the details, maybe. But Leigh Sheffield told me how things were for you when you were a kid.''

''Then…then surely you realize you can't l-love me.''

Beau gazed at her, completely stunned. She meant it! She actually thought she was unlovable because of a little speech difficulty.

''Who did such a number on you, Princess?''

''A n-number?''

''Who convinced you we all have to be perfect before anyone can love us? You're not being very fair to me. What kind of man do you think I'd be to care if you miss a few words here and there?''

His words resonated deep in her heart. He was right! She had been terribly unfair to him—grossly unfair—comparing him to Stephen and to her father. Beau was nothing like them. She had known it since the moment she met him but she had been so afraid of rejection.

He loved her. Somehow, unbelievably, this hard, abrupt, wonderful detective loved her, and she was sitting here trying to convince him he didn't, that he couldn't.

She *was* stupid. She ought to be reaching for this miracle with both hands.

''I love you, Elizabeth Quinn,'' he said quietly into her silence.

She drew a shaky breath, then she pushed away all her fears and moved across the seat and into his waiting arms. His mouth was gentle, as achingly sweet as that kiss on the Sheffield's terrace, and her tears spilled free and trickled down her cheeks.

"Once more for the record," he murmured, kissing away the tears. "In case there's ever any doubt in that brain of yours, Elizabeth, I love everything about you. Except maybe your fortune. I'd prefer it if you were in the poorhouse but I guess if you can forgive mine, I can forgive yours."

She drew back. "You have a...fortune?"

"Not much of one compared to yours. I've been trying to get rid of it for years, but I can't quite seem to shake the damn thing. Maybe you can help me with that. I understand you run the Quinn Charitable Foundation. Think you could find some good use for an extra twenty million or so?"

Her tears forgotten, she laughed at his disgruntled tone and kissed him fiercely. Oh, she loved this man. "The only thing I enjoy more than giving my own money away is giving away someone else's."

"Then my millstone and I should make you very happy."

"You do," she whispered as joy burst inside her, filling all the lost, lonely little corners with sweet, healing peace. "Oh, Beau, you make me so happy. I love you! I wish I had words to tell you how much."

His smile promised a lifetime of laughter and love. "You don't need any more than that, Princess. Those three little words are all I need."

* * * * *

Coming in April 2003

baby and all

Three brand-new stories about
the trials and triumphs of motherhood.

"Somebody Else's Baby"
by *USA TODAY* bestselling author Candace Camp

Widow Cassie Weeks had turned away from the world—until her
stepdaughter's baby turned up on her doorstep. This tiny new life—
and her gorgeous new neighbor—would teach Cassie she had
a lot more living…and loving to do….

"The Baby Bombshell" by Victoria Pade

Robin Maguire knew nothing about babies or romance.
But lucky for her, when she suddenly inherited an infant, the sexy single
father across the hall was more than happy to teach her about both.

"Lights, Camera…Baby!" by Myrna Mackenzie

When Eve Carpenter and her sexy boss were entrusted with caring for
their CEO's toddler, the formerly baby-wary executive found herself
wanting to be a real-life mother—and her boss's real-life wife.

Where love comes alive™

Visit Silhouette at www.eHarlequin.com   PSBAA

If you enjoyed what you just read,
then we've got an offer you can't resist!

Take 2 bestselling
love stories FREE!
Plus get a FREE surprise gift!

Clip this page and mail it to Silhouette Reader Service™

IN U.S.A.
3010 Walden Ave.
P.O. Box 1867
Buffalo, N.Y. 14240-1867

IN CANADA
P.O. Box 609
Fort Erie, Ontario
L2A 5X3

YES! Please send me 2 free Silhouette Intimate Moments® novels and my free surprise gift. After receiving them, if I don't wish to receive anymore, I can return the shipping statement marked cancel. If I don't cancel, I will receive 6 brand-new novels every month, before they're available in stores! In the U.S.A., bill me at the bargain price of $3.99 plus 25¢ shipping and handling per book and applicable sales tax, if any*. In Canada, bill me at the bargain price of $4.74 plus 25¢ shipping and handling per book and applicable taxes**. That's the complete price and a savings of at least 10% off the cover prices—what a great deal! I understand that accepting the 2 free books and gift places me under no obligation ever to buy any books. I can always return a shipment and cancel at any time. Even if I never buy another book from Silhouette, the 2 free books and gift are mine to keep forever.

245 SDN DNUV
345 SDN DNUW

Name	(PLEASE PRINT)	
Address	Apt.#	
City	State/Prov.	Zip/Postal Code

* Terms and prices subject to change without notice. Sales tax applicable in N.Y.
** Canadian residents will be charged applicable provincial taxes and GST.
  All orders subject to approval. Offer limited to one per household and not valid to
  current Silhouette Intimate Moments® subscribers.
  ® are registered trademarks of Harlequin Books S.A., used under license.

INMOM02   ©1998 Harlequin Enterprises Limited